SPRING
FINCH'S CROSSING BOOK 2

Amy Ruth Allen

D1714988

FINCH'S CROSSING

Spring

BOOK TWO

AMY RUTH ALLEN

Spring: Finch's Crossing Book Two
© 2020 by Amy Ruth Allen

www.amyruthallen.com

ISBN: 979-8-6303717-0-6

For Leigh, always.

CHAPTER 1

AT A REST STOP outside of Albuquerque, New Mexico, Spring Hamilton triumphantly hurled her cell phone into a garbage can by a picnic pavilion. She had wanted to throw the phone to the ground and stomp on it but decided that was too dramatic and not in her nature. Besides, there were people watching.

"That'll fix him," she said under her breath, with a toss of her long blond mane. The wind had picked up and an unpleasant dusty breeze swirled around her.

A grandmotherly woman in a lavender jogging suit walking a small terrier overheard her. "I feel your pain, honey!" she said in a sing-songy voice, and the two women laughed together. "A man?" the woman asked with a grin.

"What else?" Spring replied. "And now he's out of my life forever. He doesn't know where I am, and if he can't call me, well, then…," her voice trailed off.

"Been there, done that," the woman said, waving good-bye and following the dog as it strained against its leash.

Spring returned to her silver Mercedes Benz SUV and pulled back onto the interstate, feeling a rush of relief.

She didn't even last a mile. *What am I doing throwing away a perfectly good phone like that?* True, it would be easy enough to replace it and have her data, contacts, and apps transferred from the cloud. But that wasn't the point.

Taking the next exit, she re-entered the interstate in the other direction and headed for the rest stop. A few minutes and another U-turn later, she was plunging her hand into the garbage can, rummaging around goodness knows what, until her fingers wrapped around the familiar object. She looked around quickly to see if anyone was watching, but the rest stop was empty. Even the woman in the lavender jogging suit was gone. No wonder, the wind was whipping.

Spring knew that the outburst of impulsive behavior was counter to her organized and logical nature and was glad she had restored order to her psyche. With the ceremonial trashing of her phone, she had really just wanted to make a statement to herself. Sort of a metaphor that showed she was seriously leaving her old life behind. And, she reasoned, she had accomplished that. She would just not answer Chad when he called.

CHAPTER 1

Making her way back to her car, Spring had to shield her eyes against the wind and grit. The wind seemed to have appeared out of nowhere, accelerating from pleasant breeze to high-powered gust in a matter of moments. She had forgotten what the desert wind was like in March. She stole a glance around her and all she could see was the familiar dusty dirt and stubby brown ground covering that had accompanied her for hours along the interstate. Since leaving Los Angeles, it was all so desolate, as if the terrain reflected her own feelings. She slipped quickly into her car and let out the breath she didn't know she was holding.

Back on the road and headed more or less eastward, she had hours and hours to think about how she had ended up here, so far from her home.

A hugely successful fashion model, Spring Hamilton had played the part flawlessly, running with the beautiful and popular upper crust of Los Angeles, on the arm of her impossibly handsome and worldly boyfriend and manager. She had a cadre of beautiful friends, the kind who kissed both your cheeks whenever they greeted you. She drove an ultra-luxury car and lived in a huge custom-built and professionally decorated mansion with gorgeous views and all the latest amenities. She had a great reputation in the industry, and she and Chad could cherry-pick modeling jobs, choosing only those worthy of her considerable presence. She thought she had been happy.

Still beautiful at thirty-six, Spring knew her current career trajectory would eventually begin to curve downward, and probably pretty soon. Whether the curve was gradual or more of a plunge didn't matter. She needed to do something drastic to change direction—like leaving Los Angeles. As she grew older and her fresh face and toned body faded, she knew she would be relegated to modeling in catalogs and television commercials for pharmaceuticals to help older women with bladder control. No, thank you.

And Spring knew she was smart. Really smart. She had been told countless times that one of the things that made her so attractive was her intelligence. People could sense she was the total package, in total control. She figured Chad had her, and *their*, best interest at heart, so she pretty much went along with the career path he laid out for her, without much deviation. It had worked out fine. They were both getting what they wanted.

When she first broached the idea of branching out of modeling into perhaps fashion management, couture publishing, or even creating her own business ventures, Chad had gone ballistic, throwing up his hands and screaming at her.

He had yelled, almost trembling, "You are being so ungrateful! After all I've done for you. I made you rich. I gave you this lifestyle! And you repay me by just quitting? By leaving me in the lurch? Are you crazy?"

She could hardly believe what was happening. She had just

assumed that Chad would be all-in and that he would be as excited as she was to begin the next phase of their lives. But he was not ready to let the present chapter go.

In that moment, as he stood screaming at her from across their living room, technically *her* living room, it became evident that he was not worried about her losing *her* lifestyle. It was Chad who didn't want to lose his lifestyle: the gorgeous model on his arm, the lavish trips to shoot on location, the feeling of being a big shot, the perks like private jets and cool swag from designers. Did he even love her? Or just love what she gave him? These questions raised her hackles because, in fact, she knew the answers. Probably had known them all along. But it had only taken one instant for everything to crystallize, falling into place like the next chapter of a well-written novel. She would never forget what it felt like to have him stand before her and scream, "You wouldn't have all of this without me! I made you!" Spring seriously doubted that. It seemed much more likely that he wouldn't have anything without her.

Chad had not always been a jerk. Or more likely, he had been, but just managed to keep it well hidden. It might be better to say that his vision of the future initially aligned with Spring's. When they first met, he did seem to have Spring's best interest at heart. And she was perfectly happy to have his help in getting her modeling career off the ground and, even later, when things had really begun to take off for her. He had worked hard, but she now realized, not nearly as hard as she had. She had also been perfectly happy for him to profit more and more from her modeling income. It was a mutually beneficial, symbiotic relationship. And at first, she really thought he loved her, not really doubting that fact until recently.

Spring had been a gold mine for Chad. He had been able to parlay his suave demeanor, his boyish good looks, and the spiderweb of Los Angeles contacts he inherited from his upper-crust Los Angeles family into a fairly remarkable career as Spring's manager. And he enjoyed the added benefit of having a beautiful model on his arm as his live-in girlfriend as he fluttered around town. To be truthful, he was actually Spring's live-in boyfriend.

But Chad had no inkling of how the world, especially the world of Hollywood and Los Angeles modeling royalty, treats women—especially women like Spring, who must constantly focus on every minute detail of their being to make a living. Everything was fair game. Hair. Makeup. Style. BMI. ZIP code. Age. Carriage. Professionalism. Perfection was the expectation. Spring understood that failure to meet certain standards in too many areas could bring a career like hers to a screeching halt. She would much rather plan for this eventuality.

Chad did not understand this. His plan was to keep doing what they had been doing. He had no sense of urgency, no sense that this could not possibly go on forever. Perhaps Spring was still so beautiful and flawless to him that he just couldn't imagine her any other way. He was naive. And while he was railing against her, she swiftly and decisively made plans to untangle her life from Chad's and relocate to New York City to pursue new avenues in fashion. She was exhilarated by the prospect of what lay before her.

And now, as Spring put more and more miles between her and Chad, she was grateful that she had kept her money separate from his. Sure, she had allowed him to buy anything he wanted with her Platinum American Express card. But he wasn't a co-signer on her accounts. Their home was in her name as well.

As soon as he left, yelling obscenities all the way to the driveway before screeching away in his Range Rover—also provided by Spring—she had called her lawyer, an accountant, a locksmith, and a moving company.

A few days later, with the locks changed and Chad's belongings boxed up and packed into a single storage pod sitting in her driveway, Chad had arrived, hat in hand, apologizing, telling her he loved her, that it had all been a misunderstanding. She turned on her heels and went back into the house, leaving her lawyer, Sterling North, to oversee Chad's move. Sterling watched as Chad made phone calls and finally found a moving company that would come immediately and take the pod away. Spring had not been so heartless as to leave him without a car. She had signed the Range Rover title over to Chad and listened with relief as his tires screeched away, down the drive, and out of her life, forever.

* * *

As the miles whizzed by, Spring thought of her sister, Autumn. She thought of Finch's Crossing, and of her idyllic childhood there in her quaint hometown in the beautiful Laurel Highlands of western Pennsylvania. It was nothing like her Los Angeles neighborhood. No hillside mansions with gorgeous views. No streets choked with supercars. In her mind's eye she could vividly see her childhood home, a sturdy, painted Victorian house, in which Autumn now lived.

Spring remembered how happy she had been there growing up. Genuinely, purely happy. She remembered that she had not left Finch's Crossing all those years ago because she was not happy there. She left because she sought adventure. She was desperate, as so many in their youth are, to make her own way. To leave her mark. To show the world and everybody in it what she was made of. She had done that. She would have done that with or without Chad, she told herself. No one who knew her would disagree.

Yet she envied Autumn's strong sense of belonging to their hometown. And despite the years spent away and infrequent trips back, Spring now felt an invisible nudge back to the quirky small town of her upbringing. The closer she got to home, the stronger the feeling. She had to get back to the "happy" she felt there—back to what she thought of as "Finch's Crossing happy." She smiled brightly and glanced at herself in the rearview mirror, surprised by the swell of emotion she saw in her eyes and the pang of longing she felt for her childhood home.

Spring looked at the dashboard for the time. She could arrive in Finch's Crossing in about twenty-four hours if she drove through the night. So that settled it. Her arrival in New York wasn't set in stone. She had simply selected a date and made her plans accordingly. Her new apartment was ready for her whenever she arrived. She had sufficient financial resources to sustain herself indefinitely. So why not take an unscheduled few days and stop to see Autumn? Finch's Crossing was barely out of her way. Spring glanced at her cell resting in the passenger seat of the Mercedes. She should call to see if it suited Autumn, but decided to surprise her. Spring could hardly wait to pull into the drive of her childhood home on Loucks Avenue and see if she couldn't start getting a little "Finch's Crossing happiness" back into her life. In the hours since she had left Los Angeles, it was dawning on Spring that it had been a long time since she felt any real semblance of happiness.

She needed a distraction. Maybe a project she could plan and organize. Something where she could use her efficient and logical brain. Accompanied, of course, by her uncompromising sense of style and effortless classiness. Yes, she would stay in Finch's Crossing for a few days and take the time to map out her next move. Curled up in the familiar surroundings of her childhood home, she would be buoyed by the nostalgia of the past and her sister's tender care and nurturing ways.

Her mind jumped to Gabriel Vignaroli, her high school sweetheart, just as she had known it would. It would be impossible to think of Finch's Crossing without remembering her first love. And there it was, a memory laid out in front of her like a long-healed wound suddenly open again. The breakup with Chad, and all the ugly truths and spiteful words, were nothing compared to what Gabe had done to her almost twenty years ago. Was Gabe the reason her trips home to Finch's Crossing over the years had been so infrequent? Was she afraid that she would see him? She had long ago stopped asking her family about him, and until that moment, it had been years since she had thought of him. So why was it that even when she had successfully banished all memories of Gabe from her mind, they remained stubbornly in her heart?

CHAPTER 2

AUTUMN HAMILTON STARED as her best friend, Meg Overly, pummeled the pink bow she was trying to affix to a straw wreath.

"Just exactly when were you going to tell me that you and Ethan had set the date?" Meg asked grumpily as she abandoned the hat for an egg-shaped Styrofoam form and another bow, almost breaking the wire that was supposed to wind easily around the shape.

"Okay, Meg," Autumn groaned, ignoring the question. "You were right. You are a disaster at this kind of thing. Just put the ribbons down and no one will get hurt."

Meg did as she was told, practically flinging the pink ribbon down on the long work table in Autumn's Pittsburgh

Street art studio. "I warned you I don't have a green thumb," she said, triumphantly.

Autumn gave her an amused look. "We're not gardening, for heaven's sake. This is crafting, remember? Crafting. Making Easter decorations. I just wanted you to help me get this stuff ready for my decorating class tomorrow. How hard can it be to stick a bow on a hat?" She fingered the two decimated bows and the Styrofoam egg with its gaping holes. "Now I'm sorry I even asked." She was slightly annoyed, but also smiling. It really was her own fault. She knew better than to ask Meg to do anything that didn't have to do with dogs, food, or how annoying everyone in Finch's Crossing was, down to a person.

Autumn finally addressed Meg's question with a confused look. "We haven't set a date, Meg. You'd be the first to know. As I believe I have indicated in the past, I can't wait to find a frilly dress in fuchsia for you to wear as my maid of honor."

Leaning back on her stool and stretching out her long legs, Meg looked down at her flannel shirt, jeans, and Doc Martens.

"Can't I just wear this? How about if I promise to buy a new pair of jeans and wear a pink camo sweater?"

A gorgeous, short-haired beauty, Meg had the fresh, girl-next-door look that required no makeup or fuss.

Autumn didn't respond, so Meg returned to the topic of the wedding. "Someone better tell Heather that there's not going to be a wedding anytime soon."

"Oh?" Autumn asked, distractedly. She was planning her gazillionth trip to the Town and Country Nursery for more flowers. The entire membership of both the Finch's Crossing Women's Club and the Art Guild had enrolled in her decorating class. Plus, she was expecting a few walk-ins. Since opening a public art studio on Pittsburgh Street, she was amazed that all her crafting and studio art classes filled up so quickly, and most had waiting lists.

Six-year-old Heather was Ethan's ward. After her parents had died the year before, it came as a surprise to everyone that Ethan had been granted guardianship, even though her grandmother, Martha Kelly, was willing and able to care for Heather in Finch's Crossing. Now a lawyer in nearby Pittsburgh, Ethan had brought Heather back from his bachelor life in New York City to live in Finch's Crossing. And to be with Autumn. Autumn shivered, as she always did, when she thought of how close she and Ethan had come to losing each other.

"Why? What's Heather said now?" she asked Meg distractedly.

"Only that the only thing she wants for her birthday is for you and Ethan to get married, by her actual birthday," Meg paused. "Oh yeah, and for her Uncle Bryan to be there, too."

"How do you know this?" Autumn put down the ribbons and gave her full attention to Meg.

"I heard her tell Martha when they were having hamburgers this afternoon at the lunch counter at Hoffman's Drugstore."

Autumn could feel the blood drain from her face. "Where, exactly, were they sitting in relation to the actual counter?"

"They had the closest booth to the Sunset Boys," Meg replied, catching on. Practically all the Finch's Crossing gossip started with the group of retired men who treated the lunch counter as their man cave and gleefully ground out the Finch's Crossing rumor mill.

"And were a lot of other people there?"

Meg nodded. "It was lunchtime. There were even people waiting."

"Oh brother," Autumn wailed, burying her head in her hands. "Just a few minutes ago I stopped at Miss Elsie's Tea Room to pick up the cookies for tomorrow's class and she gave me a big hug and congratulated me. I had no idea what she meant, but I didn't want to be rude so I just played along."

"So you *aren't* getting married by Heather's birthday?" Meg clarified.

Autumn flung her an exasperated look. "Heather's birthday is only six weeks away, on April twenty-ninth. We'll just have to explain to her that it's not possible. She'll understand. And even if we could pull off a wedding in that amount of time, it would be impossible to get Bryan here. He's serving overseas and I wouldn't even know where to start."

Meg shook her head. "I don't think that's a good idea. I

heard her tell Martha that she had written a letter to Santa last Christmas and that you promised her that he would always bring her whatever she wanted."

"I meant a doll or a scooter, not a wedding," Autumn explained. "I wanted to get married in the fall because that's when Ethan and I met. We even talked about getting married in the pumpkin patch at the Town and Country Nursery where we officially met."

Meg grinned. "Yeah, where you decimated his car with baby pumpkins because you didn't like how he was treating Heather."

Autumn ignored her, blushing slightly at the memory. She had not decimated his car, exactly. She continued with her musing. "And if we get married in the fall, that's plenty of time for Bryan to ask for leave stateside."

"Look," said Meg, in her matter-of-fact tone. "Let's just say that you *are* able to pull off a wedding by Heather's birthday." Autumn began to protest, but Meg silenced her by raising her hand. "Let me just say this. If you can pull a wedding together, I can get Bryan home in time."

Autumn just stared at her friend, then burst out laughing. "Oh, Meg, that's so sweet."

Meg rolled her eyes. "It's not sweet. There's nothing sweet about it, or me, for that matter."

"I have to agree with you there," Autumn said, still laughing.

"Why are you laughing?" Meg demanded, crossing her arms across her chest. Two pink spots appeared on her cheeks.

"Well," Autumn began, "because it's just ridiculous to think that you can snap your fingers and get a Marine transferred home."

"And what makes you think I can't?"

"I guess I don't know that you can't. But I don't know if you can, either."

"Can so," Meg said, pouting.

"Cannot," Autumn responded, automatically falling into the familiar banter they had practiced since high school.

"Can so, and I am going to prove it to you." Meg hopped off the chair, threaded her way through the easels spread throughout the studio, and disappeared into Autumn's office. She came back with a wall calendar and spread it out in front of them. Her finger landed on April twenty-ninth. "If you can get a wedding together in time for Heather's birthday on April twenty-ninth, I swear to you that I will have Bryan out of his cave in some Afghan outpost and back to Finch's Crossing the day before." She planted a finger on the twenty-eighth block. "The twenty-eight, or, thereabouts, but plenty of time for him to escort Heather down the aisle. It might be tight, but I can make it happen. But you'll need to decide fast."

Autumn sized up her friend. She had never seen this side of Meg before. True, Meg had many law enforcement contacts nationwide through her work breeding German shepherds at her family's Ten Oaks Kennel. But as far as Autumn knew, Meg didn't know the chairman of the Joints Chiefs, the secretary of defense, or any other high-ranking military official who could snap his or her fingers and bring Bryan back to Finch's Crossing. How could she? It was just impossible. Or, at the very least, improbable.

"Okay," Autumn said, deciding to play along. She would need to come up with a plan to appease Heather. But in the meantime, she'd pretend she was considering it. "I'll talk to Ethan tonight and see what he thinks." She paused. "Let's just say that Ethan and I do decide to go through with the wedding. How are you going to pull this off?"

"Can't tell you. Sorry. This is the sort of thing that is 'need to know,' if you know what I mean." Meg smirked mischievously.

"What do you mean, 'need to know?'" Autumn asked incredulously. "Of course, I need to know! If we are going to attempt this wedding, I need to know."

"Whose wedding?" a voice queried behind them, and the pair turned simultaneously to see Meg's long-suffering beau, Kyle Oswald, walking toward them. They had been so engrossed in their conversation that they hadn't heard him come in. He took a stool next to Meg, kissed her cheek, and took her hand.

"So you've decided to say yes, after all, and make me the happiest man in all of Westmoreland County?"

Meg snorted her response and Autumn raised her eyebrows in surprise, speechless for a moment.

"Oh," she said in a voice that was supposed to mimic Meg's deep alto voice, "just exactly when were *you* going to tell me that you and Kyle had set the date?"

Meg pulled her hand away from Kyle's and rolled her eyes. "Because we haven't," she said blusteringly and turned to punch Kyle on his arm. "I can't even believe that you asked me. You're such a big dork. Besides, I'm way too busy to get married. I've got that new Canadian police force to work with, and the expansion construction project…"

Kyle interrupted her. "Thanks to me," he said, smiling broadly. "And, you're welcome."

Kyle had come to Finch's Crossing the previous year to bring the struggling downtown merchants into the age of social media, online advertising, and various other electronic marketing vehicles. Mayor Peggy Brightwell, who had hired him, lamented what she called "the greying" of their small town. With his help, the downtown merchants, and their shops and restaurants along Pittsburgh Street, had flourished. His efforts had worked so well that he settled down and opened his own marketing firm. And after months of convincing Meg to fall in love with him, he managed a marketing campaign for her that was so effective that Meg needed to expand the kennel where she and her family had raised German shepherds for law enforcement for fifty years.

CHAPTER 2

"Yes, I know, I know. I owe everything to you," Meg whined. "You don't have to tell me a hundred times a day. And if you think I'm going to marry you just because you helped develop my business, you're an even bigger dork."

"Am not," Kyle said playfully.

"Are too."

Autumn looked from one to the other and back again. She admired Kyle's patience and persistence. He was as kind and patient as Meg was grumpy and abrupt. But she knew that Kyle, with his oddly angled, handsome face, dark denim jeans, and white starched shirts always open at the cuffs, had won Meg's heart no matter what she said. Meg had come up with every excuse in the book not to like him—including the fact that he was six years younger—but in the end she had acquiesced, almost as if she had agreed to do something distasteful. But Autumn knew the grumpy Meg was not the only Meg. Surely, when she and Kyle were together Meg showed a softer, kinder side?

"You're thinking about getting married, and you didn't tell me?" Autumn accused them.

"Well," Meg shot back, "last year, as I seem to recall, you almost went bankrupt because you had painter's block for two years. And you never mentioned any of that."

"Okay, you got me there."

"Besides," Meg said emphatically, "whatever Kyle is going around telling people about us getting married, you need to subtract two from it, divide it by a hundred, and move the decimal five spaces."

Autumn scrunched up her face in confusion and Kyle just rolled his eyes. "It's just Meg-speak," he said. "Don't pay any attention to her." Then he kissed Meg again and strolled out the door.

CHAPTER 3

KYLE AMBLED ALONG Pittsburgh Street, gazing at the festive Easter-themed window displays and remembering his first few weeks in Finch's Crossing. It felt as if he had lived in his adopted hometown forever, but it was only last year that he had arrived, desperate to make a good impression as a contract social media and electronic marketing consultant. And just a year before, he had struggled to make ends meet. A working adult student, it had taken him six years to get through college, but he had done it. Now he had a growing business and an office on Pittsburgh Street with a small apartment above. He thought of Meg and her delicate features and beautiful figure. Even though she worked a very physically demanding job and wore men's clothes, she always carried herself like a graceful, confident woman, and he had fallen in love with her the first time he set eyes on her at the lunch counter at Hoffman's Drugstore.

As he stood in front of Miss Elsie's Tea Room, he remembered the previous holiday season and the beautifully decorated Christmas trees Miss Elsie Hixon had stuck in every available space where there wasn't a table or tea trolley. And he couldn't help but think of the previous year's Black Friday shopping disaster. As he had been hired to do, he taught the merchants the ins and outs of electronic marketing, setting up Facebook and twitter ads, radio interviews, and many other great things. Trouble was, left to their own devices, they hadn't followed through with his carefully laid-out instructions. And the few things they did manage to achieve, they executed so terribly that he felt like a kindergarten teacher herding five-year-olds that had scattered on a field trip to the zoo. But he had brought it all together in time, and all the merchants had at least tripled their sales from the previous year. And in the process, Kyle had endeared himself to the town that now embraced him as a native son.

Heading back toward Brilhart Hardware and his five o'clock appointment with Stan Brilhart, the proprietor, he passed Krop's Jewelers and the new bookstore. He made a mental note to call on the new proprietor as a potential new client.

At precisely five he walked into the hardware store and

headed straight to Stan's office at the back of the shop.

Stan greeted him like an old friend and Kyle settled into an ancient swivel chair opposite Stan's equally old and battered giant desk. Ripped and stained calendars dating back to the 1960s hung on the wall, their pages curling at the edges. Although Stan had taken to electronic marketing, he held fast to his handwritten bookkeeping records, and receipt books and ledgers were stacked high on a side table. If it wasn't for the new laptop Stan had purchased last year, Kyle would feel as if he was in a museum.

"So how goes it with the Facebook ads?" Kyle asked, pulling out a file from his leather messenger bag. "Have you seen any increase in sales?"

He watched as Stan pulled up his Facebook account, doing his typical hunt-and-peck typing with stumbling sausage-like fingers.

"I have to hand it to you, Stan," Kyle said eagerly, bursting with pride like a father watching his child take a first step or say a first word. "You are getting so adept at this, you're going to put me out of business."

"You're well worth the money we're paying you," Stan said, as he turned the laptop around so Kyle could see. "Besides, if you didn't keep tabs on me and tell me what to do and when to do it, I'd be back to my old ways in no time."

Kyle studied the screen, pleased at the huge spikes in hits on Stan's Facebook ads for his self-proclaimed "Lady Gifts"—

items under $25 suitable for women to give the men in their lives for any occasion. Boxes of drill bits, shiny red toolboxes, tool organizers, laser levels, ratchet sets, and much more were stacked in the front of the store under a special pink sign.

Stan clicked his mouse and brought up reports that showed increased traffic to his website, especially on the Lady Gifts micro website, and spreadsheets that showed ever-increasing sales.

Surprised, Kyle raised his eyebrows. "Spreadsheets? When did this happen?"

Stan smiled broadly. I knew you'd be surprised. Got myself one of those for dummies books and set up an accounting system. Not bad, eh?"

"I'm impressed," Kyle said. "You'll be selling online in no time. We can talk about setting up an e-commerce function on your website. I'll check in on you next week. I also have some thoughts about advertising your Lady Gifts promotions. It really was a terrific idea."

Kyle stood to go but then remembered the bookstore.

"Say, do you know anything about the person who opened the new bookstore last week?" he gestured in the direction of the store. "I'm wondering if the owner might need some marketing help. It's a rough time to be opening a bookstore when everyone and their brother has an e-reader."

"Coffee shop," Stan mumbled.

"What?" Kyle asked, confused.

CHAPTER 3

"It's not just a bookstore. There's also a coffee bar."

"Uh oh," Kyle said. "Before you know it they'll be putting Miss Elsie out of business. She can't be too happy."

"Nothing to it," Stan said to his hands. "He's promised not to sell tea and the only food he's serving is those hard Italian cookies that no one knows how to pronounce and those strong mints for when you have coffee breath. Other than that, there's not much to tell."

Kyle waited for Stan to elaborate, but when it was obvious that he didn't have anything else to say, Kyle readied to leave.

"Well," said Kyle, "guess I'm outta here."

"Wait just a second," Stan said, taking his voice down to a whisper. He motioned for Kyle to close the door. "There's just one other thing. You see, there's this…lady friend I met on matchme.com."

Oh boy, Kyle thought to himself as he sat back down and dropped his messenger bag on the floor next to his chair.

"So you've ventured into the world of online dating?" Kyle asked. "First electronic accounting, and now this? At this rate you'll be writing software programs next!"

"I've been a widower for two years," Stan said, ignoring Kyle's joke. "I'm only fifty years old and I have concluded that I don't want to be alone the rest of my life." Stan spoke as he pulled up the website and clicked over to a profile. Kyle found himself looking at a pretty and pleasantly plump familiar face.

"Really?" he asked, surprised. "Really? They matched you

with her?"

"Yep. I've known her all my life. We went to school together and graduated high school at the same time."

"Ducky, the mail lady? Who would have thought?" Kyle thought of the jovial, spirited woman who delivered his mail. She couldn't be more than five feet tall. "So what's the problem?" Kyle asked.

"I don't know if she knows that we were matched," Stan said. "And if she was matched with me, was I matched with her? It's all so awkward now. Do you know that I make sure I'm in the back when she delivers the mail? And I've stopped going to the post office and send Johnny or Maureen so there's no possible way I will run into her. And I took down my profile."

Kyle tried hard not to laugh, but he couldn't help it.

"This is not funny," Stan fussed at him. "I don't know what to do."

"It's pretty obvious what you should do," Kyle said. "Ask her out to dinner."

"I don't think I can do that. I haven't been on a date in almost thirty years. I wouldn't know what to say."

"At least think about it," Kyle said, standing up. "I mean, why did you put a profile up in the first place if you're just going to take it down before you've even seen if it works?"

Stan didn't reply, so Kyle patted his shoulder and headed out.

Stan watched him go and then returned his gaze to the computer screen where Ducky's face was still smiling at him. He had had a crush on her in high school but had been too shy and flustered to act on it. At six foot four and 250 pounds, Stan was a big and powerful man. Unfortunately, he always felt more like an awkward bull in a china shop, and that kept him from approaching women. Turning back to his computer, he clicked off of Ducky's page and back to another potential match, Nancy Dawson, whom he had been chatting with through emails and instant messages. He felt guilty continuing with their online relationship because he knew that at some point or another he was going to ask Ducky out. He just had no idea how. But knowing he had feelings for Ducky, he decided he shouldn't be mixed up with another woman. His hands hovered over his keyboard as he mentally prepared his "Dear Jane" letter to Nancy.

* * *

After leaving Stan's, Kyle stopped at Miss Elsie's Tea Room for an early supper of a hot turkey sandwich and cream of tomato soup. As he sat at a table near the front window and thought about Stan's dating dilemmas, he realized that over the past year he had become part consultant, part advisor, and part therapist to his clients. He thought about Teppy Tartel, who owned the Et Cetera Boutique and Christmas Shop. Earlier in the year she had confided in him that her husband, from whom she had recently separated, threatened to sue for custody of their two teenage girls because of the increased hours and workload at the shop—due, in large part, to Kyle's marketing efforts—which kept her at the shop and away from the girls.

"I'm home less and less, and he knows that when I'm home I'm doing paperwork, getting online orders ready and ordering stock," she had told Kyle. "I'm so busy with customers that I don't have time to do the administrative work during the day, and my part-time help is so unreliable. I think Roger is a little jealous of all the success of the shop and the increasing amount of time I spend there. I'm sure that's part of the reason why he left."

Ouch, Kyle had thought, feeling a twinge of guilt.

"Why don't you hire your daughters to help you in the shop after school and on Saturdays?" Kyle had suggested. "They could wait on customers and step up the social media that I'm already doing for you. I bet they'd love to set up some other accounts, like Instagram and Pinterest. And come to think of it, they'd help you attract the younger demographic you and I have been talking about tapping into."

Teppy had thrown her arms around him and there were tears in her eyes. "What would we do without you, Kyle?" she had asked, planting a heartfelt smooch on his cheek. "They'll earn some extra spending money—I'll pay them of course—plus, when the shop is slow, they'll have time to do their homework and talk with their friends! I don't think even Roger could argue with this arrangement!"

Kyle noted with satisfaction that he had seen her daughters, Jessica and Angelique, enter the shop every afternoon after school. And this evening, from his vantage point sitting by the window, he could see Roger and Teppy leaving the store together, locking up for the evening. And come to think about it, he had seen Roger come in a few times on a Saturday to take the girls out for lunch. Kyle wondered if it was the girls he was actually coming to see or Teppy. Sometimes he worried that the advice his clients sought from him, and which he offered with true affection and concern, would backfire against him. But so far, so good.

Kyle was so deep in thought that he didn't see Teppy approach his table. She plopped down on a chair, her fuzzy pink and white jacket shining with the small droplets of rain that had begun to fall outside. "Isn't it great news about Autumn and Ethan? And getting married on Heather's birthday. How romantic! Do you know where they're going to have the ceremony?"

Before Kyle could answer, or even wonder where she had heard that news, Teppy pulled a file from within the depths of her voluminous jacket and put it on the table, chattering all the while.

"I've had one of my Brilliant Ideas just a little while ago, and I had to come tell you right away because you're a big part of it. We should hold a Bridal Expo here this spring. All

SPRING

the big cities have them, with vendors coming together to promote their wedding-related services, and the brides who want
spring and summer weddings flock to them. Ours would be for
people who want to get married in a cozy, picturesque small
town during the off-season. But it won't really be off-season,
though, because we'll advertise it as if it's a great idea. Like 'fall
is the new spring.' Where better than Finch's Crossing?"

"But," Kyle finally was able to interject, "do we even have
merchants in town who could supply things for a big wedding?"

"Of course, we do," Teppy answered. "You have to think
big. I can decorate receptions and provide bridesmaids gifts
and registries. Miss Elsie can do catering and wedding cakes
and Duncan can open the Greystone Manor for ceremonies
and receptions. DeMuth's can do the flowers and Krop's Jewelers can run specials on wedding rings. See? It's all falling into
place. I told you it was one of my Brilliant Ideas," she concluded with obvious and entirely appropriate self-satisfaction.

Kyle had to admit it was a brilliant idea and another creative way to draw tourists and shoppers to Finch's Crossing.
The historic crossroads had once been a bustling and thriving
town, before falling on hard times the last few years. But all
that was changing, thanks in large part to him. And, of course,
to the downtown merchants' willingness, sometimes reluctantly, to follow his advice.

"Morris Ladies Wear can order dresses and tuxedos, and

CHAPTER 3

we could hold the entire event in the ballroom at the Greystone Manor," he said excitedly, gaining momentum as ideas
started to tumble from his mind. Built in 1912, the Greystone
was now a bed and breakfast. The entire third floor was one
large ballroom that was rarely used. It was still decorated handsomely, with gold flowery wallpaper, chair rail, and
beautiful crystal chandeliers. "And maybe we can talk the new
bookstore owner into ordering invitations," added Kyle, believing he was being helpful.

There was an awkward pause after he mentioned the
bookstore, then Teppy bulldozed over him. "Reverend Frye
can do the services in the Methodist church."

"Great!" Kyle said succinctly, knowing he probably
wouldn't get to say much more than that now that Teppy was
on a roll.

"I know exactly what you are thinking," Teppy said. "And
it's brilliant."

Kyle had no idea what else was popping around in Teppy's
mind, but he listened attentively as Teppy continued.

"We can all practice on Autumn and Ethan's wedding. She
is going to need all the help we can give her to pull off a wedding in six weeks. I think we have just enough time to pull
together something nice. And if we have the Bridal Expo the
first week in May, we'll still have time to advertise it."

I've created *monsters*, Kyle thought to himself. *Monsters.*
First Stan and his internet dating and now Teppy and her

Brilliant Idea. He had no idea how she had cooked this up in the few hours since the Finch's Crossing rumor mill had spread the news about Autumn's wedding. But she was right on the mark. He had taught her well.

Teppy stood up and pushed the file closer to him. "I've put all of my thoughts and brainstorms in here," she said, pulling her hood up over her considerable updo. "Let's get together tomorrow and plan it all out. Better yet, let's have a special meeting of the Merchants Association. I'll start the phone tree, but right now I need to get some wedding things together to take over to Autumn's. Ta ta." And with that she flounced away, like a fuzzy elf off to run an errand for the Easter Bunny.

Kyle shook his head and laughed at the wedding frenzy that had descended on Finch's Crossing in a matter of a few hours. And he found himself right in the middle of it after all. *Wait until Autumn finds out,* he said to himself. *She is going to go berserk!*

CHAPTER 4

*S*PRING EASED OFF the interstate at Mt. Pleasant, drove through the charming town's dips and rises and headed toward Finch's Crossing. In just moments, she would see the World War I doughboy statue ahead of her, on the grounds of the American Legion Post. At the thought, the tension in her shoulders that had accompanied her all the way from Los Angeles diminished a little. She let out a huge sigh of relief as she drove past the familiar statue and continued onto Chestnut Street until she turned onto Loucks Avenue. When she pulled in front of her childhood home, the tears began to trickle. And when her sister Autumn appeared on the front porch in her customary paint-splattered coveralls, a paint-brush in one hand, Spring gulped down a sob and bounded out of the car.

"Spring?" Autumn hurried off the porch.

Spring sprinted up the walk, where she embraced Autumn as if she had not seen her in decades. "You have no idea how glad I am to see you. And to be home," Spring said, pulling away from the embrace to wipe her eyes.

"Oh my gosh, Spring!" Autumn exclaimed delightedly. "I can't believe you're actually here. What a wonderful surprise."

Spring watched as her sister's happy expression changed to concern. "Are you all right?" Autumn asked. "You look awful. Gorgeous, but awful. Like you drove straight here from Los Angeles."

"I did," Spring replied, as the sisters strolled up the walk arm in arm, went into the house and settled in overstuffed chairs in the morning room. "Almost. I only slept about six hours the whole trip. I really wanted to get here."

Spring looked around the cozy room, so comforted by the familiar trimmings of her childhood. She admired Autumn's paintings on the wall, stunning flowers all rendered in hues of white and off-white and a soft, shimmery silver. "I guess I just didn't know how badly."

Spring stared at her sister and marveled at how little she had aged since she last saw her. *Wow*, she thought, *she should have been the model in the family.*

"Why didn't you tell me you were coming?" Autumn asked softly. "I would have gotten your room ready and made us a nice dinner. Well, I would have made a nice dinner for myself and thrown some lettuce in a bowl for you."

Distracted, the humor was lost on Spring. "I was going to. I really was. I can't really explain it. I guess I was afraid it wouldn't suit you. That maybe you were too busy painting or had a show somewhere. Which might have postponed me leaving Los Angeles. Which might have made me not leave in the first place or at all. Or ever."

Autumn smiled kindly and took her sister's hand. "What is it, Spring?" she asked quietly. "I've never seen you so out of sorts. It's not like you to be so indecisive."

Spring buried her head in her hands and shook her head. "I know, I know. It's hard to explain. It's not exactly a mid-life crisis. It's just. . . I want something more than what I have now. I don't want to quit modeling, but I'm not going to be an A-list model forever. And if I'm not careful, the only job I'll be able to get will be a grandmother in old-people catalogs." She shivered at the thought, then hurried to explain. "Not that there's anything wrong with that. And it could be fun even, because it's something different. But I want more. Not something better, but something more substantial. Something that will challenge me."

"I always wondered if you would realize that one day," said Autumn, who had retrieved two mugs of tea from the kitchen and handed one to Spring. "You never really used your degree from the Fashion Institute. And then you got your MBA online. Why did you do that, by the way," Autumn asked, "if you weren't going to use it?"

"I guess just to prove to myself that I could," Spring said. "To prove there was more to me than good looks and a body for a runway or magazine spread. Now I want to do more. Go into a different side of the fashion business or design clothes. Or jewelry. Why not? Other people are doing it. I know with my name recognition I wouldn't have to worry about sales." Spring threw up her hands. "I don't really know exactly what my next project is going to be. Only that there is going to be one. And it will be in New York, which is where I'm headed."

"So Finch's Crossing is just a side trip?" Autumn playfully jabbed.

"Not at all. It's just that . . . well, I just felt like I couldn't really get started in New York without visiting you. Visiting home. Recharging a little. Working on my perspective."

"Totally get it," offered Autumn. "I'm so glad you came. It's not like you to take a detour, so it's even more of a pleasant surprise."

The two women sat silently for a minute, with Spring glancing about the room, basking in the homey familiarity of everything.

"And Chad?" Autumn asked hesitantly.

"Chad isn't in the picture anymore," Spring said. "In fact, in reality he didn't like the new picture I was painting. It's funny how things change. The change is so gradual, until all of a sudden you can barely believe you didn't notice it happening all along. Anyway, I think in a nutshell Chad just couldn't understand why I wanted to do something different, why I *have* to do something different. Honestly, he used me to build a life for himself. Of course, I just let him because I was getting what I needed at the time. Hate to admit it, but Chad had a lot to do with me being so successful. Especially at first. But as my star climbed, he didn't need to work nearly as hard. Jobs would just flow my way. He kinda went into maintenance mode. Just handling the nuts and bolts of everything, enjoying the perks, living for the moment, not really considering the future."

Autumn listened as Spring detailed her story.

"We started to fight a lot. Bad fights. The kind of fights you never really make up from. Not that I really wanted to make up, anyway. It finally just hit me one day, after a particularly nasty exchange. I realized he didn't love or respect me anymore, and I didn't love or respect him, either. There was just a chasm between us. So there you go. But enough of my sad story. I am officially beginning the next chapter of my life. Chad-free. Not in Los Angeles. In New York. And, believe me, I am far more energized and excited about my next chapter than I am sad or upset about Chad or leaving Los Angeles."

Autumn put her hand on Spring's and offered a warm, understanding, sisterly smile. "What can I do to help you? What do you need?"

"Just this," Spring answered, gesturing around the room

with her free hand. "To be home. To be with someone who loves and accepts me no matter what."

Spring stood up and wandered into the living room and Autumn followed. Spring loved to explore each and every nook and cranny of the house they had grown up in, which she did every time she came home. This house, and her memory of how it was when she was a child, anchored her. It represented a peaceful and happy constant that she could always fall back on. It was her reference point. Her method for re-establishing perspective.

"You moved the couch, and that's a new ottoman," Spring said. "I like it. It opens up the room." She continued into the dining room and immediately let out a gasp of surprise as she took in the bolts of fabric, piles of colored swatches, two small stacks of china dishes, and party favors—little tins of mints, small pouches of potpourri, and matchbooks with a bride and groom on the front. And was that a wedding veil hanging over an armchair by the window? And what on earth were those large pink plastic swan statues doing on Autumn's dining room table?

Spring faced her sister. "Are you planning your wedding?" she asked, accusatorily. "I thought you weren't getting married until next fall?"

Autumn laughed nervously and waved her arm around the room. "I was planning on telling you, honestly. I wouldn't dream of getting married without you. It all happened so fast.

Yesterday, actually."

"Good," Spring responded, with a little heft in her voice. "Because if you would have gotten married without me, I would have killed you."

Spring fingered the wedding veil while Autumn explained. "So what you see here are the fruits of the labor of the Merchants Association." She told her sister about the Bridal Expo and how the shopkeepers were doing a dry run on her wedding.

Spring grimaced visibly when Autumn mentioned the wedding was just six weeks away.

"And so," Autumn concluded, "I'm really at a loss. Meg says I should just chill but I'm not so sure. Kyle—that's Meg's boyfriend—works with the merchants doing their marketing, and he thinks I'll hurt their feelings if I resist their help."

Spring interrupted, "Meg has a boyfriend?" The news of Autumn's wedding was temporarily forgotten as she imagined grumpy Meg—clad in her customary jeans and plaid workman's shirt—with a beau. With her delicate features, natural beauty, and willowy figure, that girl could have been a model. "I can't believe Meg's been nice enough to hang on to a man," Spring laughed. It felt good to laugh.

"Well," Autumn grinned impishly, "I didn't say that she was nice to him. But don't worry about that now. Back to the wedding. Teppy Tartel is on a whirlwind and she is picking up everyone in her path. Even Stan is trying to think of a way to get his hardware store involved in our wedding."

Spring nodded, her planner's mind starting to churn. It felt good to have her head in this logical, orderly space.

"Groomsmen's gifts," she said, half-listening to her sister.

"What?" she heard Autumn ask, but she didn't answer. Her mind was preoccupied with the two words that had just popped into her mind. "Distraction" and "Project." Autumn's wedding and the Bridal Expo were just what she needed to clear her head while considering her own plans. And what better place to do that than in Finch's Crossing? It had all begun here for her anyway. As a teenager she had spent hours in her bedroom, meticulously studying fashion magazines, typically at the expense of her homework. She had even taken modeling classes at an agency in Pittsburgh. Here, back in the comfort of her old bedroom—which she knew Autumn had not changed—she could wrap herself in a cocoon of self-reflection and contemplate what to do next. She could think about her own plans while she helped Autumn with hers. And six weeks wasn't too long to be away from work. She didn't have anything booked until the end of May. And while she had planned to move into her new apartment the following week, she could call the building's doorman and ask him to supervise the delivery of her belongings. She knew plenty of people in New York who would be happy to do a favor for Spring Hamilton and pitch in if needed. There was no reason not to stay.

"Don't worry," she told Autumn, picking up a tin of mints

with the word "Hitched" stamped on it, a sweet smile flashing across her face. "Leave it to me. I'll work with the merchants and before you know it, you'll have the wedding of your dreams."

Spring had a lot of work to do, if the assortment of wedding paraphernalia in the dining room was any indication. She knew the merchants—whom she had known all her life—meant well. She would have to be mindful of their feelings and employ some very tactful prodding and maneuvering. But first things first. She had to get rid of those pink swans.

* * *

Spring knew she would need to win over Teppy if she had any hope of creating a Bridal Expo committee of the Merchants Association and offer to chair it. Teppy was a formidable force and a savvy businesswoman.

Spring watched as Teppy made her way through the tables in the Greystone Manor's fine dining restaurant, raising her hand as soon as she saw Spring seated at her table.

"Hi, Teppy," Spring said eagerly and jumped up to give her a hug. Teppy was older than Spring by a good fifteen years, and they had known each other as acquaintances for as long as Spring could remember. And since Autumn was friends with just about everyone in Finch's Crossing, Spring felt she could count them—including Teppy—as friends by association.

"I was so surprised when you called, and I didn't even know you had come back to town," Teppy said, settling herself and her handbag at the table. "After you called I said to my girls, 'Now what could a famous fashion model want with little ol' me?' So, of course, I had to come find out." She turned to the waitress, who was hovering at the edge of table. "I'll have a glass of the house Merlot, please," she said smiling, then returned her gaze to Spring, expectantly.

"How've you been, Teppy?" Spring asked, taking a sip of her white wine. "Autumn was telling me how Kyle Oswald has practically doubled everyone's business in the past year."

"Is that what you wanted to see me about?" Teppy asked, wondering if the gorgeous woman seated opposite her was thinking of investing in her business. *Hmmm, she thought. Should I do it?* It would mean an influx of cash, maybe she could even expand, open another location in Mt. Pleasant, or Greensburg. She felt one of her Brilliant Ideas coming on, when she realized Spring was calling her name.

"Teppy? Teppy? Are you okay?" Spring was asking, leaning forward across the table, her hand on Teppy's arm.

"Oh yes, just fine," Teppy replied, eagerly accepting her wine glass from the waitress and taking a sip. "I was just thinking about something pertaining to my shop."

The women chatted amiably about Teppy's inventory and how she had begun to sell Christmas items online and now enjoyed a thriving Christmas business year-round.

"And, of course," Teppy said, "there's my most recent project."

"The Bridal Expo," Spring chimed in. "Of course, I heard about it from Autumn. How on earth are you going to find the time to do all this between running your shop and your online business?" Spring asked, prodding.

"I hadn't really thought about it," Teppy observed. "Whenever I have one of my Brilliant Ideas, I just go with it. Somehow it always gets done. And then there's Kyle. That sweet man makes anything he touches turn to gold."

"So I've heard," Spring agreed, "but isn't he busy getting his own marketing company off the ground and working one on one with the merchants?"

"I suppose he is," Teppy said wistfully, sipping her wine. Kyle had looked a little harried when she had approached him with the idea for the Bridal Expo. Was it unfair of her—of all the merchants—to lean so heavily on him for help?

"What if I were to help?" Spring said enthusiastically.

"Help?" Teppy asked. "How?"

"With the Bridal Expo," Spring repeated. "You have so much on your plate already."

Teppy put down her glass and gazed at Spring.

"Of course," Teppy exclaimed. "A celebrity endorsement. That's exactly what we need. You will lend cachet to the event and draw in the crowds. How sweet of you to ask."

"Actually," Spring began, "I was thinking more along the lines of helping you with the committee. I could co-chair it with you," she hurried to say. "Since it was your idea. And, of course, I would love to add my 'cachet' if you think that would help."

Teppy considered Spring's offer, gazing into her wine glass as if looking for the answer. She was overwhelmed, that was true. Between her shop, online business, and two daughters, plus her position as chairperson of the Merchants Association, she did have a lot going on.

"I think a co-chair would be quite helpful," Teppy answered, trying not to feel her Brilliant Idea slipping away from her. Spring Hamilton would be an incredible asset, certain to have loads of experience from runway shows and fashion shoots. And surely she knew many journalists and celebrity bloggers. "Let's do it!" Teppy decided.

Spring raised her glass, and Teppy followed suit. "To Teppy's Brilliant Ideas and Finch's Crossing's first-ever Bridal Expo!" The two clinked glasses, then Spring got down to business.

"Now I know you're billing Finch's Crossing as a destination wedding location for beautiful fall weddings, and that's perfect because the brides need lead time to find a venue and all the vendors." She paused to let Teppy chime in.

"That's right. And we want to show that Finch's Crossing can be a one-stop shop for all your wedding needs."

"Exactly," Spring agreed, enthusiastically. "I'd like your permission to pull together some information about all the offerings and make some marketing and other plans for the

Expo. I can present them at the next Merchants Association meeting. If you're okay with it, that is."

Teppy nodded. She knew this was the right thing to do. Having a celebrity associated with the event would be a big help, but having someone to actually help with the work was even more important.

"That sounds just fine," Teppy beamed. "And I know you're the right woman for the job."

Spring smiled in return. She was just a little surprised how happy she was that she could move forward with this new project. She could use her expertise and contacts to create a beautiful event. And it would keep her mind off of Chad. In the meantime, she would be free to consider the next steps in her career. Perhaps event planning would be among them.

CHAPTER 5

*M*EG, ARE YOU sure you can make this happen?" Autumn asked. "I mean, I know you are well intentioned and ..."

The two women were sitting at a bistro table outside Miss Elsie's Tea Room, the March day unusually warm and sunny.

Meg interrupted her best friend, holding up her hand. "Have I ever, in the twenty years we have known each other, let you down?"

Let her down? Autumn thought on that. Meg had certainly exasperated her to no end. Her blunt personality grated on her in ways that ventured into a whole new dimension. Meg annoyed her, irritated her, and occasionally embarrassed her. Yes. Meg had done all those things. But let her down? No, that had never happened.

"What's the worst thing that could happen if Bryan doesn't show up?" Meg asked. Autumn couldn't read her friend's poker face.

"Meg," Autumn said, her voice rising with concern.

"Autumn," Meg shot back.

The two friends stared at each other for long seconds before Meg winked and said, "April Fool's! Gotcha!"

"It's just that we are putting so much into the wedding and all Heather talks about is the wish she gave to Santa. And there is so much to get done in a short period of time."

Meg crossed her arms against her chest. "I thought you had a little wedding planning gang to help you?"

"About that," Autumn began, but Meg didn't let her finish.

"I think you had better just submit yourself to this one, Autumn. Kyle has created a monster and now with this Bridal Expo in their minds, the downtown merchants are completely unleashed, and I'm afraid there's no pulling them back now. Besides, you'll hurt their feelings, not to mention the momentum."

Autumn's brain filled with images of the tulle tutu in Teppy Tartel's boutique, the reindeer antlers Miss Elsie had worn at Christmastime the previous year, and the plastic flowers DeMuth's florist shop proudly displayed in the front window each winter. She shuddered.

"You're right, I guess," Autumn agreed reluctantly.

"Don't worry," Meg encouraged. "I've got that one under control, too. All you need is an infiltrator to subtly guide the group's ideas until what our spy has suggested is actually considered their idea in the first place. It's brilliant," Meg finished triumphantly.

"Infiltrator? Spy? What are you talking about?"

"Martha, of course. You tell Martha what you want and Martha will influence the merchants. She's been your neighbor and friend long enough to know your tastes. You didn't think we were going to let the merchants do this all by themselves, did you?" Meg winked again.

* * *

That evening Ethan appeared on Autumn's doorstep in a tuxedo. He had instructed her to wear the red dress she had worn the previous Christmas, and she emerged as beautiful as she had been then. And perhaps even more so. He helped her into her coat and as they headed out, Autumn called good-bye to Spring who was so absorbed with her spreadsheets and business plan that she barely lifted a distracted wave in return.

Autumn saw the horse and carriage as soon as they stepped onto the front porch.

"Oh, Ethan," she exclaimed, "where on earth did you get this?"

"Do you like it?"

"Like it? I love it. But what's the occasion?"

"Remember when I proposed last year?"

"Vaguely," Autumn joked. Then she added seriously, "You told me you had always imagined proposing to someone with a grand gesture." She squeezed his hand. "But I didn't need a grand gesture."

"I know. But it's important to me and I want you to have your romantic proposal," Ethan responded. "Or at least a romantic, after-the-fact proposal, just to check in to see if everything is proceeding as scheduled."

Autumn wrapped her arms around his neck and nuzzled him. "Ethan Rasmussen, you never cease to amaze me."

They heard the horse whinny so they climbed into the carriage, greeting the driver.

"Where did you find him?" Autumn whispered, nodding to the driver as Ethan covered their legs with a blanket.

"I was driving home from Pittsburgh a few days ago and I saw him out in the field, waxing the carriage. Turns out he used to do this in Pittsburgh but he retired and settled in Connellsville. He breaks it out every so often for special occasions. Apparently, he also has two old trolleys that he keeps in working order, too. He's a bit of a character."

"Oh, let's go see Heather," Autumn said excitedly.

"Already on our way," Ethan winked at her.

After they had gone around the block with Heather and returned her to Martha's house, the horse trotted through the neighborhood and stopped along Pittsburgh Street, behind a stretch limo.

"This is where we get off," Ethan said, helping Autumn out of the carriage.

"Oh, Ethan! This is incredible. But it must be so expensive."

"Shhh," he cut her off. "I was going to tell you over dinner. I got a promotion today. I was pretty sure I had it last week but didn't want to tell you until it was official." He squeezed her hand and helped her into the limo where champagne was chilling in a silver ice bucket next to two glasses.

"It's the same champagne you had at my first proposal," Autumn observed. She laid her head on his shoulder.

Over a candlelit dinner at the Greystone they discussed the wedding.

"I think we can pull it off," Autumn said. "And with the merchants helping…well, let's just say that will either make things easier or a lot harder. It's too soon to tell."

"I think Kyle will keep an eye on them," Ethan assured her.

"But he's not a wedding planner. I'm sure he never imagined in his life that he would be planning a Bridal Expo. In any event, there's really only one thing that I am worried about. Everything else—the reception, dress, flowers—is just window dressing," Autumn said.

"Don't tell me. Let me guess," Ethan said. "You're worried about Meg getting Bryan here on time."

"Do you trust her?" Ethan reached across the table and took her hands. Autumn nodded, and Ethan continued. "Do you think if she explained it, you really would be more comfortable? After all, whatever scheme she has up her sleeve has got to be so incredibly farfetched as to not be believable. So maybe if you did know, it wouldn't make a difference, because you still wouldn't believe she could pull it off."

"That's some kind of circular reasoning." Autumn laughed, but was still not convinced. She decided to drop the subject and was glad when Ethan went on to another topic of conversation.

"I want to talk about something else, too. Something just as important as us getting married. I've been thinking about it for a while. What would you say about adopting Heather?"

Tears welled in Autumn's bright turquoise eyes and she clasped her face in her hands. "I've been thinking the same thing, and I knew you would want it, too. I just don't know about how to approach Heather. She was old enough when her parents died that I don't think she will ever forget them."

"It's not something we have to rush out and do today. We have some time to figure it out."

Autumn raised her champagne glass in a toast. "Yep, plenty of time. Six weeks."

"Actually," Ethan corrected, "since today is about over, you really only have five weeks and six days!"

* * *

Ethan wandered into Ten Oaks Kennel, past the dog runs and into the office where Meg was on the phone. Her pet German shepherd, Spike, who didn't live up to his name, got up from his usual spot under Meg's desk and pawed over to nuzzle Ethan's knees and beg for treats.

Ethan sat down and Spike sat appreciatively next to him. They both stared at Meg who was yelling something about "getting it done fast, buddy. You think I'm grumpy now? Wait till I'm mad."

She paused before lowering her voice to say, "Okay, now that sounds better. See how easy it was?" And she slammed down the phone.

Before Ethan could say anything in way of greeting, Meg said, "I know why you're here and the answer is 'no' I'm not telling you how I'm going to get Bryan home for the wedding. The thing is, I really can't, no, *shouldn't* tell you. I've sort of given my word."

Ethan weighed Meg's comments. He had been in a similar situation when he learned that his best friends had named him Heather's guardian in their will. Having served together with Heather's father in Afghanistan, and having saved each other's lives in the course of five minutes, there was a bond between them. Ethan knew that he had to honor his friend's wish, no matter what.

"You know you're making Autumn crazy," he said. "She's worried out of her mind. I hate to see her like this. It's a happy time, but she can't enjoy it because she's worried that you can't fulfill your promise and Heather will be devastated. She's finally acting like a normal little girl. The nightmares are completely gone. I'd hate for another disappointment to set her back."

"Oh, for goodness sakes," Meg roared. "Way to lay it on thick. I can't tell you because you will tell Autumn and somehow everyone will find out, and well, let's just say that would be very, very bad."

Spike got up from his seat next to Ethan and went back to lie at his mistress's feet. Meg petted him as she let Ethan build his argument.

"You're being so cryptic, Meg," Ethan responded. "How about if you tell me, right now. And then I tell Autumn that she has nothing to worry about. Would that work?"

"I don't like it one bit," Meg said. "But you're right about Autumn not enjoying the wedding planning and Heather not being disappointed. And I know the stress I'm causing is partly responsible for that. But how will you convince her that she has nothing to worry about and get her to believe you to the point that she can enjoy herself?"

"I guess that depends on what you tell me," he joked. "Okay, seriously, though. You just leave that part to me, okay?"

"I need your word, Ethan," Meg said in a serious voice, without even a hint of her typical sarcasm.

"You have it," he answered with equal graveness.

Even Spike seemed to understand the gravity of the situation, a short whimper emanating from him.

Meg took a deep breath and began. "A few years ago, I

worked with the Washington, D.C. police chief. And let's just say that in the course of working with him, I learned some things, and saw some things—very disturbing things of a highly personal nature—that I did not want to know. If I had divulged what I knew to anyone publicly, that would be the end of his career and would cause a ripple effect throughout his family, particularly impacting his father."

She saw that Ethan was about to speak, and put him off with a raised hand. "Just wait," she said. "I'll get to that."

"So," she continued, somewhat dramatically, as she was beginning to enjoy herself. She had been itching to tell someone this story, but she had promised that she wouldn't, so she never had. She could skate around her word, by not divulging the salacious details.

"Of course, I told this police chief that I had no interest in telling anyone what I knew and I'd as soon forget the whole thing. Let me just say again that this situation was very, very bad. As a thank-you for my understanding, discretion, and generosity of spirit, let's say he told me that he 'owed me one,' and that whenever I needed something, no matter what it was, he would make it happen. He said there was no request too large that he wouldn't be able to fulfill. I have not yet called in this chit."

"I don't understand," Ethan said, perplexed. "What does that have to do with Bryan?"

Meg paused. "Remember I mentioned the police chief's father?"

Ethan nodded.

"The father is no other than the Secretary of State. And, to help matters even more, this police chief's uncle is the chairman of the Joint Chiefs of Staff. As in, the highest ranking military official in the U.S. Armed Forces."

Ethan just stared at her. "Oh," was all he could manage. "That's quite a family."

Meg smiled sweetly. "So, as you can see, I've got this under control. And if you ever tell Autumn or any other human being on earth, I will set my dogs on you."

She kept her eyes steeled. And although she was smiling—something she didn't do often—Ethan shivered, knowing full well that she meant what she said.

"Okay then," he said, getting up. "Thank you for indulging me. I can reassure Autumn and we can all continue on, happy in the knowledge that you can keep your promise."

"And don't you forget it!" Meg warned as Ethan retreated.

* * *

After Ethan was safely in his car and driving away, Meg spun the combination of the little floor safe in her office and pulled out a stack of bridal magazines and a wedding planning book, all of which she had ordered online to avoid any rumors or gossip that most assuredly would have surfaced were she seen buying them in the new bookstore. She probably could have dashed in and out of the Wal-Mart in Mt. Pleasant without being seen. But Meg didn't need the hassle. She hated hassle of any kind, like the canine trainer at the Nashville Police Department, whom she had just spoken to, who wanted her to Jump Through Unnecessary Hoops. Hassle.

She plopped down in her desk chair and eased back, crossing her legs at the ankles on top of her messy desk. She had to push a stack of file folders out of the way and then watched them fall to the floor, scattering the contents. She turned back to one of the bridal magazines and opened it to the middle.

Granted, Meg loved Kyle, in her own peculiar way. But he knew she loved him and that was all that was important. But a wedding, with a puffy marshmallow dress, dancing at a reception, and bridesmaids? That was just out of the question. Trouble was, Meg knew Kyle would want a big wedding. Coming from a broken home , he romanticized everything in his life, from the tree-lined streets of Finch's Crossing to the cozy apartment he had made for himself over his marketing office on Pittsburgh Street. If he bought one more "Live, Laugh, Love" or "Happy is the Home with Love," pillow from Teppy's boutique, she was going to take an ax to them. He even had a "Home Spooked Home" door hanger for Halloween, which he couldn't wait to use.

Meg marveled that she had attracted such a sweet and kind person, putting some truth into the "opposites attract" theory. She knew she dressed like a man, substituting comfort for fashion. She flipped through the bridesmaids section of the wedding planning book, her eyes darting from one beautifully clad woman to another. Next, the groomsmen. All so handsome in their tuxedos. She imagined a tuxedo-clad Kyle watching from the church altar as she walked down the aisle in her jeans and a loose plaid shirt. Until now, she had never considered if her choice of clothing ever bothered Kyle. In fact, she had never considered her clothes beyond putting them on in the morning and taking them off at night. She thought of Kyle in his fashionable designer jeans, which he wore so expertly it made her shiver to look at him. His dress shirts were always pressed and starched. She looked down at her wrinkled, dirt-covered jeans and then her scuffed boots. Kyle wore multiple styles and colors of Pumas and Adidas sneakers, and kept them pristine, putting them back in their respective boxes after each wear.

Meg threw down the book with disgust and slammed the magazine on top of it. She scowled at them. She shouldn't have gone there, she scolded herself. It was just as bad as googling your symptoms or heading straight for webmd.com when you have the flu. And now all of it was playing over and over again in her head. Dresses. Tuxedos. And there would be shoes. High-heeled shoes. Just exactly what she didn't need and despised. Hassle. She imagined herself at a wedding shower in Autumn's living room, surrounded by bride-themed decorations and tiny sandwiches catered by Miss Elsie. She put her head in her hands and groaned. A long, loud groan. It was all just one big hassle that would stretch out over weeks, and at the end of it she'd have to wear a big puffy dress that would make her look ridiculous. She would be the laughing stock of Finch's Crossing, the butt of jokes, and the main conversation at the Sunset Boys' gab sessions. No, thank you. She was never getting married. It was as simple, and as complicated, as that.

I just can't tell Kyle that, she told herself, wondering how long she could string him along before having to face him and tell the truth.

* * *

"Yoo hoo," Martha Kelly cooed as she walked up to the back door of Autumn's house. The Kellys and Hamiltons had been neighbors for years and had quickly beaten a path between the two properties, a path that never wavered due to Martha and Autumn's deep friendship. "A little bird told me you had a visitor," she said as Autumn opened the door and let Martha into the cozy kitchen.

"Now who could that have been?" Autumn asked, laughing, knowing full well that Teppy would have happily shared the news that Spring Hamilton not only was back in town, but was going to headline the Bridal Expo.

"Does she know yet?" Martha asked, putting a plate of cookies on the table.

Autumn shook her head and put her finger to her lips.

"Spring, there's someone here to see you," she called, and the two women walked into the dining room where Spring had all sorts of papers and colored photos she'd printed from the internet, strewn every which way.

When Spring saw Martha, she rushed to give the older woman a big hug, and the two hung on to each other for a long time. "I was so sorry to hear about Denise and Troy," she said, when they pulled back, but still clasped hands.

"Thank you, dear. And thank you for the flowers and the generous donation to the church. It meant so much to me. But now, let's talk about happier things." She gestured to the table. "What on earth have you got going on here?"

Spring moved to the table, still holding on to Martha's hand, then motioned for her and Autumn to sit down.

"I'm getting ready for the next Merchants Association meeting. Teppy has agreed to let me run the committee to organize the Bridal Expo."

"The Merchants Association has committees?" Martha asked, surprised.

"They do now," Autumn offered, "thanks to Spring."

Martha picked up a piece of paper with a bar graph on it. "What's this?" she asked and turned the paper around.

"I've made a list of all the vendors who can participate in the Expo, then correlated what they have to offer to those items essential to any wedding, then calculated the need for each of those essentials, weighing them against the percentage of offerings the vendors have."

Martha and Autumn looked at each other. "What?" said

Martha. And they all laughed. "You know, never mind," she continued. "As long as you know what you're doing, then I don't need to understand a word you just said. But I want to know about you. After just a few days, the word is already out on the street that you've left modeling and are opening a jewelry business in Mt. Pleasant. According to the Sunset Boys, Lane at Krop's Jewelers is a little more than worried. That shop has been a fixture on Pittsburgh Street in Finch's Crossing for more than seventy-five years." She stopped speaking as Autumn and Spring started laughing. "What? What's so funny?"

"As usual, those old men have it all wrong," Autumn said fondly.

"I'm moving to New York City to expand my career, and I don't know what I'm going to do yet. Jewelry designing—not selling—is just one of the things I'm thinking about. I'm also considering becoming a lifestyle blogger or running my own YouTube channel."

"Whatever those things are, dear," Martha quipped, "I know you will excel at them. You always had a head for business. I remember when you were in tenth grade and had a project on fashion merchandising, and you came into the library asking for books on psychology. I tried to steer you to the research materials your teacher had suggested, but you were adamant. You wanted books on psychology and human behavior."

CHAPTER 5

"I remember that!" Autumn exclaimed at the memory. "We all thought that she was going to totally bomb the course and get an F, because her project was supposed to be on fashion merchandising."

Spring picked up the trail. "So I decided to take a look at what makes people make decisions and choose one thing over another. And I used that as the basis for my paper. It was simply research to back up my merchandising ideas. It seemed pretty reasonable to me."

"I learned never to doubt you again. Whatever you wanted to check out of the library, I never questioned you again." Martha put the piece of paper back on the table. "I seem to remember that your paper was entered into a state competition," Martha said. "You and your boyfri…"

Martha cut herself off, but the word hung in the room, and there was an awkward silence. Martha was kicking herself for mentioning him. But, after all, it was going to come up sooner or later.

Spring pretended she hadn't heard what Martha had started to say and began arranging the papers into piles. "A head for business notwithstanding," she said, "I have a lot of research and organizing to do to get everyone on board, plot out next steps and action items, and assign tasks to each merchant. But first, I need to swing down to Pittsburgh Street and hit the shops for some supplies."

She stood and grabbed her handbag and then headed for

the back door. Martha and Autumn were close on her heels.

"Spring, before you go," Autumn began, but Spring interrupted her, a well-manicured hand on the door handle.

"Later, A," she said over her shoulder. "I've got a lot of work to do. So good to see you again, Martha. I know we'll be seeing a lot more of each other!"

"But Spring," Autumn said louder, as she followed her sister out the door. "There's something you really need to know before you head downtown."

Spring looked back mischievously. "Sis, this town has barely changed in twenty years. I don't think there's anything I don't know about it." She practically floated through the door and was on her way.

Martha put her hand on Autumn's shoulder. "You tried," she said quietly. "That's all you could do. It's not your fault she wouldn't listen."

* * *

Happy to be home, Spring decided to walk downtown, a ten-minute stroll from Autumn's house on Loucks Avenue. She walked down the familiar street, turned onto Grove, and then was in the heart of the commercial district. McCrory's Five and Dime had been her favorite store as a child. The four Hamilton sisters went there or to Hoffman's Drugstore every Saturday with their pocket money. She laughed as she remembered how different the four sisters were. Summer, the youngest and a free spirit, spent her money on the first thing that caught her eye. Winter, the oldest, looked but never bought. She saved her money until she found something of high quality that she really wanted. Autumn always headed for the art supplies. No surprise there. And Spring, being practical, organized, and logical, spent most of her money on practical things and allowed herself to splurge only once every little while. Somehow the treats she allowed herself made them all the sweeter.

She would hit the five and dime and the drugstore first, she decided. She needed to buy supplies: notebooks, pens, sheet protectors. She'd need graph paper and binders for handbooks. Each Merchants Association member would have a handbook, or "Run of Show," as it was called in the fashion industry. Once Spring was through with the merchants, everyone would know, down to the button, boutonniere, and minute what they were doing, when they were doing it, for how much, and why.

The first part of her mission completed, she was anxious to see what the new bookstore had in terms of bridal magazines and books. She remembered the shop fondly. When she and her sisters were little girls, it was called the Provident Bookstore and was run by Mennonites. Though a religious-oriented store, the sweet ladies who owned it stocked small sticker books, little dolls, book marks with tassels, tiny porcelain animals, and other treasures.

Spring stopped in front, pleased that the new owner had

kept the same large bay window to the right of the door. She looked up and was surprised to see her name on the sign, which read "Wellspring Books." Just a coincidence, she thought, as she opened the door and walked through. And in an instant, she knew it was not a coincidence, for standing behind the counter ringing up a customer, stood the man she had thought she would marry and live happily ever after with. She turned to leave, knowing he hadn't seen her yet. But it was too late. He had looked up to watch another customer leave the store and spotted her. Spring stood, holding the door open, and stared at him, not knowing what to do. He had aged since high school. After all, it had been seventeen years, but it had not affected his looks. Second-generation Italian, Gabriel Vignaroli had glossy black hair and deep brown eyes that had stolen her soul so many years before.

"Spring," he said, simply, his voice reaching her ears and almost knocking her over. "Don't go."

CHAPTER 6

REFLEXIVELY, SPRING STEPPED out of the doorway and let the store's last customer pass through before she let go of the handle.

Gabe was next to her in an instant, and he reached around her to lock the door with one hand and turn his window sign from "Open" to "Closed" with the other.

They stood staring at each other until Gabe broke the silence. His voice was thick with an emotion he had carried with him for almost two decades. "You don't know how glad I am to see you. I thought I'd never see you again."

"What did you expect?" Spring replied smartly. It wasn't like her to be confrontational and rattle off clever retorts without thinking through the consequences of her words first.

"You moved back to Finch's Crossing after twenty years and named your store after me."

Gabe reddened and Spring crossed her arms triumphantly across her chest. "Was there anything else?" she asked, cocking her head and giving him a cruel smile.

"Don't be like this, Spring," he said.

"Like what?" she spat back.

"This isn't you." He motioned at her. "This mean, abrasive person."

"And after twenty years with no contact, how do you presume to know me?"

Gabe didn't reply. She was right. He had made a mistake all those years ago when she had asked him to move to Los Angeles with her after they graduated from high school. She had some good leads with modeling agencies and if they pooled their resources and combined their incomes, they could have afforded a decent place to live. But after four years of being high school sweethearts, Gabe broke it off a few days after graduation.

Gabe held up his hands as if in defeat. "You're right, Spring. About everything. About leaving you, about not knowing you. I owe you an explanation. I've agonized over it for almost twenty years."

"You owe me nothing because I don't want anything from you," she said quietly, back to her logical self. "Whatever you've been thinking about for twenty years doesn't exist anymore.

We've both moved on. We're not those two kids anymore."

"You don't know how many times I picked up the phone to call you," he said as she turned to leave. "I got your number from your mother and carried it around with me."

"She never told me that," Spring said, turning back to face him, surprised that her loving, caring mother would withhold something that important from her.

Gabe shrugged. "She probably didn't want you to get hurt again. She probably figured that if I didn't call, you wouldn't have gotten your hopes up for nothing. I can't blame her. But here, I want to show you something."

He reached into the back pocket of his jeans and took out a worn leather wallet the color of mahogany. She recognized it as the one she had given him their last Christmas together. But that wasn't what made the tears flow. He extracted a worn piece of notebook paper, folded and refolded into tiny squares, the creases shabby with the passing of time. He handed it to her. She took it reluctantly and unfolded each square slowly until the paper expanded to its full size, and she saw her old Los Angeles phone number, still visible in faint pencil, scribbled under her name, with a heart drawn next to it. Scattered over the paper were a series of check marks. There must have been three hundred of them.

She pointed to them. "What are those?"

"Nothing," he said, taking the paper from her hands and folding it back into a tiny square.

"Listen," she said. "If you think you owe me something, then at the very least tell me what all those marks are."

He looked at her for a long moment. "Those were all the times I dialed your number and hung up before I let it ring."

"I don't understand." Spring could barely get the words out. She let the tears flow.

He pulled her close, and she let him. He whispered into her hair, "I'm so sorry I hurt you. I was a jerk. I was young. And I thought I didn't deserve you. I thought I would hold you back. I was just a boy from a working-class family. My father could barely make ends meet with his little news stand and stationery store. I was destined for a factory job or community college and you were Spring Hamilton."

She pulled away from him. "But I was always Spring Hamilton." She managed a smile.

"But suddenly you were going to be famous model Spring Hamilton. I didn't know how to handle that. I was afraid we would get to California and you would get tired of me once you saw I couldn't fit in with a fancy new lifestyle." He shook his head. "It was stupid. I know that now."

"But," she sputtered, "we had no way of knowing what would happen. It was going to be you and me together on the adventure of our lives. I never, ever gave you any indication that I thought that way. I loved you so much. You were my everything. You were my future. Those first years in Los Angeles without you were so painful you can't even imagine. Yes, I was successful and had fancy friends." She used air quotes on the word "fancy." "But those days, all I wanted was you."

"And now?" he asked, with a sly smile.

"Now?" she said incredulously. "There is no now." And she turned on her heel and left the store. But she didn't quite believe her own words. It *had* been a long time. They were adults now. But those check marks. All of those check marks. She imagined each one as a kiss between them that had never happened.

* * *

Teppy was in her display window when Ducky came in with the mail. Teppy was excited about getting her Brilliant Idea off the ground, and she didn't even mind that Spring Hamilton had taken the project over. With the growth of her online business and the increased foot traffic on Pittsburgh Street, Teppy had her hands full with the Et Cetera Shop. Yes, she was pleased that Spring had assumed ownership of the project. The rest of them could follow along and do their part.

"Greetings, Et Cetera Shop," Ducky declared as she wheeled in her mail cart and riffled through it before producing a rubber-banded stack. Ducky had the quirky habit of addressing people by the name of their business, rather than their first names. "How are you today?"

Teppy, always at the ready with a clever retort, replied, "I'm just fine, thank you. You know, getting all my ducks in a row."

"Harrumph," Ducky replied. "Toodles. Catch you on the

flip side."

"Ten four, Rubber Ducky," Teppy replied, and the two enjoyed a giggle as Ducky left and Teppy picked up the stack of mail.

She flipped through the usual coupon books, bills, and ad circulars and was pleased to see a hand-written envelope. No one wrote letters anymore, she thought mournfully. As she slid open the envelope, she had another one of her Brilliant Ideas.

I'll have a letter-writing class here in the shop and sell stationery and special pens. Miss Elsie can cater and we'll have a proper afternoon tea.

Her enthusiasm drained away when she pulled a single sheet of paper from the envelope. She clutched it to her chest and looked around the empty store, as if someone was going to jump out at her. She rushed to the front door, pulled down the shade, and locked it. She glanced out the front picture window, which overlooked the town green and Gazebo Park, where the annual Fall Festival was held. She turned her head back and forth, back and forth. She saw Ducky stroll down the sidewalk toward the Westmoreland County Courthouse. A white delivery van had pulled up in front of Miss Elsie's Tea Room across Everson Avenue, which she thought was rather strange because Miss Elsie baked everything fresh on the premises. She stared hard at the driver while he exited the vehicle and walked around back to go in through tiny O'Neill Alley, which ran behind all the shops on the south side of Pittsburgh Street. When he came back into sight, she saw that he was holding a stack of PVC pipes, and she hurriedly closed the curtains in the window and retreated to the back room.

Teppy sat on the stool at the island in her workroom. She looked at her pretty china plate with a yellow daisy chain design. She had treated herself to a slice of almond cake from Miss Elsie's, along with a cappuccino. She planned to take a break after finishing the window display and savor her treat. She might even meditate afterwards, just for a few minutes, and express a few thoughts of gratitude for her wonderful life. But now, all of that was ruined.

She had only glanced at the letter when she pulled it from the envelope, but she knew what it said. Someone had discovered a secret. Not a terrible secret, like hiding a criminal past, but still, it was something that would embarrass her in front of her friends and colleagues.

She pushed the coffee and cake out of the way and lay the letter in front of her. Pasted in the middle was a picture of Martha Stewart, the lifestyle queen of the world as far as Teppy was concerned. Teppy had read all of Martha's books and adopted a lot of her recipes and decorating ideas into her own home. Under the picture was scrawled:

"All of a sudden, everyone is going to know that you aren't Martha Stewart's cousin.

And when they do, it's boo hoo hoo for you."

Well, really, Teppy thought to herself. Yes, it was true that

Martha Stewart was not her cousin, and no, she did not go to visit her once a year at her mansion in Connecticut. She had never been to her office in Manhattan. It had happened so innocently. Someone had remarked at a Merchants Association meeting how much she looked like Martha Stewart. Teppy jokingly replied that she was Martha's cousin. Teppy didn't think anything of it until a few days later when people started arriving at her shop with books to be autographed. What could she do? She held on to them for a few weeks then returned them with forged autographs. What could it hurt? Who would ever find out?

Who, indeed? No one had ever called her on the lie. Well, she wouldn't call it a lie, exactly. It had been a misunderstanding that she simply never corrected. It was a boost to her own business, since she was selling a lifestyle as well, only on a much smaller scale. To be related to Martha Stewart was a professional accomplishment.

And now, someone knew. And that someone was going to embarrass her in front of the entire town. Teppy mentally flipped through a list of her friends and colleagues and couldn't think of even a one that would want to hurt her in this way. Not even grumpy Meg Overly at Ten Oaks Kennel. Although Meg wanted everyone to think she was gruff and tough, Teppy knew there was a softer side to the young woman. Every year during Teppy's holiday toy drive for the Marine Corps Toys for Tots campaign, Meg arranged for hundreds of dollars' worth of toys to be delivered to her store. The gift was always anonymous. But once, there was a mix-up with the paperwork and the invoice mistakenly arrived with the delivery. Teppy smiled at the memory, preferring it to having to think about how her reputation was about to be trashed across the whole town. How would it happen? Would the person sell the story to the *News-Observer?* Or announce it at the next Merchants Associations meeting? Teppy's stomach roiled as she thought of flyers being posted on telephone poles and street lamps up and down Pittsburgh Street.

Just a few moments ago she had been brimming with ideas and gratitude. Now, she felt like a deflated balloon. And what was she going to do with it? Certainly, she couldn't take it home or leave it in her office. She looked around the small workroom and settled on a Georgia O'Keefe print on the wall behind her. She took it down and carefully leaned it against the wall. Then she tucked the letter back into the envelope and taped the envelope to the back of the print.

Teppy returned the print to the wall and observed sadly that the trouble with not being able to think of someone who would do such a thing was that she would now be suspicious of everyone around her. Friends and neighbors, whom she trusted to water her plants when she was on vacation or take her cash deposit to the bank when the store was slammed with customers, were now suspects in a cruel game.

Teppy stayed in the store as long as she felt she could without arousing the suspicions of her daughters, who were no doubt at home waiting for their dinner. She saw them in her mind's eye, hunched over phones or tablets, earbuds in place. As she turned out the lights, locked the door, and made her way across the street to the municipal parking lot, she thought of the relationship she had with them. Grateful that the parking lot was empty, she tossed her purse across the console into the passenger seat and slid in after it.

Angelique and Jessica were good girls. Despite the divorce, she and Roger made an excellent parenting team. Their daughters were polite, thoughtful, and kind. They excelled in school, and Teppy was fairly certain that they confided things in her that many daughters would hesitate to talk to their parents about. She had taught her girls to be honest, telling them that nothing good came from a lie.

Teppy drove the long way home, consumed with guilt and shame. She was a terrible hypocrite. More than worrying what her friends and neighbors thought of her, Teppy's heart sagged at the notion that she had let her daughters down. What would they think of her? More importantly, could they ever forgive her? Could she ever forgive herself?

* * *

Stan was in a terrible mood. He was stuck in the back room of his hardware store because Ducky and Marlene had started chatting about the Bridal Expo and were going on and on. If he hadn't had three cups of coffee earlier, this prolonged conversation at the checkout counter would not have been a problem. But nature was not just calling, it was beating down his door. He didn't have a choice. Stan slowly opened the office door and slipped around the corner. He was almost down the corridor and out of sight when Johnny called out, somewhat too loudly, "Hey, Stan! Did you know about this new Bridal Expo? Ducky and Maureen here have just been talking about it."

Of course he knew. And Johnny knew he knew. They had just talked about groomsmen's gifts that morning. Johnny was just messing with him, having caught Stan looking at Ducky's profile on the dating website earlier that morning. Stan didn't have a choice but to turn around. He glared at the young man before turning to look at Ducky. He remembered what Kyle had said about just asking her to dinner. He wanted to, he really did. He had even broken off his online conversations with Nancy Dawson from Connellsville, and she had not taken the news very well. But he was still unsure if Ducky knew that they had been matched on the dating site. And did she know that he knew that they had been matched? He silently cursed his foray into online dating.

"Hi, Ducky," he said, rather too loudly, because he couldn't hear very well over the rush of blood thrumming in his ears. "You've got mail," he said stupidly. There was silence until Ducky slapped her leg and said, "You know, in the twenty-five years I've been delivering mail, you're the first person who's ever said that to me."

"Really?" Stan asked, pleased. His heartbeat slowed down a bit.

"Of course not," Ducky replied, and everyone in the store laughed. "I hear that at least once a month."

She must have seen his face fall, because she added, "But it still makes me laugh every time. It's a keeper."

Stan didn't know what to say. He was flustered and embarrassed, even though Ducky had tried to make him feel better. He knew she hadn't tried to embarrass him on purpose. That was just her personality.

"Okay then," he said, turning. "I'll just be…"

Before he finished, he knocked over a shelf of paint brushes. Was he ever going to get comfortable in his own body? He felt like a big bull, all left feet and shoulders as big as a barrel.

Back in his office he found another nasty email from Nancy. He was relieved that she didn't live in town and that he had never had the misfortune of meeting her.

How dare you string me along? the email began. *I have turned down so many dates because I thought you and I had something special.*

Something special? Stan thought. *Where'd she get that?* Sure, they had emailed quite a bit and talked on the phone some, but there hadn't been any commitment.

He continued reading. *I am a classy woman, you know. A lady. You don't treat a lady in this manner. You are going to be sorry!!!*

Some lady, Stan thought. He hit delete, not bothering to count the exclamation marks that danced across his screen.

After a few hours of accounting, he emerged from his office and saw another familiar face. Not exactly unwelcome, but Stan knew what the visitor wanted.

"Hello, Stan," Gabe Vignaroli said. "Can I talk to you for a few minutes?"

"If it's about what I think it is, then no," Stan replied.

Gabe shifted from one foot to another and looked nervously behind him. "Don't make me beg, Stan."

"Okay, but just for a minute. Say what you have to say and then please leave."

"Please, don't say anything about Marla," Gabe said quietly, as Stan sat down, not bothering to offer Gabe a seat.

"And why is that?" Stan snapped. "Could it be because she is your wife and you don't want anyone to know that you're married? Could it be because you don't want a certain person named Spring Hamilton to know that you are married?"

"Come off it, Stan," Gabe snapped back. "Can't you give me a break? You have no idea what's going on and what Marla and I have been through. You will ruin everything if you tell people I'm married."

Gabe gazed at the older man in front of him, cursing him for knowing his secret. What were the odds that Stan would appear in front of him and Marla just as they were leaving the courthouse on their wedding day in Norfolk, Virginia? Stan had recognized him immediately, because Gabe had worked his high school summers in Stan's hardware store. Stan had been to the funeral of a navy buddy who had been stationed at Naval Station Norfolk.

"You divorced yet?" Stan asked. "Because you parading around town pretending you aren't married is just about the same as lying." He pointed to Gabe's left hand, as Gabe nervously twisted the empty spot on his ring finger.

"You don't know anything about it," Gabe said quietly. "Things are complicated."

"I know all I need to know, and I know all the middle-aged women and widows in this town are banging around their casserole dishes fixing to make a hot covered dish for the new bachelor in town. You grew up in this town. I employed you for years, for Pete's sake. How long do you think you can keep this a secret?"

Gabe flashed his dark eyes at Stan and retorted, "As long as you don't tell anyone."

Before Stan could answer, Gabe left the office, banging the door behind him.

Stan threw down his pencil in disgust. He would keep Gabe's secret for the time being. But he would be watching him. If it looked like Gabe was going to hurt Spring again, however, well, that was altogether different.

CHAPTER 7

ESPITE HIS BAD MOOD and his deep desire just to go home and call it a day, Stan arrived at the Merchants Association meeting early enough to grab a handful of cookies from the refreshment table.

Looking for signs of agitation or sadness in Spring, he watched her place a thick white binder at each seat. Relieved that she was her efficient, bustling self, he sat down and flipped through the dividers that showed spreadsheets, timelines, and photographs. Kyle had contributed a marketing plan and instructions for something called Pinterest, which Stan thought sounded vaguely familiar.

Everyone streamed in and took their seats. The restaurateurs were the first to arrive. Laverne and Dallas Pritchard,

Texas retirees who had opened the Number One Wok restaurant, helped Miss Elsie find a seat, with Wendy James of Lucky's Pizza settling in next to her. The second- and third-generation retailers came next, sitting together in a tight knot. Samantha DeMuth, Lila Geyer, and Lane Krop had known each other since girlhood and always knew they were destined to take over their parents' Pittsburgh Street establishments. Autumn and Martha sat in the back to watch the goings-on. The remaining merchants took their seats and everyone looked expectantly at Spring.

It was easy to look at Spring Hamilton. Her face was perfection, with flawless skin and high cheekbones. Her long honey-colored hair seemed to always fall perfectly into a pre-destined place. Although she was dressed casually in jeans, a blouse, and high-heel boots, there was no mistaking who she was.

With everyone gaping at her, Spring began her presentation, pressing a button on the projector and nudging a mouse to bring her computer to life.

"I'm so glad to see everyone here," she said enthusiastically and genuinely. "I think I know all of you. Stan, my dad used to send me and my sisters to your store for drill bits because he kept breaking them. And Tim, the newspaper always sponsored our softball league."

"Still does," Tim answered proudly.

Spring continued. "Reverend Frye, I slept through a bunch

of sermons at the church, but that was before your time."

Everyone laughed, and Spring knew they were relaxing and warming to her. She wanted them to see her as the hometown girl she was.

"Mother used to bring us to Morris's for Easter dresses and she bought our crosses from Krop's for our first communions. She had our prayer books special ordered from the Provident Bookstore...." Her voice broke off as she realized what she had done.

The room went silent. Someone shuffled in their seat. A few people turned to the back of the room where Gabe was sitting.

"Well," Spring collected herself and carried on. "You get the idea. I know and love so many of you, and I'm glad that I can take a break from my modeling career to help the town I love."

She clicked the remote to reveal a drawing of a bride with the words Finch's Crossing Bridal Expo expertly drawn in cursive. "As you can see, Kyle and I have been busy. He has already developed a logo for the event, and in your binders you have the marketing and publicity plan he created. We all need to do our part and follow it to the letter. The plan only works if we all do our part."

"Oh, dear," Miss Elsie declared, as she flipped through the pages to the information about Pinterest and Instagram. "I don't have a bulletin board in my shop to pin up pictures of my cakes."

Before Spring could say anything, Kyle moved to sit next to her and took her hand. He had had to do this before, literally, hold her hand and walk her through something. "We'll do it together," he said gently. "Like we did with Twitter."

Miss Elsie's eyes brightened. "Oh, I do like that Twitter," she said, while the others tried not to laugh. "And I'm so glad the nice Mr. Twitter increased the character count to two hundred eighty. I just couldn't abide that one hundred forty."

Before Spring could return to her presentation, she heard a voice from the crowd.

"I just have to say," said Duncan Olack from the Greystone, "that there hasn't been a wedding at the Manor in more than thirty years." He wiped a dramatic tear from his eye with a polka-dotted handkerchief. "Autumn, it is my hope that you will have your wedding reception there. I offer it to you as a venue, free of charge. And catering at cost. I'll even throw in the chairs and linens."

Martha felt Autumn shift in her seat. Autumn was the hometown girl who did good. Although in a quieter and less public way, Autumn was even more successful than Spring. She made a very comfortable living as a full-time artist, with agents representing her work on both coasts. Martha knew Autumn wanted to have the reception in the backyard. But really, it was too small.

"Your garden is too small," she whispered to Autumn. "And

you know it."

The crowd began to chant "Greystone, Greystone, Greystone," and Autumn knew she couldn't say no.

"Of course I'll have my reception there, Duncan. I can't think of a more beautiful place in town," she said. This was the moment she had been waiting for, so she rose and joined her sister at the front of the room.

"I really appreciate all your enthusiasm for my wedding," Autumn began. "I want the Bridal Expo to be a success as much as you all do. But please, save your energy and resources for the Expo. Ethan, Heather, and I want a very simple wedding."

Autumn thought her declaration would fall on deaf ears. She knew Miss Elsie was planning a three-tiered cake in the shape of autumn leaves, even though her wedding was going to be in the spring. Autumn's engagement ring was a fiery red diamond, and she knew Lane Morris, who was a third-generation owner of Morris Ladies Wear, had contacted a new dressmaker in Pittsburgh to find red bridesmaids dresses and bow ties for the groomsmen. She would need to tell her, and fast, that she was only going to have one bridesmaid: Heather. Spring had agreed to walk her down the aisle. Kyle would be Ethan's best man. And Bryan? Well, she didn't even want to think about Bryan. He would be a groomsman, if he even showed up.

After the presentation, Spring watched as Kyle walked

Miss Elsie to the door. She was so impressed by the way he handled her. Spring had heard all about his social media and online advertising savvy from Autumn. She'd have to remember to scold Autumn for not telling her how handsome Kyle was.

Spring instinctively looked around the room for Meg. She still couldn't believe that this gorgeous man, who was so obviously on the ball and going places, had fallen in love with Meg Overly, of all people. Unless Meg had changed drastically since Spring had seen her a few years ago, well, she just couldn't believe it. But Spring was not the kind of woman to step on another woman's romantic interests. Kyle was, sadly, off limits. At least for the time being.

* * *

After escorting Miss Elsie across the street to her tea shop, Kyle returned to the community center to collect his things. The crowd had thinned out. It had gone well, he thought. Except for one person. He scanned the room and saw Teppy standing in a corner, her eyes darting from one person to another, like she was looking for something that wasn't quite there.

Kyle threaded his way around the tables and chairs and joined Teppy.

"What's up?" he asked. "You look like you've got something on your mind. Are you all right?"

To his surprise, Teppy pulled a tissue from her voluminous

bright orange purse and began to cry. The stragglers looked back at her, but Kyle waved them on.

"Now whatever it is, it can't be that bad," Kyle said. "Is there anything I can do? Did something happen to the girls or Roger?"

Teppy turned her head and discretely blew her nose. "Oh, nothing like that," she said, a bit nasally. "Everyone is fine. Everyone except me." Then she threw her bag over her shoulder and, gripping her binder, set off. "I have to go," she blubbered. "I'm sorry, I just can't talk now."

Concerned, Kyle followed Teppy to her shop across the street. She let herself in and turned to see Kyle standing there at the entrance, an inquisitive look on his face.

"If I'm going to tell you, you'd better come in. It'll be easier to show you what's happened."

Teppy didn't turn on the lights as they walked through the shop, and Kyle bumped into the furniture several times.

"Sorry," Teppy called over her shoulder. "But I don't want to turn the lights on in case they're watching me."

"They?" Kyle asked. "What do you mean, Teppy? Who's they?"

He followed her into the windowless office, and mercifully she turned on the desk light and sank onto a pink loveseat. She motioned for Kyle to sit next to her.

"I don't know who it is," she explained. "But someone is snooping around in my life. Looking at my secrets." She lifted the Georgia O'Keeffe print from the wall and retrieved the letter where she had hidden it. "Here," she said, handing him the envelope. "You might as well know. I guess you'll find out soon enough, along with everyone else in Finch's Crossing."

Kyle scanned the sheet of paper and then looked at Teppy, who had not taken her eyes off of him.

"Teppy," he said gently. "Are you really worried about this?"

"Of course I am," she snapped, and snatched the letter out of his hand. "Oh, Kyle, I'm sorry. I'm so on edge. I feel like I'm in a bad movie with a stalker."

"Have you told the sheriff?" Kyle asked.

"Oh no, I couldn't do that," Teppy said, mortified. "I don't want anyone to know. I only told you because, well, because I may need some damage control when this gets out. You know, some kind of PR spin."

Kyle tried not to laugh. "Teppy, my advice, which, by the way, is free, is to forget about this. It's a prank by someone who obviously lacks the courage to face you. These days, there are trolls lurking everywhere."

"Trolls?" Teppy said.

"Yes, people who lurk anonymously on the internet, posting mean comments that can't be traced back to them. They're cowards. That's what we're dealing with here. I don't think this person will carry through on their threat. They just want to get a reaction out of you."

"But this isn't the internet. It's the mail. The *real* mail."

"Same concept."

"But why?" wailed Teppy. "I haven't hurt a fly. I haven't done anything to deserve this."

"Of course not," Kyle assured her. "This is not about you. It's about the cowardly, insecure person who can't even face you."

"Really?" Teppy sniffed.

Kyle wanted to reach out and hug Teppy. She was one of his favorite clients, full of energy and enthusiasm. Her hard work promoting her store helped increase foot traffic on Pittsburgh Street and sales throughout the downtown community had skyrocketed. He hated to see her this way. Even her fluffy pink coat seemed to sag on her substantial shoulders. Her hair, always neatly coiffed into a mysterious updo, was uncharacteristically unruly, and her lipstick had faded until there was only a rim of dark red outline. Who would do such a thing to such a wonderful person?

* * *

Spring, basking in the success of her first Merchants Association meeting, raised her glass in a toast. Autumn, Ethan, Kyle, and Meg raised their glasses with her.

"To the first Finch's Crossing Bridal Expo," she enthused.

"To Spring," rang the chorus of voices around the table.

They had met after the meeting at the Greystone Manor. Heather was safely tucked away with Martha watching cartoons.

"I have an appointment to meet Duncan here tomorrow to review the space and split up the vendor tables and plan the decorations and flow of the exhibit hall," Spring said, pulling out a diagram showing where each merchant would be placed and how much space they would be allotted. She pointed as she explained. "Miss Elsie will need the space next to the kitchenette for her cake tasting. Teppy will need the larger space here to display items that can be used to decorate at receptions.

"Okay," said Ethan, rising, "that's my cue to go."

"Doesn't my future brother-in-law want to hear about the planning of his own wedding?" Spring asked in mock surprise.

Kyle rose, too. "I think I'll go find Duncan and see if he's on board with the publicity."

"Isn't it sort of late for that?" Meg asked in a biting tone.

The table grew quiet.

"Meg," Autumn admonished, "that was very rude. What's wrong with you?"

"Me?" Meg said, louder now. "What's wrong with you?"

"I just don't think you're being very nice to Kyle, that's all."

Meg shrugged. "He doesn't care."

Kyle shrugged his shoulders and left.

When he was gone and the exhibit hall layout was fully explained, Spring grew suddenly quiet.

"What's wrong?" Autumn asked, concerned. She followed Spring's gaze and saw Gabe moving toward their table.

Autumn rose and gave him a cautious hug. The Hamilton sisters hadn't quite forgiven Gabe for hurting Spring, but almost twenty years had passed, and Autumn wasn't one to hold a grudge. She hoped Spring wasn't either.

"C'mon Meg," Autumn commanded, gathering her purse. "We need to go over those fabric samples for the reception tablecloths." She pulled at Meg's elbow, literarily lifting her out of her chair.

"Geez, Autumn, take it easy," she snapped. The two friends glared at each other, each not quite understanding what the other was so upset about.

After Autumn and Meg departed in stony silence, Gabe motioned to an empty chair. "May I?"

Spring, who had decided she *did* need to hold on to her grudge just a little longer, sniffed and turned her head.

"Since that wasn't a direct no, I'll take it as a yes," Gabe said and sat down.

At six foot two, he filled the space with a relaxed presence. The confidence and charisma he exuded was palpable, as it had been back in high school. Where Spring was high-strung and obsessively neat, organized, and logical, Gabe was more easygoing and had shown her how to be spontaneous and carefree. He had balanced her. And without him as her anchor, she had drifted somewhat during her first few years in Los Angeles.

"So how long are you planning on staying in Finch's Crossing?" he asked, reaching for her hand across the table.

"Just long enough to help with the Bridal Expo," she answered, business-like, and moved her hand before he reached it with his.

"I heard you were moving to New York," he said. "You decided to take a detour?"

"And what about you?" she asked. "What brought you back? Seems a little out of character after all those years in..." she paused, remembering that she didn't actually know where he had been. Since their reunion the day before, she had been so focused on her first Merchants Association meeting that she hadn't even bothered to ask Autumn about Gabe, much less Google him.

"Virginia," he supplied for her. "After graduation I just got on my motorcycle and drove south. I got a flat tire in Norfolk and ended up settling there."

Spring took a sip of wine, allowing the amber liquid to relax her. "This whole time?" she asked.

He nodded. "I did odd jobs at first, then ended up reporting at a small newspaper. I went to college and got my journalism degree. I've been a newspaper reporter, editor, and magazine editor."

"And now you sell books and coffee in your father's old stationery store," she finished for him. Taking the edge out of her voice just a little bit, she added, "I was sorry to hear that he had died. So sad, retired to Florida for only a few years..." She allowed her voice to trail off.

Gabe nodded. "Yes, but he lived a lot of life in those two years. We could all take a lesson from his playbook. Live life to the fullest while you've still got it."

Spring rolled her eyes. "Really? That's your line? We should get back together, now, as almost complete strangers to each other, because life is short?"

"Who said anything about getting back together?" Gabe asked, trying not to smile. Inside, his heart leapt. She had actually spoken the words he most wanted to hear.

Spring reddened, two splotches forming on her neck. As cool and collected as she was, Spring had a tell. And she hated it. Gabe watched as her hand flew to her neck to cover the splotches.

"I just assumed that was what you wanted when you asked about the possibility of 'now.'" She raised her hands to form air quotes.

"You'd be right. I have never loved anyone the way I have loved you all these years."

"Oh, please," Spring rolled her eyes again.

"It's true. I think we all have that one person we never really stop loving, no matter where life takes us. For me at least, you were always with me, even though, like an idiot, I left you behind."

Spring sat silently for a moment, arms folded across her chest. "So I'm just supposed to forgive you for what you did to me? The way you broke my heart?" Spring wiped madly at her eyes, angry at herself for crying. She had promised herself that she had cried her last tears over Gabe Vignaroli years ago. She couldn't believe there were any left.

"I know you still care for me," Gabe said gently, reaching again for her hand. This time she didn't draw it back, and the familiar pressure of his big hand covering hers made her stomach flip.

"I have to go," she said abruptly, relieved that she had suddenly returned to her senses. She had an event to plan, a career to plot out, and many life decisions to make. She didn't have time to look to the past, much less to the love of her life, who had unceremoniously dumped her all those years ago. Her future was in New York. Without Gabe Vignaroli.

But the check marks. She couldn't stop thinking about all those check marks.

* * *

Gabe sat for an hour after Spring had left. In his mind, he relived every lost, lonely year without her. By the time he was a successful and award-winning journalist, worthy of her love, it was too late. Too many years had passed. He had watched her career unfold, savoring every bit of information he could find. He seldom dated, but when he did, his girlfriends always found it amusing when he bought a fashion magazine. He never dated one woman long enough for them to realize that the only fashion magazines he bought had Spring on the cover. And then he met Marla. He had pretty much given up on love, but Marla had brought him back. And now all of that was over. Their love had been bittersweet and cruel in its brevity.

CHAPTER 8

KYLE RETURNED TO the Greystone Manor early the next morning to meet with Duncan, in preparation for their meeting with Spring. They were going to walk through the third-floor ballroom, which would serve as the main location of the Bridal Expo. Kyle found Duncan in his office, his ever-present cup of mint tea sitting untouched beside him, the string pooling into the liquid. Kyle frowned. Fastidious as he was, Kyle could not imagine Duncan neglecting his tea.

As he heard Kyle enter, Duncan hurriedly shoved something into his middle desk drawer and looked up. "Oh, it's just you," he said, relieved. "I thought you might be something, someone, else."

Kyle sat, taking in Duncan's drawn face. His hair, always combed into perfect precision, was alarmingly disheveled. "Aren't you wearing the same clothes that you had on yesterday?" Kyle asked, his alarm growing with each passing second.

Duncan looked down at his crumbled blue button-down shirt, khaki trousers, and cotton yellow vest. "I didn't go to bed last night," he said quietly.

The dread in Kyle's mind grew steadier. He had seen that look before. The darting eyes, the paranoia bordering on panic. It was the same look he had seen on Teppy yesterday after the meeting.

"Duncan," Kyle began, "I am going to ask you something, and if you answer me honestly, I think I can help you with what's bothering you."

Duncan shook his head furiously. "Nope. There is no one who can help me now. I'm about to be ruined. My reputation will be in tatters. Everything I have built here is about to go up in smoke."

"Show me what's in the drawer, Duncan," Kyle said firmly. "I already know what it is."

Duncan's head snapped up and his eyes narrowed. "You?" he said in a hoarse whisper. "You sent me that awful letter? You're threatening me?"

Kyle held up both hands. "Now wait just a second. You know I would never do that."

Duncan slumped back into his chair. "Of course. I'm sorry.

I didn't mean to…"

"It's okay," Kyle interrupted. "I know what it is because you aren't the first person to receive one. It's a poison pen letter, isn't it?"

Duncan nodded, mumbled something, and robotically opened the drawer. He passed the letter over the desk and into Kyle's outstretched hand.

Like Teppy's letter, there was a photograph pasted in the middle of the paper. Kyle looked up. "What's this building?" he asked.

"It's the building that once housed the philosophy department at Carnegie Mellon University," Duncan said quietly.

"I didn't know you studied philosophy," Kyle said, impressed. "Pretty cool."

"It was," Duncan agreed, "until I had to leave school. You have to swear you won't tell anyone. Crap. Pretty soon everyone will know anyway. I cheated on an exam and got caught. I was expelled a few weeks before graduation."

Kyle looked back at the letter and read:

You're a bad, bad boy, telling one and all a tall, tall tale. You never graduated from college, yet there's that diploma hanging on your wall. Are you going to take it down, or shall I?

"You know, it's strange," Kyle replied. "These secrets, they're more like gossip. They're embarrassing, sure, but they're things that you can weather. Sure, it's less than ideal, but it's not life-and-death stuff."

He slid his phone out of his pocket, thumbed to the camera setting, and took a few pictures of the letter.

"I think it's time we went to the sheriff," he told Duncan, who snatched the letter back from a surprised Kyle.

"You can't do that," he hissed, looking around as if the letter writer might be lurking around the corner. "I have my reputation to think about. This could be really bad for my business."

"Duncan," Kyle said gently, "it would be worse for your business if you became embroiled in this person's web. If you don't do something about it now, who knows how far he might take it? They could use this information to blackmail you, and *that* would be really bad for your business."

"I didn't think about that," Duncan said distractedly.

"Trust me on this," Kyle said. "And you know the sheriff will do everything in his power to keep your secret safe."

* * *

From her kitchen, Autumn watched as Teppy, Duncan, Kyle, and Stan settled on the couch in her well-appointed living room with Spring, her organizing materials and magazines spread out before them. Autumn loved her childhood home, with its airy rooms and cozy assortment of sitting areas. While fall was her favorite season, and she typically went overboard with her decorating, she loved the delicate harbingers of spring, and had placed vases of tulips around the house and arranged small Easter bunny scenes in as many cloches as she could find in the attic. She loved the way the delicate miniatures stood vigil under the glass jars, sitting on wiry Easter grass or gazing into tiny baskets filled with miniature plastic carrots, waiting patiently as Easter approached.

"How's it going out there?" Ethan asked, coming into the kitchen and wrapping his arms around Autumn's waist and nuzzling her neck.

"Hard to tell," she answered wistfully. "They haven't really started yet. And where's Martha? She's supposed to be here watching over them to make sure they don't go overboard with our wedding."

"Relax," Ethan assured her. "She and Heather are finishing up a book report. I'm on my way over now to take Heather home for dinner. I'll send Martha right over. Okay?"

"Hmmm..." Autumn said distractedly.

"Honey," Ethan said. "It really is all going to be okay. I promise."

"But what about Meg getting Bryan here? I really want to know what's going on. I can't relax until I know."

"Don't you trust me?" he asked.

"Of course, it's just that..."

"You don't trust Meg," he finished for her.

"Oh, I don't know. She's my best friend and she's never let me down. But this whole thing about her being able to bring Bryan home is just too good to be true. I'm more afraid for Heather than for myself. And I'm trying not to be mad at Meg. Every time I even hint about wanting to know how she's going to do it she gets huffy with me. And I've been getting huffy back."

"Like you said," Ethan reminded her, "you've been friends for a long time, and you've been through a lot together. You've got to trust her. And me. It is going to work out."

Ethan let himself out the back door just as Kyle and Meg came in the front carrying cake boxes, with Miss Elsie bringing up the rear.

Autumn hurried into the foyer to help them bring everything into the dining room. She had brought out plates, cocktail napkins, and forks for the cake tasting. When Autumn heard Martha bang in through the kitchen door she breathed a sigh of relief. At least something was going to go right this evening.

With everyone assembled in the living room, Spring began to review everyone's suggestions for Autumn's wedding. She signaled for Teppy to go first.

Teppy lifted out a few items from her oversized canvas shopping bag and arranged them on the coffee table.

"Crystals and clear glass are in this year," she explained. "I'm going to offer several reception decorating packages, and this is the one I've selected for Autumn and Ethan. First, each table will have a round mirror in the center, with three vases holding assortments of clear glass pebbles, crystals, and a votive candle floating in the middle."

So far so good, thought Autumn.

"Teppy, that's wonderful," Spring said, then turned toward Duncan.

He brought out a series of sketches to show how the ballroom would be laid out for the reception.

"I thought it would be very romantic to offer a seating arrangement with chairs and cocktail tables arranged in the shape of a heart." He held one of the sketches aloft. "Of course, that will only work for a cocktail reception with heavy hors d'oeuvres, so there is the possibility of heart-shaped tables, as well."

The room was quiet until Martha stepped in, with her lovely way of smoothing things over.

"I think those heart-shaped tables would be tricky, Duncan," she said, "as fun as they are. Leg room would be a bit awkward. Especially with the older crowd."

"Oh, I see," Duncan said flatly. "Yes, of course you're right. The third option is classic round tables, head table at the front, buffet lines at the back, with room for a DJ." He passed around the final drawing.

"Duncan, you are a class act," Martha gushed, trying not to overdo it. "Leave it to you to make the traditional new again. It's perfect for Autumn's wedding!"

Spring was about to ask Stan to discuss his groomsmen's gifts when Gabe's head poked out from the kitchen. "I knocked, but no one answered," he explained.

Spring shot Autumn a "who invited him?" glance, to which

Autumn just shrugged.

Kyle stood up. "So great you could make it, Gabe," he said.

"I wasn't sure I would be welcome," he responded, looking directly at Spring.

When Gabe settled on the couch with his invitation books and boxes, Spring suggested he go next.

"As you know, my father ran a newsstand and stationer's store where I now have my bookstore and coffee shop. He always offered wedding invitations on order, and I know a good many of you ordered your invitations through him back in the day. I was able to track down some of his original vendors that are still in business. They agreed to give us some special pricing for anyone who purchases them as a direct result of the Bridal Expo."

"Oh, that's wonderful, Gabe," Spring interjected, before checking herself and remembering she was angry at him. She forced a scowl back onto her face.

Gabe looked at her, amused. "And, finally, I know it's old-fashioned, but I'd like to offer At Home cards, too."

"Actually," Spring jumped in again, "that's really a good idea because these days you don't know if the bride is keeping or changing her name. At Home cards take the guesswork out of that."

"Why thank you, Spring," Gabe said and winked at her. Red blotches appeared instantly around her neck.

She ignored him and continued. "The At Home cards

should be sent with the thank-you notes, which you can also stock. It's very au courant, very Martha Stewart."

At the mention of Martha Stewart, Teppy choked on a cookie, then spilled her glass of lemonade all over herself. Spring leapt up to help her.

"Oh, I'm so sorry, Spring," Teppy said, and Spring saw that there were tears in her eyes.

"It's okay, Teppy, really. It's just a little spill," said Autumn, who had come into the living room with paper towels. "Why don't you go to the ladies room. There's a hand towel in there you can use to soak up the lemonade on your skirt. I'll do the rest."

Grateful for an excuse to leave the room, Teppy practically hurled herself out of the living room and was relieved when she could close the restroom door behind her. She leaned against the door and closed her eyes. Could Spring be behind the letter? Was it a coincidence that Spring's arrival coincided with the letter? Teppy shuddered, not believing that it could be true, but not totally dismissing the idea, either. Spring would have been the last person Teppy would have suspected. But who else could it be?

Teppy returned to the living room and Autumn watched her closely, then looked at each of her guests with renewed interest. Was it her imagination, or were people on edge? Teppy seemed distracted, and Duncan kept staring at everyone, scrutinizing each person as if he had never seen them before. And

Stan, usually ready with a joke or a riddle, was subdued. He had prepared an assortment of groomsmen's gifts to choose from, but usually enthusiastic about tools, he couldn't seem less interested if he tried, despite Spring's enthusiasm about having the tools engraved with the men's initials.

When Stan had finished his presentation, the group moved to the dining room where Miss Elsie was fussing with the cake tasting. Meg had already managed to make her way through a quarter of the samples. While this would have typically just mildly irritated Autumn, this particular night it made her furious.

"Do you have to be such a pig, Meg?" she hissed. "This is my wedding, remember? Just because you can't get yourself married, doesn't mean you have to ruin my wedding."

The room went silent. Meg's fork hung in the air, with her mouth ajar.

"Oh, I'm so sorry, everyone," Autumn apologized, then ran out of the dining room into the kitchen where she grabbed a dish towel and wiped her eyes.

What has come over me?" she thought to herself. *This isn't me.*

"What are you waiting for?" Kyle asked Meg. "Go after her."

Instead, Meg crossed her arms over her chest, harrumphed, then left by the front door, slamming it so hard that the photos on the occasional tables rattled.

The rest of the group disbanded soon after, but Gabe lingered in the front foyer, hoping to catch a moment alone with Spring. However, she didn't even look at him as she walked back into the living room to collect her planning materials and laptop. He stepped in front of her as she made her way back to the kitchen.

"Will you sit with me for a few minutes on the porch swing?" he asked, boldly relieving Spring of her burden and placing the items on a nearby table. He moved aside, and Spring surprised him by walking out in front of him and settling on the porch swing.

"This brings back good memories, at least for me," he said, sitting close to her, pleased when she did not move away from him.

"For me, too," Spring admitted. "I don't have bad feelings or any regrets about the time we spent together," she said softly. "I don't want you to misunderstand. It was just such a shock to see you. I wasn't prepared. You took me totally off guard."

"I would have thought Autumn would have told you," he mused.

"I think she tried to," Spring laughed. "Right before I walked into town that day and into your store. But my head was so full of my project and plans that I didn't let her talk. I was preoccupied with my own problems.. . ." Her voice trailed off.

"Problems?" Gabe asked quizzically. "What kind of problems? I thought everything was going well for you. Sounds to me that you have it all planned out, just like the Spring I knew and—"

Spring cut him off before he could say "knew and loved," and began to explain about her diminishing career options and breakup with Chad.

When she was done, Gabe brushed a strand of hair behind her ear. "I can't believe that anyone could turn away from you."

"*You* did," she said without thinking, and instantly regretted it. It pained her to see his face fall. This was the man she had loved with all her being seventeen years ago. The man she had planned to spend her life with. Yes, he had hurt her. But was that a reason to hurt him back? To be unkind? Now that Gabe was back in her life she couldn't reconcile her moral self with the unkind things she was saying to him. With horror, she realized that, as with Chad, she didn't like the person she was when she was with Gabe. But this time, it was *her* fault. With Chad, she was reacting to his bad behavior and cruelty. With Gabe, she was the instigator, saying nasty things when all he was doing was being nice to her.

"When are you going to forgive me so we can move past the hurt feelings?" she heard him ask her, and she emerged from her reverie.

Spring looked at her hands. "I don't know, but I want to."

"I'll take it," Gabe said, grinning, then added, "for now. Now about this modeling problem of yours. Don't you know about Elon Musk's mother? She's like ninety and still works as a model. Sounds like there's hope for you after all."

"First, she's in her early seventies. But you're right, she's a total inspiration for aging models. And by the time I'm her age, I want to be able to say that I've left some kind of mark on this world, something other than magazine covers and teenage girls with poor body images."

"Is that how you see yourself?" Gabe asked, surprised to hear the uncertainty in Spring's voice. It was a side of her he hadn't seen before.

"That's why I'm branching out. I want to start something new, from the beginning, something that is totally my own."

"Is that why you got your MBA?" he asked.

Spring was stunned. "How did you know about that?"

"*Glamour* magazine, I think it was April 2013. You were the cover story, and it was all about how you decided to pursue your MBA."

"I don't know what to say. How could you possibly know all of that?"

"I have read every magazine article about you for almost twenty years," he said, not at all embarrassed. "And I still have them. I am probably your best bet for finding any back issues you might need for your portfolio."

"Silly," she laughed, and playfully hit him on his arm. "There's no such thing as a paper portfolio anymore."

He grabbed her hand and held it tightly.

"I'm not going to let you go this time, Spring," he said, kissing her hand. "We're meant to be together, and you know it. How many people get a second chance at their first love?"

CHAPTER 9

*S*HERIFF BUDDY LANDRY sat at the lunch counter at Hoffman's Drugstore on Pittsburgh Street enjoying his chocolate cream pie. With his wife out of town on a girls' weekend, he felt confident that he could sneak in a slice or two without her knowing. His waitress, knowing his situation, had given him an extra-large slice, and he would return the favor by leaving an extra-large tip.

Buddy loved Finch's Crossing. He worked for his sister-in-law, Mayor Peggy Brightwell, and thoroughly enjoyed his job. Currently on an extended second-honeymoon cruise, Peggy was celebrating her cancer remission, which was something worth celebrating. With pie. Things were peaceful in his hamlet, just the way he liked it. Oh, there were always a few drunk

CHAPTER 9

and disorderlies, some petty theft, and even some domestic violence cases from time to time, but it was nothing he couldn't handle.

When he saw Kyle Oswald making a beeline for him, he could tell by the grave look on the young man's face that something was amiss, and the peace and quiet he had been enjoying was about to come to an end. In the year since Kyle had moved to Finch's Crossing, the young man had become something of a son to him. He saw something of himself in the hip young man who had adopted Finch's Crossing as his hometown.

"Hey, Sheriff, I need to talk to you. It's important," Kyle said, getting straight to the point.

Buddy motioned for him to take the seat next to him at the counter, but Kyle cocked his head, indicating they should take the back booth that was out of earshot. Buddy grabbed his pie and coffee and they settled across from each other.

"You look worried, son," Buddy said.

Kyle nodded. "There's something going on. I'm not exactly sure what, but it's not good."

He slid out his phone and brought up the pictures of Duncan's letter and the one of Teppy's, which she had reluctantly let him take.

"I promised them that you wouldn't reveal their secrets to anyone," Kyle told the sheriff. "I hope that was okay."

Buddy looked at the photos. "Should be," he said. "It's not the content of the letters necessarily that is important, but the fact that they received them in the first place. How did they arrive?"

"They both came in the mail. Mt. Pleasant postmark. The letter writer used a love stamp."

"That's pretty sick," the sheriff responded.

"So what do you make of it? Are you going to take fingerprints?" Kyle asked eagerly.

"Now before you go all junior detective on me, son," Buddy warned, "you need to understand that this is now a criminal investigation. It's not fun and games. Someone has a vendetta against people in this town."

Kyle was surprised at how seriously the sheriff was taking it.

"One on its own is nothing to be terribly concerned about," he said. "Two is a pattern and definitely something to pursue. And you can rest assured there are others out there. I'd bet my pie on it." As if for emphasis, he took an extra-large bite. Nothing was going to keep him from finishing his hard-won treat.

"What are you going to do next?" Kyle asked.

"Besides getting the letters and envelopes fingerprinted, I want you to get ready to come to an emergency meeting of the Merchants Association. When the rest of the letters hit, we're going to have to drill deep into this. And I want to be ready."

"Why the Merchants Association?" Kyle asked.

"Because it looks like someone is targeting our business community."

* * *

As soon as he had completed his conversation with Kyle, Buddy headed back to the office, a second slice of pie tucked neatly away in a to-go carton, and dialed Teppy's number, instructing her to initiate the Merchants Association phone tree to bring everyone together at the community center in one hour's time.

Teppy's heart fell when she heard the concern in the sheriff's voice. Instinctively, she knew the meeting had to be about her poison pen letter. She had considered the possibility that there were other letters besides hers. She knew the town hadn't seen the end of this problem. She toyed with the idea of starting the phone tree, and then escaping to Mt. Pleasant to sit in the corner café and have a pity party over a chocolate sundae.

Pull yourself together, she commanded herself. *There are children starving. Pets are shivering out in the cold. This could be a whole lot worse for me.* Even though she said the words to herself, she only half-believed them.

At the appointed time, Teppy made her way to the community center off Gazebo Park, next to the sheriff's office.

Teppy remembered the many happy times she had enjoyed here with her fellow business owners. The community center was the site of so many of her Brilliant Ideas. She remembered the time they celebrated Kyle's social media marketing success and the time Melissa Overholt announced that she would open the Burnt Orange antique shop. When the McCrory's

Five and Dime experienced a devastating fire, the merchants gathered at these very tables to assign clean-up tasks and refreshment duty. She remembered when Miss Elsie, sixty-five years old, newly retired from teaching school, decided to open a tea shop. Her first order of business had been to join the Merchants Association, and she brought fresh cookies for her very first meeting. In the twenty-five years since, Miss Elsie had not missed one meeting, regular or emergency. And she never showed up without treats.

Teppy looked over at the refreshment table and the platter with assorted cookies and tiny cakes. A lump formed in her throat, and her stomach clutched, like a fist squeezing a tennis ball. Her stomach was such a jumble, she bypassed the refreshment table and took a seat in the back, hoping to be as invisible as possible.

Everyone arrived seemingly at the same time. Stan helped Miss Elsie set out the coffee urns. Melissa chatted with Lila Geyer from Morris Ladies Wear. Their stores were side by side, and they could often be found chatting at one or the other's counter, gossiping almost to the point of neglecting their own shops. Local customers knew that if one of their shops was empty, the proprietor was most likely next door.

Sheriff Landry strolled in at exactly six o'clock, with Kyle and a dejected Duncan in tow. He instructed them to sit in the front row.

"No doubt you are wondering why I have called this emergency meeting," he said, and the crowd vocalized their agreement. "Before I go into very much detail, I have something very important to ask all of you. Over the past few days, have any of you received anonymous letters threatening to expose some secret or another?"

No one moved. Then Duncan, in the first row, raised his hand but hung his head.

The sheriff looked out over the room and nodded as more hands were raised. Melissa, Lila, and Lane Krop raised their hands. Then Maureen from the hardware store tentatively raised hers. Teppy was the last, and half-raised her arm. Maybe if she didn't extend her arm fully, the problem would only be half-bad.

He was relieved that Miss Elsie did not raise her hand. And he wasn't ready yet to share that he, too, had received a letter. Everyone in town already knew his secret, so he was confused why the letter writer would think it was something he was ashamed of. But that was an important clue that he would tuck away for later use.

"Okay, everyone. I am grateful for your honesty. Now I want you to know that I have no intention of sharing your secrets. And honestly, the contents of these letters, while mean and vindictive, are not life-and-death. Of course, if you think otherwise about a particular letter, please let me know. But nonetheless, I have opened a criminal investigation. For now it's not the *what* of these letters that concerns me but the why.

Furthermore, I don't know how many of you know this, but sending threatening letters through the U.S. mail is a federal crime. If things escalate, I will have to contact the Postal Inspection Service and maybe even the FBI."

The room exploded into gasps and surprised chatter, but he continued. "And this is why I have asked Ducky to tell us a little more about what this means, because she is delivering the letters.

As Ducky made her way to the front of the room, the doors opened and Autumn, Spring, Meg, and Gabe appeared, whispering their apologies for being late. Meg made her way to the front and sat next to Kyle. The others took their seats in the back.

The sheriff briefly explained to the latecomers that many merchants had received letters in the mail threatening to reveal unsavory or embarrassing secrets.

"Does anyone find it too much of a coincidence that these letters started arriving the same week Spring Hamilton came back to town?" asked William Porter, the town curmudgeon who was known for being contrary for the sake of sowing discord.

"Nonsense and fiddlesticks," Miss Elsie chirped in her high, shrill voice. "I've known those girls since they were in school with me. Spring would never do such a thing."

"Yeah," Lila echoed. "What would she have to gain by that?"

The crowd tittered as William continued, "And I bet she

hasn't received a letter yet, have you, Spring?"

"That doesn't mean anything," Spring replied, growing very uneasy. She wasn't concerned that the merchants thought she had sent the letters. They would come to their senses when they had all calmed down. But she couldn't help but think about the lengths to which Chad might go in a vendetta against her. Had she talked enough about her hometown and its beloved inhabitants for him to have ammunition to terrorize her neighbors in this way? Over the years, Autumn had kept her apprised of local gossip and comings and goings. She just couldn't remember how much she had told Chad.

"Listen, people," Buddy spoke loudly above the din, and everyone turned back around in their chairs to face him. "Now is not the time to turn on each other. The letter writer obviously has some kind of vendetta against the town or the merchants as a group. Or maybe the person is wreaking havoc to retaliate against one particular person. I want you to go home and ask yourselves who might have it in for you. Don't get paranoid, just put your thinking caps on."

"I still think it's quite a coincidence that the first letter arrived just a few days after Spring came back," William muttered.

"Oh, just drop it for Pete's sake," Meg barked from the front row next to Kyle. "If she was gonna mail those letters, she could have done it just as easily from California. This is the way nasty rumors get started, and that's no way to live. Now stop it before I send one of my dogs around to your house. If they sniffed around the woods on your property long enough, I bet they'd find some of the special concoction your cousins like to make in their basement."

"Wait just a minute," William said, but the crowd's laughter drowned him out.

"Yeah," Melissa pointed out, "you've got a lot of nerve accusing Spring of doing something."

"Yes," Miss Elsie chimed in. "People who live in stone houses should not throw glass shards at each other. Someone could end up getting hurt." She was pretty sure she had butchered that particular metaphor. But it didn't matter.

"Enough!" the sheriff boomed from the front, desperate to wrangle the merchants into some kind of calm. He motioned at Ducky, who had dressed for the occasion in a pretty pink sweater set and black pants, and had waited patiently next to him for her time to speak.

Ducky knew everyone in the room. In fact, she had known most of them all of her life. She looked out over the faces until she saw Stan. He immediately looked away, and her face reddened. She had never had to speak in public before, and as soon as the sheriff had asked her to attend the meeting, she googled public speaking tips. One tip said to find a friendly face in the audience and pretend that you were just talking to them. The other tip said to imagine everyone in their underwear, but that was out of the question. As the town's only letter carrier, she had seen more than she had wanted to when she brought packages up onto people's porches. So she'd have to settle for talking to Stan's head. Stan was the nicest man she had ever known. She knew he had been sweet on her in high school, but he had never approached her for a date. And now they had been matched on a dating site, and she was sure he would make his move. But weeks had passed. She knew he knew they had been matched. That's how it worked.

"Ducky? Ducky?" She heard the sheriff calling her name.

She had momentarily forgotten where she was. She cleared her throat and began, pulling out a set of index cards from her pocket, and pivoting herself so she was facing Stan. "I would like to read the following to you from the U.S. Postal Service Inspector General's website:

"It's a serious federal crime to use the mail to threaten a person. It's one of more than 200 postal crimes that Postal Inspectors investigate. These mailings may threaten a person's reputation or involve blackmail or extortion. Or it may be a direct act of coercion where the action is proposed to elicit a negative or fearful response. Threats are communicated attempts to inflict harm, fear, or some form of loss on another individual.

"Postal Inspectors investigate extortion and blackmail when demands for ransoms or rewards are sent through the U.S. mail. Inspectors also strictly enforce laws prohibiting mail that contains threats of kidnapping, physical injury, or injury to the property or reputations of others.

"The United States defines and classifies threats based on how they are delivered and the likelihood that they will be acted upon. For instance, federal law criminalizes specific…

"C'mon, Ducky, get to the point," William called rudely from the crowd. "You're going to bore me to death."

Stan's head shot up, and he momentarily locked eyes with Ducky, whose shocked expression told him she didn't expect him to realize she had been staring at him.

"That's enough William," Stan said, standing up. "Ducky is doing us all a favor by providing this background information. I, for one, find it not only helpful but also very interesting. So shut up and let her finish."

The room exploded into applause. Stan took a bow, motioned for Ducky to continue, and took his seat.

Ducky had turned pink, and she looked back at her index cards for help.

"Okay, now where was I?" she muttered. "Oh yes, I was going to turn it back over to the sheriff to tell you about the penalties. Thank you."

She resumed her seat and the sheriff stood up again. "Thank you, Ducky. Pursuant to U.S. stalking laws, sending threatening letters via the mail can translate into ten years in prison. One last thing before I dismiss you. I've asked Kyle to talk with you about how your social media presence might be contributing to these letters."

CHAPTER 9

Kyle twisted around in his seat. "I know that I have encouraged you for the past year to use social media as much as possible to promote your business," he said. "And for the time being, I want you to continue to do that, but I want you to suspend any posts or pictures about your personal life. Furthermore, as new people like your pages, follow you, or otherwise engage, I want you to email me their names so I can check out their profiles."

The group disbanded with far less enthusiasm than when they had come together. Kyle watched them go and felt as deflated as the merchants looked.

* * *

After a long day painting in the studio, Autumn invited Spring to the Greystone Manor for dinner.

"With pleasure," Spring declared, getting up from the bed in her childhood bedroom. Papers and photographs were scattered around her. She had been fingering fabric samples when Autumn poked her head in the door.

Once ensconced in a cozy booth at the Greystone and reviewing their menus, Spring addressed a critical subject.

"You are going to have to start looking for a dress, you know. It's the most important part of the whole day, the centerpiece, if you will. All eyes will be on you."

Autumn sighed. "I know. I've just been so busy with the art classes and my own work. You know Scottie has a new show for me in Philadelphia. It's a while away, but I want to see if I can come up with some new work for it."

"As long as you get started soon, you'll be okay," Spring assured her.

She brought out a few fabric swatches from her purse and laid them on the table between their place settings. "Let's talk about the color palette. I finally convinced Teppy that we shouldn't go with Easter egg colors, like pink, yellow, light blue, purple, and so on."

"Thank goodness for that," Autumn said, a shiver running through her.

"I know, right? It wasn't easy but I pointed out that a theme of the greening spreading across the town would be spectacular, and before too long, I convinced her that it was one of her Brilliant Ideas."

"You're the brilliant one," Autumn replied. "Once Teppy gets going, it's hard to talk her down."

"Okay," Spring continued, fingering a light green piece of fabric. "This is the color I have in mind for the tablecloths, and we'll match them with crisp white napkins. Duncan has beautiful place settings with a thin silver band around the edge. Very elegant. He doesn't have enough silver, though, so we'll have to use the flatware from the restaurant." Spring paused. "You aren't terribly disappointed are you? It won't look as nice."

"Are you kidding?" Autumn said. "You saved me from an Easter egg theme, so flatware is looking pretty good." She picked up the other two fabric swatches, one a darker green, and the other a pale sage.

Spring pointed to the darker one. "That's the color of the greenery DeMuth's is going to supply for the centerpieces. We aren't actually using a fabric that color. She'll add baby's breath and white roses to the greenery, and Teppy will put the whole thing in glass bowls with crystals lining the bottom."

"Sounds beautiful, Spring. You have no idea how grateful I am that you're here to help with this. Or should I say, to do everything. Now what about this light color? It's beautiful."

"I found tulle in that color and we'll use it, and some more white roses, to decorate the pews at the church. Ethan and Bryan will have white rose boutonnieres, and DeMuth's will also make a corsage for Martha, and they'll use some tulle in it, as well."

"Do you know what Martha is wearing yet?" Autumn asked, suddenly feeling the pinch of time. As Spring talked, Autumn realized how much there was left to do. She fought back the urge to panic. She didn't need any more stress on top of how much she was worrying about Meg keeping her promise. And that stress was compounded because she was trying to hide the fact that she was stressed.

Her sister could see right through her.

"I know you're worried about Meg, but I think you need to trust Ethan when he says she's got it under control."

"Wow," Autumn answered. "You're the last person I'd think

would stand up for Meg, of all people."

Spring smiled. "I guess you could call it that. Let's just say I have faith in Ethan because you have faith in Ethan, so that transfers over to Meg. Somehow. Anyway. Back to what Martha is wearing. She and Heather have gone to Morris's and ordered what Heather is calling "surprise dresses.""

"Oh boy," Autumn mused. "I don't think I need any more surprises."

"No worries," Spring assured her. "Martha knows the color palette. She's got it under control. No gaudy Easter egg colors, I promise."

"I feel so badly we've been talking so much about me and the wedding, I feel like I haven't checked in with you enough," Autumn said, changing the subject. "You and Gabe spent a lot of time out on the porch swing the other night after the Bridal Expo planning meeting."

"Yes," Spring answered, toying with the silverware in front of her. "It felt like old times," she almost whispered.

"That's saying a lot, sis," Autumn replied quietly. "Are you thinking of giving him another chance?"

Spring thought about this question, though she knew, deep in her heart, that the answer was yes. Gabe's explanations, his confession, his obvious regret, all were tugging at her. She knew him so well, she thought, even now. His reasoning, about being intimidated by her potential, was not out of character with the Gabe she knew and loved so many years ago. She knew then that he felt he wasn't worthy of her because he was from a working-class family and the Hamiltons were wealthy and educated. But that had not mattered to Spring. And it certainly had not mattered to her parents, who had genuinely adored Gabe, and never missed the chance to tell him so throughout their time together. She remembered all the times he had come to dinner or accompanied them to church on Christmas Eve or on a family outing to visit museums and shops in Pittsburgh. How could he not have known that he was a beloved almost-member of their family?

Spring snapped out of her reverie as she heard Autumn call her name several times and motion to the side of the table.

"Oh, sorry, yes," she said, noticing the waitress at their table. "I'll have the tomato basil soup and the house salad. Dressing on the side, please." She folded her menu and handed it to the young woman.

"I'll have the same," said Autumn, "but you can put a huge portion of ranch dressing right smack on the middle of my salad."

Spring laughed.

"I don't have a modeling career to return to," Autumn observed, also laughing. "So back to Gabe and the second chance," Autumn prompted.

"I guess so," Spring said.

"Don't sound so excited about it," Autumn exclaimed, raising her eyebrows.

"No, it's not that I'm not excited. I want to give it a go again, but I don't want to get my heart ripped out again. He was the love of my life and he hurt me, really badly. I think that makes it worse now."

"What makes it worse?" Autumn asked.

"That we were so incredibly close. We were like one person. I couldn't have in a million years ever imagined that he would leave me the way he did."

"Unlike Chad," Autumn observed.

"That's right. Chad was…" Spring's voice trailed off. "Well, I don't know what Chad was. I think whatever he started out as, well, let's just say, he didn't end up being that person. And Gabe, with all his faults, and what he did to me, is still so authentic. And the connection I felt with him, the chemistry, that's still there. It's as if no time has passed. At all. We're completely different people, but seventeen years later, my feelings are still the same."

Spring hadn't realized all of this until just that moment when she said it aloud. The thoughts, the emotions, the way her stomach flip-flopped when she thought of him, all of those sensations made her shiver.

"Just take it slowly," Autumn suggested. "There's no reason to be in a hurry. I think you're right to be cautious. What's your next step?"

"I want us to spend some solid time together," Spring said, perking up. She could feel her heart flutter in her chest, and her palms grew clammy. All of a sudden she felt like a school-girl, waiting by the phone for Gabe to call her for the first time. "Maybe I'll suggest we go to Pittsburgh for lunch, away from prying eyes, if you know what I mean. But I do worry about the logistics. Him living here, me living in New York. How would that work? What does that look like?"

Autumn was shaking her head. "You just need to let it play out the way it's supposed to. If it's meant to be, the logistics will work themselves out."

"You are such the romantic," Spring observed. "You are Mother Earth."

"And you are Father Time," Autumn responded, "always wanting everything planned to the tiniest detail, everything in its orderly, logical place."

"There's nothing wrong with that," Spring said, proud of her efficiency and can-do attitude. After all, her analytical mind had served her well throughout her career. But oh, how she wished it had served her better during her personal life.

"Don't get me wrong," Autumn was saying, "I love your sensibleness, how you reason everything out. Sometimes I wish I had some of your common sense."

"And I wish I had some of your carefree spontaneity."

"Like throwing together a wedding in six weeks?"

"Exactly," Spring said. And then was quiet.

"There's something else on your mind, Spring, I can tell," Autumn said, as the waitress returned with their meal. Autumn paused until she had left the table. "Something other than Gabe."

Spring looked to her right and then to her left, as if expecting someone, or something, to jump out from behind a chair. "Those nasty letters people have been getting. I'm afraid they're from Chad."

Autumn looked aghast. "Your Chad?"

"Yes," Spring whispered. "And keep your voice down. Someone might hear you."

Autumn looked around at the half-empty dining room, then back at Spring. She pushed her salad plate out of the way so she could lean forward across the table. "What makes you think it's him, of all people?"

"One thing that Chad loved was gossip," Spring explained. "He wanted me to tell him all of the gossip at the fashion shoots, and I did, to make him happy. Then, when I didn't have any L.A. gossip, well, I gave him some from Finch's Crossing."

"Oh my God, that's awful. And you think he's found you and is sending the letters?"

"That's exactly what I think," Spring said, nodding her head vigorously.

"But how would he know where you are? And what could he possibly know about Teppy and Duncan and the others that he could write nasty letters about?"

"We don't know what's in the letters, do we," Spring observed. "Only that people have gotten them. And Chad may be a jerk, but he's not stupid. I wouldn't put anything past him."

She observed the concern in Autumn's voice as she asked, "Do you think you need to go to the sheriff?"

Spring shook her head and looked at her sister, reaching for words to reassure her. "You know, I'm probably being silly. I'm totally paranoid. And you're right. How could he have found me here? Last he heard I was going to New York. The only person who knows that I'm here is my lawyer. Everyone else just knows I won't get to New York for a few weeks."

"If you're sure," Autumn said, and Spring knew she wasn't convinced. "At least promise me you'll be careful."

That night, tucked away in her childhood bedroom, Spring dreamed of a younger Gabe and Spring, sitting hand in hand on the front porch swing. And she dreamed that the vindictive Chad was outside her window, yelling obscenities. She awoke in a cold sweat, and couldn't help but smile at the irony of the sweet and sour of her dreams colliding inside her, just as it was in her waking life.

CHAPTER 10

*I*T HAD BEEN A rainy week, and Spring was enjoying the respite and small rays of sunshine poking out of the clouds. She sat on the front porch, her laptop in her lap and a glass of cucumber-infused water sitting on the table next to her. She was feeling confident that the merchants were doing all they could to make the Bridal Expo the success she knew it would be, and everyone was on board for Autumn's wedding, now just a few weeks away. Spring was so lost in the intensity of her work that she didn't hear Ducky approach, her mailbag slapping against her leg.

"Hi there, Springy girl," Ducky called cheerfully.

A little too cheerfully for someone who is delivering poison pen letters, Spring thought.

"Hi, Ducky. It's nice to see you again. Anything good for me?"

"I'm sorry to have to tell you, but you got one of those letters."

Spring held out her hand, expecting Ducky to hand it to her, but instead she just gave her some circulars and other junk mail."

"Where is it?" she asked, trying to bite back her dread. Maybe Chad was the letter writer after all.

"Sheriff's orders. He said to deliver the letters to him and send the recipients down to the station to open them. It's a federal offence to open mail not addressed to you," Ducky added sternly. "Oh, and Gabe got one today, too."

But Spring wasn't listening. She grabbed her purse from under the table and ran down the porch steps to her car. She wasn't going to waste any time getting into town.

She screeched to a halt in front of the Borough Building and stomped into the sheriff's office.

"Now calm down, Spring," Buddy said, rising as he heard her approach. "I've not opened your letter, but I wanted to fingerprint it before it was delivered to you." He reached into his desk drawer and pulled it out. "Now I want you to open it and we'll fingerprint the letter. I won't reveal the contents to anyone. You have my word."

Spring looked at him a long while, then nodded. She opened the envelope and read:

Roses are red and Spring should be blue, because you-know-who has already said "I do."

She read it aloud to Buddy. "That's cryptic," she said. And he nodded. "What do you think it means?"

Before Buddy could answer, Gabe came in the door, out of breath and somewhat disheveled. He stopped when he saw Spring.

"What are you doing here?" he asked.

"What are you doing here?" she responded.

"I got one of those letters," he said. "I've come here to pick it up."

"That's quite a coincidence, because I got one, too," Spring said.

"You did?" Gabe asked warily, and he felt beads of sweat on his brow.

Spring held out her letter. "I didn't understand what this meant until just now, when you walked in." She shoved the letter toward his chest when he refused to take it. "You're married, aren't you?"

He didn't reply.

"Aren't you?"

Finally, he affirmed, nodding his head.

"You're a piece of work, do you know that? Don't you ever speak to me again, or I'll get a restraining order against you." Spring turned to Buddy. "You're my witness, right? I don't want him anywhere near me."

Eyes blazing, she handed the letter back to the sheriff, and without looking at Gabe, she stormed out of the office.

For a moment, Gabe and Buddy stood like silent sentinels, just staring at each other over the expanse of the secret that had just entered the room. Without a word, the sheriff reached back into his desk for Gabe's letter. He gave the same instructions, and watched as Gabe opened the envelope and slipped out the paper. He read aloud. There wasn't any use trying to hide it. He was pretty sure he knew what it was going to say.

Roses are red, and Spring is blue because now she knows you've already said "I do."

* * *

Spring wiped wildly at her eyes, uselessly trying to stop the flow of tears. They were coming so quickly, she could barely see. As soon as she turned off Pittsburgh Street and out of sight of the bustling street, she threw herself into a full-out sprint, up the street and over to Loucks Avenue. She had forgotten that she had driven downtown and was making her way home on foot. Her purse slipped on her shoulder so she held it against her chest. She had run the steep hill on Loucks Avenue hundreds of times, preparing for track and field meets. She let the adrenaline that shot through her the moment she read her letter propel her up the hill. She stumbled out of one shoe but kept going. All she could think about was getting home, flinging her belongings into her suitcase, and leaving. She could be on the road in ten minutes if she didn't bother to fold her clothes. She slowed as soon as she saw the house, trying to get a hold of herself. She straightened her blouse, returned her handbag to her shoulder, and limped up the walk and through the front door. Autumn was sitting in the morning room with a cup of coffee and jumped up as soon as she saw Spring.

"Oh my God! What happened to you? Are you okay? Is it Chad? Did he attack you? Are you hurt?" Autumn sprang to Spring's side and started to feel her arms and neck, looking for injuries.

Spring imagined that she must look like a wild woman and regretted that she had given in to her emotions and made such a scene, but it was too late. She was a full-on mess. She couldn't stop crying.

"It's Gabe," she blubbered. "He's married." And then she fell into Autumn's arms, sobbing, just as she had done seventeen years earlier when she realized that Gabe had walked out of her life. She had sat on the curb in front of the house for hours, waiting for him, before she got in the car and headed to California, on her own.

* * *

Autumn followed Spring up the stairs and stood outside her bedroom door, watching as her sister pulled her suitcase from under the bed and hauled it onto the bed. Wordlessly, Spring began opening drawers and hurling the contents into the bag.

"I know the last thing you want is to see Gabe again. I get

that," Autumn said gently. "But you can't leave. You've made a commitment to the merchants to help them with the Bridal Expo. At this point, it's too late to bring in anyone else to help them. And besides, there's no money to pay an event planner. They need you."

Spring moved to the en suite bathroom and tossed toiletries into her makeup bag. "I can pay someone to take over the planning," she said and came back into the bedroom.

"Oh, some horrible LA person like Chad?" Autumn asked, trying not to lose her temper.

"Of course not," Spring snapped. "I know tons of event planners. I can hire one of them to help."

"Yeah, because all the glitzy event planners you know have just been dying to get their hands on a small-town Bridal Expo to sink their teeth into."

"That's not the point." Spring sighed, fingering the luggage tag and not looking at her sister. "If I pay someone enough they wouldn't care if I asked them to do an Amish wedding in Lancaster County."

"And how do you think Miss Elsie is going to fare with a froufrou event planner? Or Stan, with his Lady Gifts? The only person who would eat it up is Teppy. Everyone else would be miserable. And you know it. And whether you like it or not, you are part of this now. You asked for this, remember?"

"But that was before I knew Gabe was married," Spring whined, and hearing her childish voice just made her angrier at herself. And at Gabe.

"So what?" Autumn asked. "That doesn't change the fact that Miss Elsie needs you to help her with Instagram. And you promised to help Lila with a window display of bridesmaids dresses. Whether you like it or not, this isn't about you."

As Autumn's words sunk in, Spring stopped packing and sat on the bed. She balled up a silk blouse and tossed it onto the floor. "You're right, of course," she said quietly. "But I'm just so mad at that man, I don't ever want to see him again. How am I going to avoid him in a town this small?"

"You're not," Autumn said, matter-of-factly. "You're a grown woman. You're going to get a hold of yourself, hold your head high, and ignore him when you see him."

"Geez, you sound like me," Spring said, not quite sure she had heard her sister correctly. "That's a very logical way to approach the situation. I expected you to suggest that we go egg his house and bust out his shop windows."

"Well," Autumn said with a grin, "I haven't ruled that out yet."

"But how am I going to face everyone?" Spring moaned. "By now, the whole town knows what a fool I am, letting Gabe burn me not once, but twice. They are going to think I am such an idiot."

"Quite the opposite," Autumn reassured her. "Everyone in this town has a lot of respect for you. You are the celebrity in their midst. Besides, it's Gabe that everyone is going to target with nasty looks and the cold shoulder. They will have nothing but sympathy for you."

"I don't want their pity," Spring cried, horrified at the mere thought of people hugging and petting her and assuring her that everything was going to be all right.

"It's not pity," her sister corrected her. "It's empathy. One human being reaching out to another human being, offering comfort and kindness."

As Autumn spoke, Spring returned her clothes to the drawers and closet. She took her toiletries and makeup back into the bathroom and organized them on the vanity table. Only then did she look up at herself in the mirror, willing the tears to stop as they fell down her face. And for once, Spring didn't even care that her mascara ran in streaks like ribbons of black mourning.

* * *

Perched on Meg's desk in the Ten Oaks office, Kyle was choosing his words carefully.

"So you know how much I love you," he began.

"Mmm," Meg responded, not looking up from her computer screen. "I do. You tell me, like, three thousand times a day."

"And you've already said that you will marry me, right?"

Meg's hands, poised over the keyboard, froze in midair.

"Do we really have to talk about this now?" she asked, trying to hide her exasperation, but knowing she was failing miserably.

"Why not now?" Kyle asked, feeling his voice rise an octave. "You never want to talk about it. And I want to talk about it."

"Well, I don't," Meg threw back.

"You don't what?" Kyle barked, now on his feet. "You don't want to marry me, or you don't want to talk about it?"

"Stop twisting my words around. I never said that."

Kyle crossed his arms over his chest, the truth finally dawning on him. "You know, you've never actually said the words 'marriage' or 'engagement' or 'wedding.' All this time, and you've never uttered one of those words."

Meg sighed. "Why can't we just keep things the way they are, just for the time being?"

"Because I want you to be my wife. Because I want to have a big wedding to show all my friends—and yours—that I am the luckiest man in the world because Meg Overly has consented to be my wife. I want to shout it from the rooftops. 'I love Meg Overly. I want to marry Meg Overly.'"

By this time, Kyle's face was red and he was flapping his arms in the air. He looked like a puffed-out bird and Meg couldn't help but laugh.

Suddenly, he stopped moving. "You think this is funny? All of this. Getting married. My love for you. You know, I don't even know if you love me. I've only ever heard you say it once, when I asked you to marry me. I say it to you every day." He paused, looking down at his feet and shaking his head. "Maybe we're just not right for each other. We want different things."

Silence hung between them. Meg was miserable and now she knew she was making Kyle miserable, too. It was obvious he didn't want to be with her if she wouldn't marry him. And at least for the time being, Meg only wanted to be with him if they didn't get married.

"Maybe you're right," she said contritely, fighting back tears. "Let's just call it all off." She pulled off his engagement ring and held it out to him. When he didn't take it, she dropped it into his shirt pocket and stood staring at him. Finally, Kyle turned and walked away.

CHAPTER 11

EVERY TUESDAY AND Sunday since moving back to Finch's Crossing, Gabe made the half-hour drive to Arbor Commons in Greensburg. He had moved Marla there when their savings had run out. The facility cost one-third of what he had paid in Norfolk. He retired early from the newspaper, taking a generous payout, and moved her. Because Gabe now owned his father's building outright, there was no mortgage, and he lived in the apartment upstairs. No one else knew about Marla. It wasn't any of their business. Especially not Stan Brilhart. Gabe hit the steering wheel in anger as he remembered the scene earlier in the week. He knew Stan meant well, but he didn't understand the circumstances.

At the intersection of U.S. 199 and Pennsylvania Highway

CHAPTER 11

819, Gabe felt the all-too-familiar somersault in his stomach, the sign that he had almost arrived. He never knew which Marla would be there. There was the sweet, intelligent, talented Marla he had fallen in love with. And there was the stony-faced Marla whose early-onset Alzheimer's was slowly eating her life away. More and more it was the latter, and the doctors had recently told him it was now just a matter of weeks until Marla would no longer have any lucid moments, no longer recognize him, not even for a moment. Each time he came, he dreaded that it would be the last time he really saw her. And he wondered if she would have the opportunity to see *him* one last time, or if that time had passed them by.

He parked outside the building and walked into the lobby, greeting the receptionist, then made his way down the hall to the Alzheimer's ward. Locked at all times, he had to wait for someone to let him in. Today it was his favorite nurse, Bea, a matronly woman in her sixties who treated Marla as the most important person in the world.

Her face glowed as she opened the door. "Come on in, Gabe," Bea said. "She's been waiting. Hurry."

"Really?" He brightened.

"Yes, she knows you're coming today, and she had me curl her hair so it would look just the way you like it."

He hurried, following Bea down the hall into room 162. "Gabe's here," she said brightly, "right on time."

Gabe went inside, full of the hope and expectation that he

SPRING

hadn't allowed himself to feel in a long time. "Hey, babe," he said. "Bea says you're doing good today." He kissed the top of Marla's head and felt it move back and forth under his lips.

She looked up excitedly, eyes shining. "Hi, Daddy, did you bring me a dolly?"

Gabe sank into the sofa beside her, buried his face in his hands, and wept. Bea sat next to him. "I'm so sorry. It gets shorter and shorter each time. She was just here not five minutes ago."

Gabe couldn't respond and Bea continued. "In fact, she asked me to give you this," Bea said gently. She pulled a thick envelope out of her smock pocket and held it out for him.

"What is it?" he asked, afraid to even touch it.

"It's her final gift to you," Bea said contemplatively. "At least that's what she called it. I'll leave you alone. If you need me, I'll just be down the corridor at the nurses' station."

Gabe nodded mutely, fingering the envelope. Beside him, Marla sang softly to herself and wound a strand of hair around her fingers. Gabe put his arm around her shoulders and she leaned into him, resting her head on his shoulder. When she had fallen asleep, he rose gently so as not to disturb her and went to stand next to the window. Marla loved looking out over the garden and could sit for hours staring at the rose bushes and potted geraniums.

With trepidation, Gabe slid his finger under the lip of the envelope to unseal it and pulled out its contents. He had to unfold the thick stack of papers, and a small envelope with his name on it, written in Marla's neat handwriting, fell to the floor. He picked it up while he read the large print at the top of the papers, DECREE OF DIVORCE was written in solid black capital letters. Through his tears, he read the note from his wife. It had been dated nine months earlier, on the day he had moved her into Arbor Commons.

My darling Gabe,

Today was a good day. We came to this place together and you settled me in, fussing over me like an old hen. You made sure I had my crossword puzzles and my favorite pen, and you arranged the boxes of Oreos in my dresser drawer and told Bea to make sure I got a few every day with a glass of milk. I don't remember your leaving, which is probably a good thing. I knew that the next time you saw me, I might not know you. How brutal that must be for you, my dear, sweet husband.

Tomorrow, our lawyer is going to file divorce papers for me. Remember last Christmas, when I was still lucid enough that I could stay at home alone? I went to see her one day while you were at work and instructed her to file the papers.

This is my last gift to you, my darling. I want you to be free. When the time is right, when I no longer know you, that is the time to sign them. And you must promise that you will. I made Bea swear that she would extract that promise from you.

Never doubt my love for you. It is because I love you that I am setting you free. We will always have our time together. Nothing will change that. In the time I do have left, when I can think and feel like my old self, it will give me so much peace to know that you are taken care of. That you can go on with your life. Who knows how long I will linger on, oblivious to you or anything else. I don't want you to sit and wait, year by year, for me to release you. You are released, my dear, sweet love. Not from a cage, but from an untenable situation. This disease does not have to destroy us both. I want you to live your life. To love again. To be happy. You deserve that. I do not think for a minute that you will stop your visits. I know you too well. After you sign the papers, even after you fall in love with someone else, I know you will still come to brush my hair and give me cookies. And the thought of that brings me peace, even though I will probably not even know you are here. Knowing it now means the world to me.

Your loving wife,

Marla

Gabe stood for a long while, watching Marla sleep, gazing upon her lovely, childlike face that more and more just looked blankly at him, without seeing him. He heard someone come into the room and looked up to see Bea, who enveloped him an immense, motherly hug.

"Come on, sugar. We'll go sit in the garden for a time and talk. You'll still be able to see Marla, and she you, when she wakes up."

Bea led him out onto the patio and they settled on a bench.

"What do you know about this?" he asked, handing her the divorce papers.

She looked at them a long time before answering. "I suspected this is what it was," she said, "but Marla never told me and I never asked. Like I said, she said it was her final gift to you. When she was feeling herself, she would ask me to get the envelope for her and she would set it on the bureau for a while. I think just knowing what it was made her feel good."

"There is no way I am going to sign these papers," he said, emphatically, wiping away tears. "What kind of person would I be? Divorcing my wife who was struck down by Alzheimer's in the prime of her life? What kind of monster does that?"

"Exactly," said Bea, nodding her head.

"What do you mean?" he asked. "I don't get it."

"You aren't the kind of man who would divorce his wife under these circumstances. And Marla knew that. So she did it for you. This is like her last will and testament. You need to honor her wishes. You need to honor her."

After Bea left, Gabe stayed another hour in the garden, watching Marla through the window. She had barely moved since he had left the room. Finally, he collected the papers and went back inside. He sat with her for another hour, simply holding her hand. When it was time to leave, he kissed her on the cheek. "See you Tuesday," he said. Knowing she would not answer, he left and quietly closed the door.

* * *

Autumn was surprised to see Scottie Lambert, her agent, skulking around her back garden, then rapping on the window of her studio. She watched him say "Let me in" several times, but she pretended not to understand and watched as he wildly pointed and mimed that he wanted in. Finally, she took mercy on him and opened the glass door that led from the studio into the flower garden. Scottie stomped in, huffing, and the two made their way to the kitchen.

"I haven't heard from you in a month, and when you don't return a call I get nervous that you've had another breakdown," he said accusingly.

"I did not have a breakdown. I had a breakthrough," Autumn retorted.

Scottie waved his hands in the air in circular flourishes. "Breakdown, breakthrough, whatever. You still are avoiding me and you are my favorite client, so I had to come to see you, and you know how much I hate leaving the city for small-town America. How you do not languish and waste away from sheer boredom, I have no idea."

"Scottie," Autumn warned. "Don't start. You know that badmouthing my lovely hometown is strictly off limits."

"Okay, okay. We'll table that discussion for now and move on to why I am here. You haven't given me new work in twenty-nine days. That's almost a month, you know." He accepted a cup of tea from Autumn and sat down dramatically on a kitchen island stool.

Scottie was Autumn's highly successful agent, and she credited him with keeping her work selling and relevant and with making her name known in the finest art circles.

"It's Meg," Autumn said. "She promised she could get Heather's Uncle Bryan here in time for the wedding."

"What's wrong with that?" Scottie asked. While he abhorred Meg's unbelievably terrible taste in clothes, and almost criminal unwillingness to fix herself up, he was quite fond of her, and there was something in Autumn's tone that made him want to stick up for Meg.

"Bryan is a Marine serving in some far-flung classified outpost in the Middle East."

"Oh," was Scottie's succinct response. "Go on."

"Meg finally told Ethan how she would accomplish it because I was getting so anxious, but she won't tell me. And she made Ethan swear never to tell anyone. Sometimes I wish my husband-to-be wasn't so honorable."

Ethan wandered in to refill his coffee mug and joined them around the kitchen island.

"Them's fighting words, missy," he said playfully, nodding a hello to Scottie. "But I'll forgive you. What's up?"

"I'm just telling Scottie about Meg's strange behavior," she explained. "I'm so worried about the whole Bryan thing."

"Honey," Ethan said, putting his hand over hers, "I really believe that she's going to come through. You just have to trust me about that."

Scottie raised his eyebrows. "I'm with Autumn on this one," he said. "And in the immortal words of movie star president

Ronald Reagan, I encourage you to, 'trust, but verify.'"

"That doesn't make me feel any better," Autumn said. "And actually, now I feel worse because all we can do is trust. There is no way to verify."

* * *

Spring had taken her sister's frank words to heart. Autumn was right, of course, and as the tears dried and her mind cleared, Spring acknowledged to herself that the only thing to keep her mind off of Gabe was to keep going with the Bridal Expo. She'd see it through to its successful finale and then be on her way to New York, to start her new life.

After their "come to Jesus" conversation, Spring rallied, even convincing herself she had no feelings for Gabe and could carry on as before, oblivious to his very existence. It wasn't like it had been seventeen years ago, when she had fallen apart. He no longer held that power over her. And in fact, she recognized triumphantly, neither of the men in her life held any power over her as long as she didn't let them.

Besides, she had business to take care of. When she had taken over the coordination of the expo, Kyle had warned her that some of the merchants would need some hand-holding. When she walked into Hoffman's Drugstore, she saw Kyle at the lunch counter, and he motioned for her to take the stool next to him. She pecked him lightly on the cheek.

"Thanks for meeting me," she said. "You sort of scared me when you said the merchants might need some hand-holding."

"Not all of them," Kyle interjected, "and not with everything. Teppy and Melissa at the Burnt Orange Antique Shop are on top of their social media and their stock. All Stan has to do is change his 'Lady Gifts' sign to 'Groomsmen's Gifts.' DeMuth's Florist and Krop's Jewelers are okay, but it wouldn't hurt to keep a closer eye on them and help them take their game to the next level." He paused. "So that just leaves…"

"Miss Elsie," they said together.

"Yeah, she's going to need a lot of help with logistics. She's got the staff to help, but a few nudges in the right direction will go a long way."

Spring took out a notebook from her binder and started taking notes, scribbling furiously. "I'd like the window displays to be spectacular," she said. "Something unique and creative in each window will draw people in for certain."

"Yeah, I think you should put a lot of your time there," Kyle agreed. "Concentrate on Krop's and DeMuth's. The jewelry and flowers are front and center for any wedding. And get Morris's to get some new mannequins, if you can. The ones she has are like stick figures and the old-fashioned dressmaker's forms."

Spring groaned. "How did we get from only Miss Elsie needing help to redoing all the merchants' windows?"

"Let's split it up," Kyle suggested. "If you will help Lane get the jewelry window sparkling, talk with Samantha about the flowers, and do something with Lila and her mannequins and dresses, I'll work on Miss Elsie and her cardboard cakes and fake cookies and old-fashioned teapots. And I'll go into the Burnt Orange Antique Shop and help Melissa pull together a bridal theme for her shop window. With everything she has jammed in that store she's bound to have something other than those old pieces of furniture and hat stands she has in her window now."

Sandra appeared before them with her pad and pencil poised to take an order. "Your usual, hon?" she asked Kyle, who nodded. She turned to Spring. "I'm guessing you'll want a salad and diet drink? Gotta keep that girlish figure," she laughed.

"You can read me like a book, Sandra," Spring admitted. It was so nice to be back among people who knew her. Knew what she liked. What was good for her. What wasn't good for her.

She turned back to Kyle. "So how did Meg snag you?" she asked abruptly, causing Kyle to cough up his water, turning his face red. Spring slapped him on the back until the coughing stopped.

"I'm charming, handsome, and I created a free website for her," he admitted, not ready to admit to Spring or anyone else that Meg had broken up with him.

"I've known Meg all my life," Spring informed him. "She's selfish, barely civil, practically a barbarian. I just don't get it."

"The good thing is you don't have to," Kyle answered curtly.

"Don't have to what?" Spring asked.

"Get us. Me and Meg. As long as we get each other, that's all we need. And please refrain from calling my girlfriend a barbarian. She has a kindness that you probably don't see because it's private."

"You're right," Spring apologized. "I shouldn't have said that, and I am sorry."

"So what about you?" Kyle asked. "I heard you left your boyfriend in Los Angeles."

"I did," Spring answered as Sandra put their plates in front of them and slid the check between them. Spring quickly picked it up and set it by her plate. "My treat," she said. "A peace offering."

"Accepted," Kyle said. He poked a french fry into a puddle of ketchup. "The sheriff told me about the letters you and Gabe got," he said quietly. He felt Spring stiffen beside him.

"Yep, lucky me. Fool me once, shame on you. Fool me twice, shame on me."

"He seemed like such a nice guy," Kyle said. "It just surprises me to find out he was lying to you."

"You and me both," Spring mused, picking at her salad. "You and me both."

CHAPTER 12

*S*INGING A HEARTY rendition of *Here Comes the Bride,* Scottie pointed his red Mini Cooper toward the other end of town and Ten Oaks Kennel. It was time to have a little chat with Meg. Her argument with Autumn was hurting Autumn's productivity, not to mention his productivity and potentially his bottom line. And there could be no more of that.

He parked next to the smallest mud puddle he could find, and although he gingerly folded himself out of the car, carefully watching where he stepped, he still managed to get his loafers wet.

The things I do for art, he said to himself, and instantly was surrounded by so much barking he felt he was in a horror movie.

"Dear Lord, have mercy," he exclaimed to no one in particular, as he opened the door—ignoring the closed sign—and wandered past the dog runs and toward, he hoped, Meg's office.

He stopped in the doorway and rested his elbow on a stack of dog food bags, then thought better of it and removed his arm. The barking continued and he stood there waiting for Meg to notice him, but she was so consumed by her task that she didn't see him at first, then she hollered, her back toward him, "We're closed. Didn't you see the sign?"

"Not for me you're not," Scottie said, his eyes on the bride magazines that Meg was shredding. He had concocted an excuse to stop by so as not to make Meg—who could smell fear and phonies as if she possessed a German shepherd's nose—suspicious. "I wanted to ask you about a wedding gift for Autumn and Ethan, but that can wait. What on earth are you doing? You know, there is such a thing as a recycling can."

To her immense horror, Meg felt tears sting her eyes. One even rolled down her cheek. She could feel her nose turning red. "I don't want anyone to know that I was reading these ridiculous things," she told Scottie, then turned back to her task.

"Honey, you could've just waited until it got dark and tossed those things out the window of your truck speeding down Highway 119."

Meg sat back on her heels. "I didn't think of that," she said. "I've not really been thinking straight these days. Not since

Kyle and I broke up."

Scottie helped her up from where she had been crouched by the shredder and steered her toward the couch, sitting down beside her.

"Everyone's going to be mad at me when they find out. They're already mad at me because they think I'm going to ruin Autumn's wedding."

"Are you?" Scottie asked, raising an eyebrow.

"Of course not," Meg snapped. "I'm too busy ruining my own." And she burst into tears.

"Meg, you obviously love Kyle, and he adores you, though God knows why since you dress like a bum and talk like a sailor."

"If you're trying to make me feel better, it's not working," Meg said, wiping her nose on her sleeve.

"I'm trying to help you," he admonished. "Just exactly what is the problem? Why won't you marry Kyle?"

"You know," Meg said, "I bet you'll be the only person to ask me that. Everyone else will just assume it's because I'm crabby and just changed my mind."

"I'm not everyone," Scottie said gently. "Tell me. I know I can help."

Meg gestured to the half-shredded magazines scattered on the floor around them. "Look at me, and then look at those dresses," she commanded. "What do you see?"

"I don't know what you mean," Scottie said. "Stop being so

CHAPTER 12

cryptic and just say what you mean."

Meg admired Scottie's directness. "I'm going to look stupid in one of those big marshmallow dresses, and everyone in town will laugh at me. Plus, there will be photographs."

"What about your bridesmaid dress for Autumn's wedding?" he asked. "Aren't you afraid of looking silly in that?"

"Autumn decided that the only bridesmaid is going to be Heather. And Spring is going to walk her down the aisle, so I'm off the hook. But my own wedding's different. I can't get out of it."

"So don't wear one of those marshmallow dresses," Scottie said, exasperated and throwing up his hands. "Wear one of those sleek numbers, like a sheath dress. Simple, elegant." He picked up one of the magazines that hadn't yet made it to the shredder and flipped through the pages, then held it up for her to see. "It's beautiful."

Meg groaned. "I don't want to wear any dress. Don't you see, it's the dress. I don't feel comfortable in dresses. I feel awkward and silly."

"So don't wear a dress. Wear a pretty white silk pantsuit. You don't even have to carry a bouquet. And you can have your dogs walk down the aisle with you."

"What are you talking about?" Meg shrieked. "That's insane!"

"No more insane than not marrying the man you love because you're afraid you'll look silly in a dress. It's *your* wedding. Do whatever you want. Go to the courthouse. Or elope."

"I know Kyle is going to want some big froufrou wedding with all that tulle crap that Autumn puts all over her Easter decorations. And the vows. Oh crap. I didn't even think about the vows. I can't get up there and say all that mushy stuff in front of all those people. It's embarrassing."

Scottie took Meg's hands in his. "Look. You know that I love you, despite the fact that you have no fashion sense, are mean as a snake, and can barely say anything nice. Go talk with Kyle. Tell him what you're worried about. He will understand. Then the two of you can work out a simple ceremony that doesn't involve a dress or tulle. Or flowers. Well, that's pushing it. You have to have flowers somewhere."

"Do you think so?" Meg hiccupped.

"Darn tootin'. Look at how much he's put up with so far. Do you think a few changes to the traditional wedding ceremony will send him packing? He adores you, though God knows why."

"Okay, you can stop insulting me now," Meg snapped. "You're like a tiny dog with a Bernese Mountain dog complex."

"There she is," Scottie said as he got up to go. "That's the Meg I know and love." He moved to peck her on the cheek. "Let me know when you're ready to pick out your wedding attire, whatever that may be, and I'll take you shopping."

* * *

CHAPTER 12

The revelation that Gabe was married hung around Spring like a cruel fog. No matter where she went or what she did, there he was, figuratively and literally. She tried to follow Autumn's advice to put on her big girl pants and get on with it. From a logical perspective, Spring knew this was the correct course of action. But her heart, which had always done as it was told, now rebelled against Autumn's instructions.

To make things worse, the stress caused by the poison pen letters threatened to disrupt the planning of the Bridal Expo. As she went from store to store to consult with the merchants on various aspects of the event, Spring noticed how closed off they were. Now wary of their friends and neighbors, they had become islands unto themselves. When Spring tried to get Teppy to collaborate with Melissa on the centerpieces, making a sample that had an antique-esque flair, Teppy had looked away, shuffled the papers next to her cash register, and said she was too busy to try anything new with the decorations. Samantha at Krop's Jewelers had flat out refused the idea that Teppy, Melissa, and Gabe could contribute items to give her shop window a bridal flair. Only Miss Elsie—God bless her—responded enthusiastically to Spring's idea that she use the leftover sample wedding shoes from Lila's store as table centerpieces in the tea shop the week leading up to the Expo.

After a raw afternoon of tension and rejection, Spring stopped by Kyle's office and collapsed into one of his guest chairs opposite his desk.

"It's a disaster," she declared. "All of our careful planning and strategizing has been dismantled in one stroke of a poison pen. And I don't know what to do about it."

"It can't be that bad," Kyle offered. Spring admired his enduring optimism and recounted her afternoon rounds to the merchants, admitting that her visits had netted virtually nothing.

"What you need to do," Kyle said, leaning back in his chair, "is to bring in someone from the outside. Surely you must know someone in New York who would pop down to give a presentation or something to generate some excitement. I can call a special meeting of the Merchants Association."

"If they'll even come," Spring mused. "They're all tied up in knots wondering who the letter writer is. I'm not sure they'd cross the street, much less come to a meeting."

"That's where you're wrong," Kyle chided her. "They may be suspicious of each other, but they know that they have to do their part to make this event a success. And since they don't want to have anything to do with each other, maybe they'll be more inclined to listen to an expert from out of town who can help each one of them individually. Look at it this way, what harm could it do?"

"All right," Spring agreed. "I trust your judgment. "If you think they will respond positively, I'll get something going right away. And I know just the person. She's very elegant but down to earth. I'll send her some of the details of what we're doing so far and ask her to find a way to make connections between what each merchant has to offer. Easy peasy."

* * *

Poppy, a wedding planner from New York, was a tall, painfully thin brunette with a black pixie cut and red lipstick that matched her red wool suit.

Spring handed the remote to Poppy and sat down in the front of the room as Poppy began her presentation to the group of merchants assembled in the community center.

"Spring sent me photographs of some of the items you plan to showcase during your Bridal Expo and asked me to go through and evaluate each one, telling you whether or not I think your ideas are worthy of pursuing."

Spring half-stood in her chair and responded. "Poppy, that's not exactly true. What we need are some words of wisdom and encouragement about how to take what we already have in place and improve on it."

Poppy waved at her dismissively and clicked the remote. "Exactly what I just said."

A picture popped up of three flower arrangements lovingly arranged by Samantha DeMuth, a third- generation owner of the iconic Finch's Crossing flower shop, and was the first to receive Poppy's wrath.

"I don't know what amateur created this monstrosity, but it has to go. Instead of these horrible pussy willows, I encourage you to purchase some curly willow. It's very dramatic.

Very au courant. And stop with the baby's breath already. It is so gauche. No one uses that anymore."

The room sat in stunned silence, as if watching a car accident and not knowing exactly what to do or say. Oblivious to the response of her audience, Poppy clicked the remote again and a sample of Ducky's calligraphy appeared.

"This has got to be the worst calligraphy I have ever seen, and believe me, I have seen a lot." She clicked again, and a blow up of several words appeared. Poppy turned on the laser pointer feature and moved it around the words. "See here, the way the ink has bled? Completely unacceptable. Any of my clients would send these back in a heartbeat."

Spring stood to say something, but Stan beat her to it. He rose to his full six foot four inches and stormed to the front of the room, looming over Poppy, who defiantly stood her ground and jutted out her chin.

"Now you just wait a minute, lady," Stan boomed, as he switched off the projector. "What gives you the right to come here and insult us?"

"Why, Spring asked me to come here and help. I'm doing this out of the goodness of my heart as a favor to Spring. To whom much is given, much is expected. And I am here to help the unfortunates of this town."

The crowd began to boo and chatter nervously as Spring sprang to the front of the room, standing next to Stan.

"We've had quite enough of your 'help,'" she told Poppy,

using air quotes around the word help. "I think it's time for you to go. Now."

Poppy whirled around to face the room. "Well, I have never encountered such a group of ungrateful people in my life." She gathered her things and as she walked out shot back, "And don't get me started on those hideous table centerpieces and stupid groomsmen gifts. And those overdone wedding cakes. I can't even tell you how awful they are. And see if I ever do another favor for you, Spring Hamilton!"

Spring called after, "That won't be a problem, Poppy. The world doesn't need any more of your favors."

When Poppy slammed the door on her way out, the room came to a standstill. Every face turned toward Spring.

"I am so sorry, everyone," she said, and she felt her cheeks flush. "I hope you know that I would never ask Poppy to come here and criticize you."

But the room had exploded into chatter again, and no one was paying any attention to her.

Miss Elsie had her arm around Ducky, who was holding a handkerchief to her eyes. As she had for the previous Merchants Association meeting, Ducky had dressed carefully, this time selecting a pretty light-blue shirtdress and dark-blue loafers. She had even put on pearl earrings that had belonged to her mother, and a splash of Shalimar perfume.

"I just don't understand how someone could be that mean," she was saying, between sobs.

"Now you just don't give that woman another thought," Miss Elsie commanded. "She had to blow up your writing ten times to find one tiny flaw in it. That's just nonsense, and we all know it. It was all just nonsense."

Sitting behind her, Teppy stood. "You are absolutely right, Miss Elsie." Her eyes sought Samantha DeMuth, and when she found her shrunken into a chair on the far side of the room, Teppy headed straight for her. "Samantha, you have been making beautiful arrangements for my shop for years. You are a talented and gifted artist. And, as a matter of fact, I am going to double my floral order at Christmas. And I want all the arrangements to have pussy willows and baby's breath in them."

The crowd broke out in cheers and laughter. Spring watched as Stan hovered next to Ducky, and wondered if she had even noticed that Stan had been her champion. She watched Melissa hurry over to where Miss Elsie sat and put her arm around her.

She said, to no one in particular, "Miss Elsie made a beautiful cake for my wedding. Remember?" She didn't wait for an answer. "Roy and I wanted an ivy theme, because ivy represents fidelity. You made the most beautiful strands of ivy with green candy licorice and leaves made out of icing. I still have the pictures. Everyone said it was a beautiful cake."

Miss Elsie teared up and she patted Melissa's hand. "Thank you, dear. I remember every cake I make and the special people I make them for. Each one is as unique as my friends."

As Spring watched her friends and neighbors compliment each other and offer words of comfort and cheer, she couldn't help but smile and congratulate herself. True, bringing Poppy to Finch's Crossing to help advise the merchants had been a disastrous idea. But she was beginning to see an unanticipated side effect of the ordeal. Where there had been, just moments before, discord and mistrust between the merchants, there was suddenly camaraderie. No longer suspicious of each other, the merchants were banding together once more.

Then all of a sudden, Miss Elsie stood, her knees creaking and her hands firmly clutching the chair in front of her. As was her custom, she was dressed for the coming season, in a turtleneck featuring Easter bunnies and eggs.

"I have debated long and hard with myself about whether or not to share this with you, or the sheriff," she began, her voice as strong and clear as ever. "And if I do, well, I might as well share it with all of you. I have lived among you my entire life as your friend and neighbor. Some of you know how old I am, and the rest of you, well, you can just keep on guessing."

Samantha DeMuth rose to make her way over to Miss Elsie, but the elderly woman held up her hand to stop her. "Thank you for the support, Samantha, but this is something I'll do on my own."

"We love you, Miss Elsie," Stan called. Teppy and others echoed the sentiment.

"I have received one of those awful letters," Miss Elsie continued. "And instead of waiting for the other shoe to drop, I will tell you myself about the secret I have kept for years. I've kept it so long, in fact, that when I received that poison pen letter, I almost thought that it was meant for someone else. For so long, I had believed what you all have believed, so much so that when the truth was in front of me, I barely recognized it. You all know that my Earl and I spent almost a lifetime together before he died some twenty years ago. We lost two children, raised three others, and kept ourselves to ourselves. He was a deacon at Christ United Methodist Church and I was mistress of the Ladies' Society for a long time. We raised money for scholarships and to help others less fortunate than ourselves. Many of you attended Earl's funeral. If you look at his tombstone you will see it says 'Loving husband, father, and friend.'"

She took a deep, ragged breath, and then sat down with something of a thud, but still faced the crowd. "But you see, Earl and I weren't married, not in the legal way of standing before the preacher and filling out a marriage license at the clerk of the court."

The room, already quiet as Miss Elsie spoke, sank into a silence so hard even old Mrs. Ward at the library had never experienced such quiet. Spring, unable to stand by and do nothing any longer, retrieved a glass of water, which Miss Elsie accepted gratefully.

"You see, he was already married to a Canadian nurse he met in Korea. It had been a whirlwind romance and they had only known each other a few months. Her family was devoutly Catholic, and when they found out she had married a Protestant, they intervened and brought her home. One day she was there, the next, she had just vanished. Earl never saw her again, and not for want of trying. At first, all he wanted was to find the woman he loved. Then he simply just accepted his fate. And then he and I met, and our fate became our secret."

"I wanted you to hear this from me, and not from the Finch's Crossing rumor mill. With all due respect to the Sunset Boys," she added, referring to the group of retirees who fed the Finch's Crossing rumor mill from their booth at the lunch counter at Hoffman's Drugstore.

The audience flowed toward Miss Elsie. To them, what Miss Elsie had revealed was of no consequence. It did not diminish her accomplishments in their minds. And it never would.

CHAPTER 13

*S*PRING LEFT THE community center, overtaken by mixed emotions. She thought of Autumn's upcoming nuptials, of how Meg refused to get married, and of Miss Elsie making a life as much as a wife as any other woman in Finch's Crossing, yet without the paperwork that made it legal. How was Miss Elsie any less of a wife than a woman who had been legally married? The idea of marriage suddenly seemed elastic in Spring's mind. Miss Elsie and Earl were Finch's Crossing legends. Their love and generosity helped their friends and neighbors through hard times. Earl had been a Marine, loyally serving his country, while Miss Elsie had served the community.

And what of Spring's own relationship with Chad? Why

had they not married? They had lived as man and wife in almost every way for ten years. Yet there was a feeling, deep inside of her, that had kept Chad at a distance, just far enough away that she would never become one with him.

And then there was Gabe, who was already married but who inexplicably pursued her. What had brought the two of them together again in the same time and space? She had decided at the last minute to come to Finch's Crossing. If she hadn't, she probably would not have seen Gabe again. He would remain a distant memory, and the hurt she had finally overcome would never have returned.

What she did know for certain was that Chad was not the author of the poison pen letters. Spring had known about Teppy's fake connection to Martha Stewart and that Duncan hadn't graduated from college. She was certain that most of Finch's Crossing knew these things and just overlooked them. However, she had not known Miss Elsie's secret, so she could not have inadvertently passed it on to Chad, the way she might have done with the other secrets. Another thing Spring was certain of was that she was grateful for how the merchants came together to support each other, and most importantly, to support Miss Elsie, who was, without question, the town matriarch.

Spring strolled through Gazebo Park, in the center square of the town, named for the white clapboard gazebo that was the site of many summer concerts and ice cream socials. Gazebo Park was ringed by the community center, the Borough Building housing the sheriff and mayor's offices and assorted other town offices, and the Senior Center on the far side.

The gazebo had always been one of Spring's favorite spots in Finch's Crossing. The Hamilton family gathered with the other citizens of the town for the opening of the Finch's Crossing Fall Festival, which was a forty-year tradition. And thanks to Kyle, and his social media savvy, the once-flagging festival had returned to its former glory, attracting people from the surrounding counties and as far away as Pittsburgh to shop the many vendors and enjoy the parade, dog show, and live music.

During the fall, yellow, orange, and white mums bloomed all around Gazebo Park, with hay bales creating amphitheater seating. Veterans, many so old that they stumbled along, brought in the colors to officially open the festival, accompanied by a sole trumpeter playing "Taps." Spring's grandfather Hamilton had been one of those veterans.

But that evening, Spring soaked in the pink azaleas blooming throughout the quaint park. The cherry blossoms were starting to bud, and the weeping willows began to take on their bright green canopies. Spring climbed the steps to the gazebo and sat down.

It was so ironic, she thought, that she had come home to Finch's Crossing just in time for the spring season. And wasn't she in her own private spring? A place where she was shaking off the old in search of the new? It was ironic, too, that she found herself in a town full of secrets. She had run away from her secret but discovered that it would always be with her, and she would take it to New York in just a few weeks. She was still considering all of her options, but in the past days she had forgotten that before she had seen Gabe again after so many years, she had been enthralled with the idea of starting anew in New York. The excitement of a possible career as a designer or fashion editor had consumed and driven her. And now, when she should be thinking about her own future, she had allowed Gabe to rip out her heart and stomp it to pieces. Again. She should be thinking about how to start a YouTube channel or hire on as a fashion commentator at one of the networks. But instead, she was musing about an old, faded love that was destined only to hurt her.

She looked out over the park, the brown grass already overtaken by the green, and remembered two young teenagers—fresh-faced and in love—running through the shadows and up into the gazebo, so many years ago. It had been their freshman year of high school, and Spring had asked Gabe to the Sadie Hawkins dance. Afterwards, he had brought her to Gazebo Park and kissed her tenderly as they sat shoulder to shoulder on one of the benches. That kiss had sealed their fate, and for the next four years they were inseparable.

Spring furiously shook her head at the memory that had come unbidden into her mind. It had interrupted her musings about the future and what she would do next.

Gabe. He was a part of her past, just as Chad was. Two men who had meant so much to her at different points in her life. One had broken her heart. The other had never really loved her, not for who she was as a person, and had just used her for his own gain. Wasn't it time that she left these two men behind her for good? Certainly she had washed her hands of Chad. That was a no-brainer.

But where, if anywhere, did Gabe fit into her life? Even in the face of the indisputable fact that he was married, Spring had her doubts. She had known him so well when they were teenagers. Known his heart and seen into his soul, where there was only goodness and kindness. The Gabe she knew would never have pursued one woman while married to another. It didn't make sense.

The air turned chilly, and she gathered her things to leave. But as she stood in the middle of the structure, surrounded by the white latticework and gleaming white banister and rails, she paused and turned full circle around the gazebo, taking in the structure with new eyes.

If the gazebo had been the centerpiece of so many community events over the years, why not fold it into the plan for the Bridal Expo? The original plan was to limit the entire Expo to the Greystone, where attendees would visit each vendor's table, then enjoy complimentary refreshments in the Greystone's formal parlor or outside in the gardens, if weather permitted. There was plenty of room to continue with that plan, of course. She turned again in the gazebo and stopped, facing the municipal parking lot. Her hand shot up to her forehead. Parking. No one had considered that the Greystone did not have enough parking for the event. Spring hurriedly sat down and pulled a pencil and sketch pad out of her purse, flipping past sketches of dresses, pantsuits, scarves, and earrings. Her pencil strokes were quick but decisive.

She drew the gazebo in the middle of the page and sketched in the municipal parking lot behind it. In the center of the beautiful structure, she drew a bride and groom. What a wonderful place to hold a wedding.

At the edge of the page she placed the Greystone Manor and plotted in the streets that lay between the gazebo and the event venue. Even if Duncan allowed visitors to come in the back entrance, it would still be six blocks to the Greystone Manor. Too far for people to walk. But this wouldn't stop Spring, who truly believed that there was a solution to any and every problem.

* * *

After her 'aha' moment in the gazebo, Spring slipped into the kitchen door of Autumn's house and was immediately surrounded by the pungent aroma of roasting garlic and simmering tomatoes and onions. She set her purse and Bridal Expo planner on the kitchen counter and kissed her sister on the check.

"Grandpa's tomato sauce?" Spring asked, practically drooling at the thought, carbs be damned.

"Oh yeah," Autumn responded. "Is there any other kind of spaghetti ever made in this house?"

Spring grinned. "Did you remember the ground cloves?" she asked.

Autumn nodded. "And the whiskey. We should all sleep soundly tonight, what with that and the red wine I tossed in." She turned to look at Spring. "You're in a good mood," she observed. "You've got a spring in your step, so to speak. The meeting went well?"

Spring groaned at the cheesy joke. "It didn't start out so well. Poppy didn't exactly give the presentation I thought she would. She was a little...harsh."

Spring waited for Autumn to say "I told you so," but instead she just shot a glance over her shoulder and raised her eyebrows.

Spring put up her hands and said, "You were right, when you said I shouldn't leave because the merchants needed me. But curiously enough, what started out as a potential disaster, turned into a heart-warming moment."

Spring recounted how the evening unfolded and concluded with Miss Elsie's confession.

Autumn dropped the wooden spoon on the floor, and if Spring hadn't had such good reflexes, the basket of garlic bread would have quickly followed.

CHAPTER 13

"I know," Spring agreed. "It's a shocker. It just goes to show how you never know how someone else is suffering."

"Poor Miss Elsie," Autumn mused. "Is she okay?"

Spring nodded. "I think she will be." When I left, everyone was gathered around her as if she was a rock star."

"We'll go see her in a few days, after the hubbub has passed," Autumn said. "She's a strong old bird, and I know she's weathered a lot of hard times, but this is bound to have shocked her to the core." Autumn wiped away a few tears, and Spring gave her a quick hug.

"Okay, so now that's out of the way," Spring said brightly, ready to transition to the plans she'd made in the gazebo just a few minutes earlier. "I have to get a handle on the flow of traffic. If the Bridal Expo is to be as successful as we want it to be, we need to consider where all of those people are going to park. Instead of people going directly to the Greystone Manor and the Expo, we want people to see Finch's Crossing's quaint shopping district. If they go directly to the Expo, they will by-pass Pittsburgh Street altogether."

Autumn dumped the spaghetti noodles into a colander and shot a glance at her sister over her shoulder. She shook the colander to release the water.

"That's a good point," Autumn agreed. "Plus, there's not a lot of parking at the Greystone," Autumn said. "I don't know why I didn't realize that sooner."

"Same here," Spring said. "But I have an idea that will

solve everything. You told me that the man who drives the horse-drawn carriages resurrects his business for special occasions. Maybe he would do that for the Expo, especially if Ethan asks him."

The kitchen door banged and Ethan walked in. "Especially if Ethan asks who what?" he inquired, planting a kiss on Autumn's proffered cheek.

"You're back early. I wasn't expecting you until later," Autumn said with obvious pleasure.

Spring admired the relationship they had, built on genuine love and mutual respect. She hadn't experienced that with Chad. And it had taken her a long time to realize that. Too long.

Spring rushed to explain about the parking issue around the Expo.

"You know," Ethan said, snatching a piece of garlic bread off the counter, "those carriages are pretty small. You could only take four people at a time. Why don't you just ask him if he'll run his trolleys."

"Oh, that's right," Autumn chimed in. "I forgot that he has two working old-fashioned trolleys."

Spring's mind began to turn again. "Even better. Let's go visit him tomorrow when you get home from work."

Satisfied with her progress, Spring offered to make the dinner salad, when her cell phone rang. She answered it cheerily. "Finch's Crossing Bridal Expo, Spring Hamilton speaking. Oh, hi, Sterling. Ah ha. You're kidding. What does that mean?"

Autumn noticed that her sister's voice was shaking and ushered Spring to sit down in a kitchen chair. After everything that Spring had been through in the past few weeks, Autumn hated to see that perhaps something else was wrong.

When Spring ended the call, she sat in stunned silence.

"Spring, what is it? What's wrong?" Autumn asked and reached across the table to take her sister's hand.

With her free hand, Spring reached for a dinner napkin and wiped her eyes. "That was my lawyer, Sterling. Chad is suing me for alimony, claiming we had a common-law marriage."

Ethan piped up. "But California doesn't recognize common-law marriages. He has no claim to your assets."

"I know," Spring said and hiccupped. "But Sterling said that's just the beginning of what he's doing. He's also going to sue me for breach of contract."

"Did you have anything in writing?" Ethan pressed, as Autumn looked on, concerned.

"Honestly, I don't know. I always let Sterling handle everything. And I trust him, so I don't think he would have let me sign anything that wasn't in my favor. Plus, he just told me he never liked Chad."

"There's a lot of that going around," Autumn said, trying to lighten the mood, and squeezed Spring's hand.

"Spring, I don't think you have anything to worry about," Ethan tried to assure her.

"I know, and you're right. But Sterling said Chad is set on getting revenge and even though he doesn't have any legal claims, he can make my life miserable with these bogus claims and lawsuits."

"That's certainly accurate," Ethan said. "You can always find an attorney who will file frivolous lawsuits, either for the publicity or whatever price their client is willing to pay. There's no law against filing unwinnable suits. People do it all the time to tie up someone's personal life in red tape indefinitely, either to avoid paying child support, or getting revenge, as in your case."

"That's despicable," Autumn said, retrieving a bottle of wine from the pantry. "Here, I think we could all use a soothing glass of wine. It will go well with dinner." She winked at Spring. "And if you have a second glass, it might just take Chad off your mind for the rest of the evening."

Spring smiled wanly. She could always count on Autumn to come to her emotional aid. But then something occurred to her, and she turned to Ethan.

"Wait, how do you know so much about California marriage law?" Spring asked her soon-to-be brother-in-law.

Ethan looked sheepish. "It occurred to me that Chad might pull something like this, given everything you told us about him. I wanted to give you some peace of mind, if it should come to this, so I did a little research."

Spring felt tears in her eyes. But for the first time since she had learned that Gabe was married, she was crying tears of joy, thankful for Ethan's kindness and generosity of spirit.

Of all her sisters, Spring was closest to Autumn, who was an earthy, generous, nurturing soul. The Hamilton sisters had been named after the seasons of the year by their bohemian parents. Autumn, Summer, and Spring went by their given names. Only Winter, an architect in Pittsburgh, who was as hard and cold as her name implied, went by a nickname, Win.

After their father passed away (they had lost their mother eleven years earlier), each of the Hamilton girls had chosen what she wanted to keep from their parents' significant estate. There had been no fighting or bickering or hard feelings that so often occur when families attempt to divide money, property, and keepsakes. Autumn had wanted their childhood home and furniture. Spring had taken the lion's share of their mother's significant silver and crystal collection and all the heirloom jewelry, which included many one-of-a-kind Tiffany pieces worth tens of thousands of dollars. Summer and Win had split their parents' considerable remaining cash assets.

Only Autumn had chosen to stay in Finch's Crossing, and Spring understood that Autumn was intrinsically linked to their childhood home. She couldn't imagine her sister living anyplace else. That day in particular, she was glad that, largely because of Autumn, she had her childhood home to go back to. At that very moment, being in the house felt like a comforting embrace.

CHAPTER 14

WHEN KYLE OPENED the door to his apartment that evening, he tried not to smile. He wasn't surprised to see Meg standing on his doorstep. But he was surprised that it hadn't taken her very long to change her mind. And this thought warmed his heart. But he still had to teach her a lesson so that this never happened again. He was going to have some fun at Meg's expense. His beautiful, cranky, and gruff girlfriend was about to meet her match. He hung his head and shook it slowly, then he pretended to wipe away a tear.

"I've changed my mind," Meg said matter-of-factly and without emotion. "I will marry you after all. And I'm ready to set a date. We can get married as soon as you want. But it has to be after Autumn's wedding. And I have a few requirements."

"I don't know, Meg," Kyle said quietly. "This is a big decision. If you weren't sure you wanted to marry me last week, what makes you think that you can really commit? What changed your mind?"

Meg wasn't about to tell him about her fear of the marshmallow dress, snickers behind her back, and her general mortification and loss of her reputation of being as tough and fierce as the dogs she raised. And she sure wasn't going to tell him that Scottie had helped her figure out that she could wear a simple pantsuit.

So what could she tell him?

For the first time in as long as he could remember, Kyle found that his beloved had nothing to say. No clever comeback. No sarcastic joke. No needling. No teasing. *Wow. This is going to be easier than I thought!*

"I think I'll have to think about it for a few days and let you know," he said.

"Think about it?" Meg screeched. She had apparently found her voice. "What's there to think about?"

"Exactly," Kyle said slyly. "You've been 'thinking about it' for over a year now."

Meg crossed her arms over her chest and stuck out her chin. "Oh. I see how it's going to be," she said very smoothly. "Okay then. You think about it. You know where to find me." She turned to leave and added, "Call Sammy when you're ready and he can make an appointment for you to see me. I'm very busy, you know, with the recent expansion and all."

If Kyle had had a cowboy hat on, he would have thrown it to the ground and stomped on it. How did Meg always manage to get the better of him, even when it seemed like he had the upper hand?

* * *

"Now you just leave the talking to me," Autumn told Spring as they turned off Mulberry Street and drove up the long driveway to Ten Oaks Kennel. "You know how prickly Meg is. We have to play it just right."

"Fine by me," Spring complied. She knew this trip was a futile effort. Meg would never give up her secret. She was as stubborn as a mule. And as far back as Spring could remember, Meg had always been that way. When they were in high school, Meg refused to wear anything but jeans, even to gym class. She would not go to any dances, even though Autumn had begged her.

Spring did an internal inventory at the status of her current relationships—or more accurately, lack thereof—as Autumn parked the jeep. Her relationship with Gabe was a non-starter. Worse, actually, but not as bad as her relationship with Chad had been. Autumn's relationship with Ethan was amazing. He was the man of her sister's dreams, but she couldn't enjoy her engagement because her best friend was driving her crazy. So it seemed that only cranky Meg—the source of that stress—was enjoying a stress-free relationship with a gorgeous and kind-hearted man who adored her.

As they approached the front door to the kennel, the dogs started barking immediately.

"How does she stand all that noise?" Spring asked, as she took in the tidy rows of kennels to the right, the neat shelves and storage cubbies in front of them, and the long hallway that she supposed led to the offices, to the left. She was correct. Autumn turned to the left and Spring noticed walls lined with photos of law enforcement officers and their dogs, many holding medals and contestant ribbons. She supposed they had all been bred by Meg's family. Most of the photos were fairly recent, probably since the Overlys had retired to Florida. Spring had to hand it to her. Meg might have been a grump, but she was obviously a talented businesswoman and respected in her field. She could probably learn a thing or two from Meg, Spring thought.

They arrived at the office, and Autumn knocked on the doorframe. Meg looked up and half-smiled, half-scowled in the way that only she could manage.

"Come to check up on me?" she asked, as she motioned for them to sit on the guest chairs in front of her desk. She returned to her chair and sat facing them. "I would have expected this little stunt from Spring," she said sadly, "but not you, Autumn."

"What are you talking about?" Spring asked innocently.

"I know very well that you are here to ask me to tell you how I'm going to get Heather's uncle to your wedding in time."

"We aren't," Spring said, as Autumn said, "Of course not."

Meg folded her arms across her chest. "Okay then, so what are you doing here?"

Autumn and Spring looked at each other, and Spring chastised herself for not having concocted a cover story. Another reason to curse Gabe. He was taking her off her game. If she were in the stages of mourning, she had definitely left grief behind. She was now in the full anger stage.

"We just came by to, to..." Autumn began, and Spring jumped in, "to see if you would host the wedding shower here."

As soon as she said the words, she realized how absurd they were. And so did Meg.

"I'm not even going to dignify that insane suggestion with a response, Spring. You know very well that you or Martha will host the shower and it will be all froufrou and ladylike. You probably won't even invite me because you think I'll spoil it."

"As long as you bring a gift, you're invited," Autumn teased, hoping to steer the conversation in a different direction.

"Okay, you two. Spit it out," Meg insisted, with a long sigh. "Just tell me what you came here to say and then be on your way. I've got work to do."

"Well," Spring began gently, paying no attention to Autumn's glare. After all, this was just a straightforward situation that needed a logical analysis. Being a businesswoman who had a bottom line to consider, surely Meg would understand the concepts of risk management and return on investment. Spring continued. "This is really a simple matter that I think we can resolve quickly and amicably."

"Uhhuh," Meg said, picking at a fingernail. "Go on."

"We all want the same thing, right? We want Autumn to enjoy her engagement, have the wedding of her dreams, and make a little girl's wish come true." Spring ignored Autumn's shoe rubbing against her shin. "So what do you say?"

"About what?" Meg asked.

"About telling us how you are going to get Bryan to the wedding in time."

"Oh, that. No can do," Meg answered matter-of-factly and rose from her chair. "Now, if that's all, I think it's time you go."

Spring started to speak, but Autumn kicked her again and they got up to leave.

"It's okay," Autumn said. "I trust Ethan. And if Ethan says you're going to come through, then I'll just have to be satisfied with that."

All of a sudden, Autumn let out a little gasp. "Meg, you're not wearing your engagement ring!"

Meg immediately wedged her left hand into her pocket. "I don't wear it when I'm working," she lied.

"Of course you do," Autumn corrected her. "I've never seen

you without it since you got engaged. Not once. Now what gives? Spill."

Meg didn't say anything, but she didn't have to because the gears in Spring's logical mind had clicked into place.

"You broke up with him, didn't you?" Spring cried, wanting to hurl the stapler or the tape dispenser at Meg. "You broke up with that wonderful, sweet man who you don't even deserve."

"It was a mutual, uh, understanding," Meg fudged.

Autumn got up and leaned on the desk next to Meg. "Are you okay?" she asked her best friend, with genuine concern.

"Of course she's not okay," Spring practically squealed. "She must be insane if she let that nice man go. He must be a saint to put up with you and your grumpy ways and rough-and-tumble act. You don't know what a catch he is."

"Spring, that's enough," Autumn commanded.

Spring took a step back and covered her mouth with her hand. "Oh, Meg, I'm so sorry. I shouldn't have said any of those things. I'm so, so sorry."

"It's okay," Meg mumbled, much to the sisters' surprise. "You're right. And I knew as soon as I did it, well, maybe a couple of hours later, that I had made a mistake. So I went to his apartment. But he wouldn't take me back."

Autumn and Spring looked at each other, dumbfounded.

"What did he say?" Spring asked, now feeling incredibly guilty for having lashed out.

"He said he had to think about it," she responded. "Which

basically means no."

"Not necessarily," Autumn said, trying to sound hopeful.

"If he has to think about it, that means he's not sure. And if he's not sure, then that means part of him is saying no. So that's that."

What had started out as an attempt to de-stress Autumn had turned into yet another thing for her to worry about.

"But I don't understand why you broke up with him," Autumn said gently.

"It all happened so fast. He was pressuring me to set a date to get marr...marri—"

"Married," Autumn finished for her.

Meg nodded and Spring rolled her eyes and said, "So what's the big deal? If you plan on marrying him, then why not set a date? Unless," Spring paused. "Unless you planned all along that you weren't going to marry him and were just stringing him along, prolonging the engagement indefinitely."

Meg squirmed and tried not to look guilty. There was no way she was going to tell Autumn and Spring about her freak-out over the marshmallow dress and flowers and high heels. But then again, she didn't want them to think she was capable of stringing Kyle along, when they both knew—at least Autumn knew—that she really loved Kyle.

"It's not like that," she finally said. "You wouldn't understand. Now if you don't mind, I'd like to be alone."

* * *

"You weren't very nice to her in there," Autumn scolded Spring as they drove home. "Even if Meg doesn't show it, she's hurting inside."

"That's her own fault," Spring snapped. "What on earth was she thinking?"

"For all her faults and simple, no-nonsense lifestyle, she can be complicated," Autumn explained. "And it doesn't help that she bottles it all up inside."

"Do you think Kyle really told Meg that he had to think about whether or not he would take her back?" Spring asked.

Autumn grinned at her. "I'm sure that he said it. But what I don't believe for a second is that he meant it."

"Really?" Spring asked. "What do you mean?"

"I think Kyle is giving her a taste of her own medicine. He's going to string her along like she did to him."

"But you heard Meg," Spring insisted. "She thinks it's over. I wouldn't be surprised if she wasn't going through her phone deleting all of his photos and their text chains. She's probably blocked his number."

"She still uses a flip phone," Autumn responded, laughing. "It doesn't even have a camera. At least I don't think it does. Anyway, if it does, I'm sure she doesn't know how to use it."

"That's a discussion for another time," Spring responded, exasperated. "I think I know where you're going with this. And I like it."

"I'm not going anywhere, except home. Ethan, Heather,

and Martha are coming over for dinner, remember?"

"No, that's not what I mean," Spring insisted. "I mean where you are going, figuratively. We can help Kyle get back at Meg and teach Meg a lesson at the same time."

"Why would we do that?" Autumn asked, surprised. "I can't believe you would think about doing something so mean."

"Don't think of it as mean," Spring responded, cringing at the thought of the mean girls who had tortured the Hamilton sisters all through school, teasing them about their unusual names. "It's more like we're doing this for Meg's own good."

"It doesn't feel like you have her best interest at heart," Autumn observed.

"Not directly," Spring agreed. "I'm more interested in helping Kyle, but in the end, helping him means helping Meg, so what's the difference?"

Irritated by her sister's innate goodness, Spring approached the situation from a logical position. They were faced with a problem that needed solving. Kyle needed to win back Meg in such a way that she would never abandon him again. No more of this wishy-washy stuff.

"Are you sure you aren't projecting, even just a little bit?" Autumn asked, carefully.

"What on earth do you mean?" Spring tried not to sound as defensive as she felt.

"What I mean," Autumn explained, "is that you're in a very vulnerable position right now. First you broke up with Chad and then Gabe broke your heart. Sure, you're committed to helping Kyle, but it sure seems like you want to hurt Meg in the process. I'm not sure you're the right person to be masterminding a reconciliation between these two particular lovebirds."

Spring grudgingly admitted to herself that Autumn was right. She was grinding the ax she wielded for Chad and Gabe against Kyle and Meg's relationship.

"Well," Spring said to her sister, working on a compromise in her mind as Autumn pulled her jeep up to the curb in front of their home on Loucks Avenue. "What if I promise to help Kyle but not enjoy it?"

Spring watched as her sister slid the gear into park and turned to face her, rolling her eyes. "All I ask is that you be careful."

Spring raised two fingers to her forehead in a mock salute. "Don't worry," she promised. "Before you know it, Kyle and Meg will be back together. Besides, we need them happy and functioning if she's going to get Bryan here in time for the wedding."

* * *

Kyle had the back door of his apartment cracked open ever so slightly, and he watched through the crack with considerable pleasure as Martha's Toyota Camry crept slowly down the alley toward the back parking lot. Martha guided the car into a parking spot, put it in park, turned off the ignition, and forced herself to not look behind her toward the back seat. If she had looked, she would have seen Autumn and Spring slumped down, leaning toward one another, giggling, making sure that no one could see their heads sticking up. Martha looked toward Kyle's apartment and was pleased to see his handsome young face smiling at her. He nodded, which Martha took as permission to allow her covert passengers to disembark.

Martha didn't turn around. She just said, "Okay, girls. Kyle is ready." She glanced around her. "I don't see anybody. Make it quick."

At Martha's command, the sisters exited the driver's side passenger door, and keeping their heads down like movie stars dodging the paparazzi, made a dash for Kyle's apartment. After Kyle stood aside to allow them to enter, Martha got out of the car and calmly walked toward Kyle's, not giving any hint that she has just transported a pair of willing and talented conspirators.

Kyle had called this meeting. He needed help in what he called "Meg matters."

"What can I do to get Meg to realize that she really does love me and we should be together? I know she loves me. She's just so tied up in knots about this marriage thing. I don't know what to do."

It was Spring who had had the eureka idea that they had gathered to discuss. "I have the perfect thing," she said. "We'll make her jealous. Insanely jealous. Then she'll realize what a catch Kyle really is."

More than intrigued, Kyle asked, "And just how do you plan to do that?" Not much got by Meg, and she could outwit, out-best, and out-boast anyone.

"Fake dates, of course!" Spring responded triumphantly. "We want to set you up on some fake dates. Dates with really attractive girls. Model types. And we want Meg to see you out. We want her to get jealous. Really, really jealous. So jealous that she realizes that she is supposed to be on your arm. And nobody else."

Kyle's mind raced as he considered the plan, and he stroked his chin, then smiled like a Cheshire cat, and declared, "I like it!"

* * *

Ethan parked his Jaguar in front of the entrance to Ten Oaks Kennel. It had rained earlier and he was damned if he was going to drive his car up the hill and park it in a mud pile next to a mud puddle. He knew Meg was busy with the new business generated by the expansion, but she really needed to get the parking lot paved. He avoided the puddles gingerly and walked in. The dogs began to bark furiously as soon as they heard his footsteps.

"Hello," he called. "Meg? Sammy? Hello?"

And she really needed to hire some extra help. He walked around the counter and toward a muffled voice coming from

Meg's office. He heard her say, "Of course I'm worried! What do you think will happen if I can't deliver? It will be the disaster of the century."

Ethan stopped in his tracks when Meg paused. When she started talking again, he crept forward.

"That's no help, dimwit," she barked. "You promised you could make this happen and if you don't, I'm coming after you hard. This is my reputation we're talking about, buster."

Ethan heard Meg slam the phone down and before he could slink away, Meg stomped out of her office and nearly ran into him.

"Geez, you scared me!" She hurled her words at him like an accusation. "What are you doing out here sneaking around?" She narrowed her eyes at him, which made him shrink back. "You're checking up on me, aren't you? Spring and Autumn couldn't get anything out of me so now you've come for a progress report. Everything's fine, so you don't have to worry, and you can stop acting like Nancy Drew. You're terrible at it, by the way."

"It didn't sound okay to me," Ethan said quietly, and there was a long pause before Meg said anything.

"What? That?" she pointed behind her. "That conversation just now that you were eavesdropping on? That had nothing to do with Bryan. Not. One. Iota."

"Meg," Ethan said slowly, as if speaking to a child. "It's nothing to be embarrassed about, you know. None of us really thought you could pull it off anyway. It's time to come clean and let Autumn know. There's still time to make this right for Heather."

Meg took a step toward him and spoke under her breath, mimicking his tone. "Are you out of your mind? Embarrassed? No one thought I could pull it off? Make it right?"

"Now, Meg, just calm down."

"Don't you dare come into my place of business, Ethan Rasmussen, and tell me to calm down. I have given you my word that I will have Bryan here in time for your wedding, and I will. I don't know what else you want me to say."

Ethan shrugged his shoulders. "I just want you to tell us the truth, Meg. That's all." He turned to leave, then paused. "You know I'm going to have to tell Autumn about this."

"Don't you dare," Meg warned Ethan. "You have no idea what you're talking about. That conversation was about my expansion further into Canada. And not that it's any of your business, but I am having troubles with customs and there's a certain Mountie I know who promised to help but is having second thoughts. He's not willing to, er, gloss over a few things for me."

Ethan shook his head, laughing. "A Mountie? What is this, nineteenth-century Canadian *Little House on the Prairie?*"

"They are called Mounties, Ethan. The Royal Canadian Mounted Police, also known as Mounties."

"And you just happen to know a random Mountie, like you

happen to know the Chairman of the Joint Chiefs of Staff."

"No," she replied tersely. "I don't personally know the Secretary of State or the Chairman of the Joint Chiefs of Staff, and you know that. Because I explained all that to you."

Ethan now wished he had not put so much faith in Meg. He knew she meant well and that she really thought she was going to be able to do it. Maybe she would, after all, but to him it was seeming less and less likely.

* * *

Spring, Autumn, and Martha waited a few days before they descended on Miss Elsie with a light picnic dinner and a bottle of Miss Elsie's favorite sherry.

"Just hold on there now," they heard Miss Elsie say from inside her cottage after they rang the bell. "I'm old and slow so don't go scurrying off. I'll be along directly."

The women smiled at each other warmly, and when Miss Elsie saw her friends gathered on her stoop, smiling cheerfully, tears formed in her eyes.

"My dear friends, can't say I can think of a more welcome surprise than to find the three of you at my door." She held the door open and stepped aside to allow them in.

Martha and Autumn had been in Miss Elsie's cozy cottage on Grace Road before, as it was just up the street from Loucks Avenue, but it was Spring's first visit, and she took in the sparkling interior. A chintz sofa and matching chairs faced a corner fireplace in the front room. The walls were lined with bookshelves, holding a lifetime of cookbooks. In the kitchen, which formed the rest of the downstairs, the three could smell cinnamon and cloves.

"Don't just stand there," Miss Elsie commanded, "come on into the living room. I'm guessing you have some bread and cheese and fruit in there, and maybe some cheese straws, if I'm lucky."

"You are lucky, Miss Elsie," Martha said and put the picnic hamper onto the coffee table in front of the fire. The three of them made themselves comfortable, and Miss Elsie took the chair closest to the fire.

Spring let herself step mentally away from the cozy scene to consider the circumstances to date, the gears in her mind turning her famous logic into motion.

She was beginning to suspect that one person in Finch's Crossing was the source of the letters, but not the actual letter writer. If Spring herself had casually known Teppy's and Duncan's secrets, someone else could know them, and others, too.

Spring looked around the table, mentally calculating the number of years they had all lived in Finch's Crossing. Both Autumn and Martha were born and raised in the town and had never lived elsewhere, except for when Autumn went to college. Miss Elsie had lived most of her adult life in Finch's Crossing. And what about the other life-long residents of Finch's Crossing? A person could come across a lot of secrets as years passed.

"You know," Spring began slowly, "I think we've been looking at everything all wrong. For us, letters and secrets are incredibly emotional, but that's not the only way to look at them."

Autumn popped a brie-topped cracker into her mouth, chewed, and asked, "What other way is there to look at it? So many of us have had our innermost secrets revealed. It's an incredibly emotional experience."

Martha and Miss Elsie nodded in agreement and Miss Elsie chimed in. "You don't know how hard it was for me to bare my soul the other day at the Merchants Association meeting." She felt for a handkerchief in her pocket and dabbed at her eye.

Martha took her other hand. "You have always been a brave soul, dear friend. Losing two children, then your husband, starting a business after you retired. You'll weather this rough patch, too."

"You're right of course, Martha," Miss Elsie responded with a weak smile, but a smile, nonetheless. "And no one has treated me any differently since my revelation. It's as if it never happened."

Miss Elsie returned her gaze to Spring. "Now go on, honey, we went down a rabbit hole, me and my good friend here." She squeezed Martha's hand.

Spring wished she had a flip chart so she could plot out what she was thinking. Instead, she cleared the remains of the picnic from the coffee table and looked around the room. When she spotted Miss Elsie's salt and pepper shaker collection, she stood up and walked over to the curio cabinet.

"Miss Elsie, I think I can explain what I'm thinking if I can use these salt and pepper shakers. I'll be careful, I promise."

"That's fine, just fine, honey. You go right on ahead. I've not had them out in ages. They'll be a sight for my sore, red eyes. My dear husb…" Miss Elsie stopped in mid-sentence and the tears started to flow again.

Martha squeezed her friend's hand again and offered words of comfort. "As far as we're concerned, and as far as the entire town is concerned, Earl was your husband. And that's that."

Miss Elsie took a deep breath and continued. "My husband gave those to me over the years, for birthdays and Christmases. I've not looked at them in ages."

She stood and joined Spring at the curio cabinet and directed the younger woman which items to take, telling the trio that they were her favorites—the Amish couple, the hen and rooster, the toothpaste and toothbrush and two windmills.

Spring sat on the floor at one end of the coffee table and carefully placed seven shakers on the table. "These represent the people we know of who have received letters so far," she explained.

Autumn interrupted her. "You better make that eight," she said quietly, looking down at her hands.

"Oh, Autumn," Spring exclaimed. "Why didn't you say anything?"

"Because it was so incredibly stupid that it didn't warrant mentioning," she said. "But now that I think about it, the fact that I got one is the important thing, not what it said."

Spring nodded in agreement as she added an eighth salt shaker to the table. "I think you should tell the sheriff anyway. It's an important part of a pattern."

Autumn nodded and motioned for Spring to keep going with her theories.

"So if we look at this logically," Spring continued, "we need to establish a few facts or at least make a few observations about what we're dealing with. First, based on what the letters look like, in terms of handwriting and the insides having a big picture stuck in the middle, I think we can safely assume that the letter writer is one person."

The other women nodded in agreement, and Spring went on.

"So far, we haven't asked ourselves, or anyone else, what the letters say. By now, everyone knows Miss Elsie's secret and Gabe's. But we don't know the others. I think if we're going to try and track down the letter writer, we need to pool our collective knowledge and put all the secrets out in the open."

"Good luck with that," Autumn mused. "I can't see anyone willing to do that. They're already embarrassed and snarking at each other, suspicious of people they've known for years."

"That's exactly my point," Spring said excitedly and then reminded them again of the scene at the community center where Poppy's insults had brought everyone together and to each other's defense. She described how Stan had stood up for Ducky and how Teppy had doubled her DeMuth's floral order.

Spring continued. "I can't imagine that anyone in this community sent those letters. I think they were sent by an outsider with the intent of sowing discord and just generally being disruptive and mean-spirited."

"Who on earth would do such a thing" Martha asked. "And furthermore, how on earth would they have known all these secrets?"

"Because there is a single source inside Finch's Crossing who is feeding the stories to someone who in turn is sending around the poison pen letters. Think about it. I'll admit that I knew two of the secrets, and I haven't even lived her for almost twenty years."

Autumn picked up the thread. "But that would mean that someone in Finch's Crossing already knew all the secrets," she said. "How is that possible?"

Miss Elsie piped up from her chair next to the fire. "If you've lived long enough in one place, like I have, you do tend to pick up on things, even secrets. Sometimes you're just in the right place at the wrong time and happen to overhear something you weren't meant to hear." She blushed a little.

"So you're saying that you know all of these secrets?" Martha asked her friend.

"Oh gracious, no. I just knew three of them. She held up her hand in a stop signal. "But don't even bother asking me what they are, because my lips are sealed." She made the motion of locking and throwing away the key on her lips.

"But that's exactly my point," Spring said, revving up again. "You only knew a few secrets, and you didn't tell anyone. Our source is one person who knows all the secrets. Someone who's lived in Finch's Crossing their entire life."

"And long enough," Miss Elsie chimed in enthusiastically, "to know my secret, which, let's face it, is as old as the hills."

"So what do we do now?" Autumn asked as she poured the sherry in Miss Elsie's small glasses and passed them around. "Should we tell the sheriff?"

"Eventually," Spring answered. "But first I want to tell you my secret."

"Your secret?" Autumn asked, gasping. "But your letter was about Gabe's secret. Not yours."

"That's because no one in Finch's Crossing knows about it. And I've been so ashamed about it that I never told anyone, not even you, Autumn, which should tell you the level of embarrassment I've felt all these years."

Autumn reached for her sister's hand.

Spring added another pair of salt and pepper shakers to the mix, placing them on the other end of the table.

"These represent me and Chad, out in California," she said

with a shaky voice. "For the longest time, I thought I was nothing without him."

"But nothing could be further from the truth," Autumn interjected, appalled at her sister's revelation. "He was nothing without you."

"Yes," Spring agreed, "but for years he told me that without him I would have nothing, and I believed it. Every day for years he berated me with insults and told me I was stupid. He knew what buttons to push. He would tell me I was fat or that my complexion was fading. And I believed him. At first, it was because I was so young and naïve, and after I guess I just was so used to the mental and emotional abuse that it barely registered as being anything but normal. It was just what my life had become."

Spring went on to explain how he had pumped her for gossip, no matter where it came from.

"Well, you're rid of him now and on your own two feet," Miss Elsie said. "No one can take that away from you. And you know, don't you, honey, that no person—not even you—is what someone else says or thinks you are."

"Thanks, Miss Elsie," Spring said between tears and accepting a tissue, which Martha pulled out of her cardigan.

"But back to the poison pen letters," Spring continued. "At first, I thought that Chad was behind them and that he had tracked me down to Finch's Crossing and set out to make life miserable for me."

Autumn picked up the trail. "And that's where you got the theory that the letters are the source of one person feeding the stories to an outsider, who then turned around and used them to sow discord."

"Exactly," Spring responded with renewed vigor.

"So what made you decide it wasn't Chad?" Martha asked.

"Simple," Spring responded. "I didn't know Miss Elsie's secret or Gabe's. So I couldn't have been the source. Thank goodness. I was really sweating it there for a while. You have no idea how relieved I am!"

Spring then moved the salt and pepper shakers that represented her and Chad closer to the others. "So now these represent the Finch's Crossing insider and the person they're feeding the gossip to."

"And you think they're closer to home, not like you, out of state and far away," Autumn suggested.

"Yeah," Spring agreed. "It's just a feeling, but I'd bet money on it."

* * *

The three women walked the short distance back to Loucks Avenue, and Martha said good night and went inside. Spring and Autumn sat on the front porch swing, where once they whispered secrets to each other about the boys they liked, and their dreams for marriage and careers. It was a cool evening, and they brought out the blankets Autumn kept in the wicker ottoman for just such an occasion.

"You okay?" Autumn asked her sister.

Spring tilted her head back to look at the stars. They looked the same as they had seventeen years ago. And they wouldn't change for another seventeen years. That was the thing Spring loved most about Finch's Crossing. It never changed. And right then, it was the balm she needed.

"Yes, I am now," Spring responded softly. "But I could kick myself for the years I wasted on Chad."

"Don't," Autumn said gently. "You are the person you are today despite him. And that says a lot about you, about your strength and resilience. Do you want to talk about it? What can I do?"

"Thanks, sis," Spring said, smiling. "But I really am okay. Just keep on being you. That's all I need. That, and I think I'll sit out here a while longer."

Autumn rose to leave and kissed Spring on the cheek.

Once Autumn was inside, Spring stared at the stars, then at the silent trees that lined the slate sidewalk along the front of the house. How many secrets had been made or shared in their presence over the years? She looked to the right, down the street, and then to the left, pausing to look at each house, glowing with lamplight, and she thought of the people inside and wondered about their secrets and what burdens they might be carrying. She had felt lighter almost immediately after sharing her secret earlier that evening. She didn't go to Miss Elsie's with the intention of sharing it, but it had felt right. And she did not regret it.

And she could finally admit to herself that her visit to Finch's Crossing had been much more than a detour on her way to start her new life. She had needed the familiarity of home. Here, she could go back to the way things had been before Chad. She could connect with the young, enthusiastic Spring. And now, she would find her old self again, and meld it with the stronger, wiser person she was today.

CHAPTER 15

*T*HE NEXT MORNING feeling vigorous and renewed, Spring rose up early. She donned her running clothes and sneakers and went out for a five-mile run—her first real exercise since she had arrived in Finch's Crossing. It felt good to crisscross the silent streets, and with each stride she felt her old confidence returning.

When she arrived back at the house, Autumn and Ethan were so deep in conversation sitting at the kitchen table that they didn't see her come in.

"I think maybe Meg can't pull it off after all," Ethan was saying.

"You can't be serious," Spring said, wiping her face with a dish towel.

Ethan and Autumn turned in unison to look at her.

"Oh, I didn't hear you come in," Autumn said, obviously uncomfortable.

Ethan repeated what he had overheard Meg saying on the phone, and Spring watched her sweet sister physically grimace to have to listen to his words again. How Spring resented Meg at that very moment. And how pleased she was that they had cooked up a plan to fix her wagon.

"Are you sure you heard her right?" Spring asked, getting down to the business of analyzing the situation from various perspectives and preparing to offer advice and solutions.

"Oh, there was no mistaking it," Ethan said firmly. "She said 'You promised you could make this happen and if you don't, I'm coming after you hard.'"

"That sounds like Meg," Autumn agreed.

"What did she say when you confronted her?" Spring asked, joining them at the table.

"She denied it of course." Ethan said. "She made up some story about a Canadian Mountie, then threatened me with bodily harm before throwing me out."

"That definitely sounds like Meg," Spring said.

"I honestly don't know what to do," Autumn said. "I'm thinking about postponing the wedding until we know Bryan can be here."

"You can't call it off," Spring balked.

"I didn't say call it off," Autumn said patiently, "I said postpone. As in a few weeks or months."

"And what are you going to tell Heather?"

Autumn looked pensive. "I haven't gotten that far yet."

I'm going to tell you what you told me," Spring said, getting to her feet and standing in front of her sister. "You're a grown woman, and you're going to get a hold of yourself."

"I said that?" Autumn asked distractedly. "When?"

"When I wanted to leave after I found out Gabe was married."

"I don't know what would be worse," Autumn mused, playing devil's advocate, "having the wedding without Bryan in time for Heather's birthday or waiting to have the wedding so Bryan can attend." She buried her head in her hands. "Oh, I just hate to disappoint that sweet little girl," she sniffed. "She has been through so much."

She lifted her head and looked into Ethan's concerned eyes. "I can't believe I let Meg talk me into this. I should have considered the consequences, should have thought through what would happen if she couldn't come through."

Ethan reached across the table and took her hand. "Heather is resilient, you know that. Look at the way she bounced back after her parents died."

"She didn't talk for six weeks," Autumn corrected. "That's not bouncing back."

Spring moved her head slightly and Ethan took the hint. He got up to leave, saying, "It's your call, babe. Whatever you decide, we'll make it work. And we'll figure out how to make this something Heather can understand."

After she heard the front door open and close and Ethan's car backed out of the driveway, Spring moved to sit next to Autumn at the table.

"Meg and I have never kept anything from each other," she started to say, then corrected herself. "Only that one time when I was struggling with my painting. But that was different. There wasn't anything at stake. There wasn't a fragile little girl involved."

Spring broke down her sister's words and brought them out to examine logically. "I think we're talking about two different things here," she said. "You're worried about how Heather is going to react if the wedding doesn't happen and Bryan doesn't show. But I think there's more going on here. I think this is more about you and Meg than it is about Heather. Because Ethan's right. Heather's resilient. She'll bounce back."

Autumn sighed and sat back in her chair. "You're right, of course," she laughed with mirth. "Way to get to the heart of the matter, sis. I hate it that Meg won't tell me how she is going to get Bryan to the wedding."

Suddenly, Spring jumped up and ran out the kitchen door reappearing two minutes later with a harried Martha.

"What is it?" Martha asked, looking around wildly. "What's wrong?"

"Oh, Martha, I'm sorry Spring scared you. Nothing's

wrong." Autumn glared at her sister.

Spring just shrugged and said, "The only thing that's wrong is Meg is driving everyone—especially Autumn—crazy. She won't tell us how she's going to get Bryan here in time for the wedding. And I can't believe I just now thought of this." She ushered Martha to sit down, who did so with an uncertain look on her face.

"Thought of what?" Martha asked, accepting the cup of coffee Autumn poured for her.

"If anyone knows about what's going on, it's you," Spring exclaimed. "After all, you are Bryan's mother."

"Hold on, girls," Martha said. "I know what Meg has told you. And I know that Ethan knows what she's doing, and how she's doing it, but is sworn to secrecy. And let me tell you, that man will take the secret to the grave. He's that honorable. So I wouldn't waste your time trying to get anything out of him."

"It's not Ethan we want to talk to," Spring said, having quieted down and settled back in her chair. "It's you, Martha. You must know something."

"I really don't," Martha protested, "and honestly, if I knew I'm not sure whether or not I would tell you if I had promised not to tell."

"Martha!" Autumn exclaimed, hurt. "You're one of my best friends. I can't believe you wouldn't tell me if you knew." She paused. "Do you know?"

"Of course not," Martha said, gentling her tone. "The point

is moot anyway. I don't even know exactly where Bryan is serving. All I know is that he is somewhere in the Middle East."

Autumn piped up, "Meg said he's in a cave somewhere in Afghanistan."

Martha raised her eyebrows. "I have no idea how she would know that. Bryan never tells me where he is. I think revealing his location to anyone would be tantamount to treason."

Martha and Spring exchanged glances. "Then how does Meg know?" Autumn asked. "And more importantly, do we think that Meg actually knows, which would be strange but promising, or do we think that Meg is just blundering her way through this?"

Martha stood up to leave. "You'll have to excuse me. I've got the Sixty-Plus luncheon to get ready for," she said, referring to the retiree social club she belonged to. "Now don't take this the wrong way, but you girls are thinking way too much about this. You've gone and got yourselves wrapped inside a mindbender inside a quandary. You have to decide once and for all what you're going to do and then leave it at that."

Spring and Autumn watched Martha leave, closing the kitchen door behind her.

"Now I don't know what to think," Autumn said quietly. "This is either really good, or really bad."

"Yeah," Spring agreed. "Or maybe both at the same time."

CHAPTER 16

EG FLOUNCED INTO the chair opposite Spring at the Greystone Manor restaurant. "Okay, I'm here. What's so important that you had to see me in person? And it better not be about Kyle. And I don't want another mean lecture either."

Spring picked up her wine. "I want to talk to you about Autumn," Spring answered, moving her chair slightly to the left, leaving a clear line of sight for Meg to see Kyle and Alyssa sitting across the room.

"Here we go," Meg sighed. "What about her? She doesn't believe that I can have Bryan here in time because Ethan overheard a conversation that had nothing to do with that. She'll probably disinvite me from her wedding."

"I think you mean 'un-invite' you," Spring corrected. "So what did Ethan hear?"

"He heard a totally different business arrangement I was making with the Royal Canadian Mounted Police," Meg explained patiently. "But I'm sure you already knew that."

Spring shrugged and waved her hand dismissively. "Okay, well, all that is beside the point," she said.

"Beside what point?" Meg retorted. "What are you talking about?"

Spring leaned forward in her chair. "I know you don't want to tell Autumn how you're going to get Bryan home, but at least tell me how you know that Bryan is in a cave in Afghanistan."

"What are you talking about?" Meg asked, annoyed. "I have no idea where he is. How could I?"

Spring shook her head in solemn disagreement. "Autumn distinctly remembers you telling her when you cooked up this crazy scheme that Bryan was in a cave in a remote Afghan outpost."

Meg rolled her eyes. "I wasn't being literal, for Pete's sake. I was being...what's the word?"

"Figurative?" Spring offered.

"Exactly. Everyone knows he's in the Middle East somewhere. I've heard Martha talk about it. It's no secret. So that's all I meant."

"But you said 'cave in Afghanistan,'" Spring pressed.

"Which means somehow you have access to some sensitive information." She let her voice trail off.

Meg picked up the thread. "Which, if I did have, might make Autumn feel better about the wedding?"

Spring nodded. "Martha said there was no way that you could know his location because it's classified. How could you know if Martha distinctly says you can't know? Unless, somehow, you do. And if you say you know, then how do you know?"

"Spring," Meg said impatiently, "you are thinking too much and talking in circles. So just stop." She paused. "You're filling Autumn with all these crazy speculations, aren't you?"

"She's talking about postponing the wedding," Spring said.

"That's not my problem or my fault," Meg retorted. "And it would be a real shame if these people went to all the trouble of getting Bryan home and it turned out there wasn't a wedding after all." Meg leaned back in her chair, a self-satisfied smirk on her face.

Spring's ears perked up. "These people?" she asked. "What people?"

"What do you mean, 'what people?'" Meg asked, exasperated. "The people who are getting Bryan home." She stood, readying to leave. "And the people you will never know about."

Spring knew that Meg would head for the exit any minute, and she had to put the plan in motion before Meg made for the door.

"Oh, look, is that Kyle over there?" Spring asked innocently, looking over her shoulder. "Don't look now, but he's two tables behind us. He's with Alyssa Porter. She's the sales manager at the *News-Observer*. And they're sharing a bottle of champagne, and there's a red rose next to her place setting."

Meg leaned her torso so far to the side that she bumped the table and the water glasses, and silverware shook.

Spring continued her rehearsed words. "They must work very closely together since Kyle buys advertising for the merchants. I'm guessing they spend a lot of time together?"

"How should I know?" Meg asked, drumming her fingers on the table, obviously perturbed at the sight of Kyle on a date.

Good, Spring thought, *it's getting to her!*

"I'm just going to pop over and say hello," Spring said brightly. "It wouldn't be polite to ignore them. Coming?"

"Of course not," Meg snapped.

"Suit yourself," Spring answered, "but if you leave, you'll let him know that you care what he's doing."

"Well, I don't," Meg said, shaking her head, the image of Kyle and Alyssa sitting tete-a-tete stinging more than she ever imagined it would.

That didn't take very long, Meg thought. *My God, I may have really lost him for good.* She turned back to Spring and bumped the table again in her haste to leave. "I have to go," she hissed. "Right now."

She didn't wait for a reply. Once Meg was out of sight,

Spring ordered another glass of wine and joined Kyle and Alyssa.

"Is it working?" Alyssa asked. "I couldn't tell because my back was to her."

"Oh, it's working all right," Spring said and raised her glass to clink with Kyle's.

"Do you think we went too far?" Kyle asked. "With the champagne and rose? Was it too much? I don't want to hurt her, you know."

"Of course not," Spring answered. "You have to show her what she's missing if she's ever going to come around for good. Trust me, this will work."

* * *

"Only a few more weeks until Uncle Bryan is here!" Heather exclaimed to no one in particular as she made her appearance on Martha's doorstep on Easter morning. Jack, who had arrived early to help Martha put the finishing touches on the ham dinner, held the front door for her, welcoming her with a bright smile. Heather flitted straight over to Martha, who also had a big smile on her face, along with a snug hug for her granddaughter.

"Where's Autumn?" Martha asked.

"And Ethan?" added Jack.

"Oh, they're just slow," Heather declared.

Jack peered out the door expecting to see Autumn and Ethan just as Kyle and a woman he thought looked familiar but couldn't quite place, came up the walk. Jack smiled at the couple, but didn't really know what to say, so he just held the door for them.

"Hey, Jack," Kyle said. "How are ya?"

"I'm just fine," Jack managed, maintaining a sideways look at Kyle's date.

Kyle recognized Jack's confusion. "Jack, I'd like you to meet my, well, my good friend Alyssa. Alyssa, you probably know Jack from Town and Country Nursery."

"Of course," Alyssa beamed. "My family has been going there for years. Nice to see you, Jack."

Jack was now officially the doorman, as Ethan and Autumn had finally collected everything to be transported from next door over to Martha's, and were struggling up the walk laden with Easter goodies. Martha had specifically told them not to bring anything, but Autumn, being Autumn, couldn't help herself. Jack held the door for them as well, and they said their "hellos" and found their way to the kitchen.

Martha smiled as they entered. "Now what did you go and do?" Martha scolded. "I told you not to bother with anything!" Feigning irritation, she pecked first Autumn on the cheek, then Ethan.

"Oh, it's nothing, really. Just a coconut cake and a chocolate chess pie. There might be two of them, even. And you know how Ethan loves cheesecake."

Now feigning exasperation, Martha directed, "We'll just

put all the desserts on the far end of the sideboard. Sheesh, we're gonna have enough food to feed a platoon of Marines!"

When Martha said the word "Marines," Autumn and Ethan immediately glanced at each other, each knowing that the other had an uneasy feeling in the pit of their respective stomachs, because they feared they might eventually have to tell Heather that they were postponing the wedding.

Just then Spring entered, carrying nothing, but offering instead her unmistakable beauty. Her hair was gorgeous, and she was wearing a pale pink pantsuit that caused everyone who saw her to do a double-take. Seeing Spring wearing her full complement of the makeup she had eschewed since she had come to Finch's Crossing, Martha gasped, then went over to give her a warm hug and kiss.

"You look lovely," she said to Spring.

"Aww, Martha. Thanks. I am so, so happy to be here!"

Martha had heard that Miss Elsie's family was not going to make it for Easter, so she had invited her to join the group.

After all the guests had arrived, Martha corralled everyone into the dining room. She and Jack had hand-drawn the place cards the day before. Jack had actually drawn a flower he thought best represented each guest. Martha had been so impressed with Jack's artistic ability but then realized she shouldn't have been. Everyone who visited the nursery knew Jack was a true artist, his medium being plants and flowers.

Martha stood in the entrance between the kitchen and the

dining room, smiling at her guests. "This year, Heather will offer the Easter blessing," she announced.

Heather, who had apparently been hovering in the kitchen just behind Martha, entered the dining room. She rounded the table, stopping at her place card, which was at the chair between Autumn and Ethan. She was holding a piece of paper in her hand. Glancing down at the page, she began.

"Happy Easter, everyone!" All at the table echoed her sentiment. You could tell that Heather was a little nervous, but in remarkable control for a six-year-old.

"Easter is when spring gets to shine," Heather declared in a loud, steady voice, and Spring felt a shot of adrenaline in her chest, as if Heather was delivering a message just to her.

Heather continued. "All stories have really good times and really bad times and some times when everything is just okay. For me, this is a really good time. My Uncle Bryan told me he would always be my biggest fan. That's what we all need. A biggest fan. And he's coming soon."

Heather crossed her hands and bowed her head. The guests followed suit.

"Lord," she began, "thank you that everyone gets a spring. Thank you for my grandma Martha. And for Jack." She opened one eye, not wanting to miss anyone, and went around the table, continuing her prayer. "And for Kyle. And for . . ." Kyle immediately helped out by whispering, "Alyssa." Alyssa, head bowed, smiled to herself, and Kyle found himself wishing deeply that it was Meg by his side. Nothing against Alyssa, who was fine, but it was Meg who was supposed to be there.

Heather resumed. "And for Alyssa. And for Autumn. And for Ethan. And for Spring. And for Miss Elsie. And for Uncle Bryan, who will be here soon. Lord, thank you for Easter because the food is good and Jesus is good. Amen."

Everyone around the table looked up and smiled at Heather, who scooted out her chair and took her seat as Martha made her way to the head of the table and sat as well.

"That was just lovely," Autumn beamed. "Just so lovely."

Dishes were passed around, delicious food was consumed, and the conversation drifted in and out, mostly concerned with the weather or what was happening in town. When it did drift toward the wedding, Autumn and Ethan deflected the conversation away from their upcoming nuptials. They were feeling worse and worse about the Uncle Bryan situation and knew that the likelihood they would have to disappoint Heather grew stronger with each passing day.

CHAPTER 17

ABE TURNED THE "Open" sign in his shop window to "Closed," locked the door behind him, and hustled down the street to Autumn's studio. Things had reached a breaking point. Spring wouldn't even remain in his company for more than a few minutes, much less talk to him. He needed to bring in reinforcements to help him. He needed to talk to Autumn, though he was unsure of where he stood with her. He guessed he was probably on shaky ground.

When he opened the door and stepped inside the gallery, the bell chimed merrily, and Autumn looked up and greeted him somewhat coldly.

She had barely changed in the last seventeen years, he thought to himself, as his mind reached back into the memories of what happened after high school—memories that were still so painful.

"I want to tell you what's going on with me," he said, getting right to the point. "I hope when you hear my story that you'll help me win Spring back."

Autumn eyed him suspiciously. "There is no way I am helping a married man win back my sister." She crossed her arms over her chest and glared at him incredulously. "Especially a man who broke her heart two decades ago."

"I totally get it," Gabe rushed in to say. "I would be suspicious, too. But just hear me out. First, I want you to read these." He handed Autumn the letter from Marla and the divorce papers he had signed just minutes before leaving his shop.

"What's this?" Autumn asked, flipping through the pages. "You're divorced now?"

"Yes. Well, I guess I will be when I file the papers at the courthouse. Right now, I think I'm not married but not divorced, either. Just read the letter first. *Please,*" Gabe pleaded.

Autumn sat down in her desk chair and donned a pair of reading glasses, and Gabe stood in front of the window that overlooked Pittsburgh Street. He had spent so many happy times here as a child and later as a young man. He saw Spring everywhere he looked because she had walked the same streets and shopped in the same places with him. He was so engrossed in his thoughts that he didn't hear Autumn come up behind him until she cleared her throat, causing him to turn around.

"I don't know what to say, Gabe," she said quietly and handed the papers back to him. "It's so incredibly sad, but beautiful at the same time, that Marla wants you to be happy. It takes a special person to do what she did."

"Marla and I found each other just a few years ago," Gabe said. "She was an incredible person, so full of life and so fun. We had a blast together. She could make anything an adventure. The Alzheimer's started pretty soon after we were married." He turned back to look out the window. "At first the drugs worked, but they quickly lost their effectiveness, and I had no choice but to put her in a facility."

"But why did you come back here?" Autumn asked gently.

"The care costs a fraction of what I was paying in Virginia. Plus, I owned the store and apartment here that I inherited from my father. It made sense not to pay a mortgage when I had a perfectly good place to live and work for free."

"Did you expect to see Spring when you came back?" Autumn asked.

"I guess I didn't think it through," he responded. "I knew she lived in California, of course. I assumed she would come home every once in a while, for holidays and such, and we'd run into each other sooner or later."

"But you never expected to run into her while she was on an extended visit home," Autumn finished for him.

"Exactly. And I never expected that all my old feelings would come screaming back to the surface so quickly and so intensely. From the second she walked into my bookstore a few weeks ago, I knew I had never stopped loving her. I knew that she had always been 'the one.'" He used air quotes to make his point.

"You know you hurt her pretty badly when you left," Autumn accused. "She was devastated for a long time. Part of me doesn't want to forgive you for the pain you caused her. I can't tell you how many late-night calls we got, with her sobbing so intensely I thought she would break in two. Mother and Daddy even went out to California not long after it happened. They were all set to bring her back home, but after seeing her, they decided that the last thing she needed was to be in a place that reminded her of you."

"I didn't know any of that," he said quietly.

"You don't know a lot of things," Autumn retorted. "And you can't just waltz back into Spring's life and expect that everything is going to be the same as it was before."

"I don't expect that," Gabe protested. "I respect the person that Spring has become. She's incredibly strong and capable. I know it's not like high school when we were so desperately in love with each other that we couldn't imagine life without the other."

"Look," Autumn said. "I don't know why you left the way you did, and you don't have to tell me. But what I do want is your promise that you will not hurt Spring again. I know she seems strong to you, and she is, but she's also very vulnerable right now."

Gabe turned to look at her. "Is she okay?" he asked, suddenly worried, incapable of thinking that he was going to lose her again.

"She is, or at least she will be," Autumn reassured him. "But I want you to make me a promise. If Spring doesn't want you back, I don't want you to pressure her. If she rejects you, that's that. You have to walk away and let her go."

The thought terrified Gabe, but he agreed, knowing that it was the only way that Autumn would help him.

"Okay," she said, as if reading his mind. "What is it exactly that you want me to do to help you?"

"Can you talk to her for me?"

"Do you want me to tell her about your wife? I mean Marla. And about the letter and the divorce?"

Gabe thought hard. "No, I think I should be the one to tell her about those things."

Autumn stared at him, finding herself genuinely wanting to help him. "So, I ask again, what exactly do you want me to do?"

Gabe's mind scrambled for a strategy. "Can you talk to her and tell her that I came to see you and that I told you something that makes you think she should at least hear me out? Can you tell her I have something really important to tell her and persuade her to listen?"

He entertained the thought of how devastated he would

be if Spring refused to see him. He simply could not let that happen.

"Can you tell her that you think that if she refuses to see me she may regret it? That is, if you truly believe it yourself. You know, that she'll regret it if she doesn't at least give me a chance to explain myself? Just one chance. Not as a threat. Not like that at all. Just as a sister who loves her sister and wants what's best for her."

Autumn looked squarely at Gabe, and all she could offer was, "Gabe, I promise I will think about it." But in her mind, she was already preparing the words necessary to convince Spring to give Gabe what he wanted, what he so desperately needed—a second chance.

* * *

That evening, Spring and Autumn arrived home at just the same moment, to Autumn's great delight.

"Hey, sis," Autumn said. "How goes it?"

"All good," Spring shot back cheerfully.

"Guess what?" Autumn announced. "I was moving some stuff around at the gallery yesterday and I found a bottle of pink Moscato gathering dust. So of course I brought it home, and I am happy to report it is now properly chilled and awaiting our perusal."

"Our perusal?"

"You know, it's waiting for us to drink it," Autumn said smiling.

"What's the occasion?"

"Oh, no occasion really. I just thought it would be nice for us to sit on the porch and enjoy a glass of sparkling wine together. You in?"

"You better let me check my calendar," Spring replied sarcastically. She held her palm in front of her face, as if glancing at a page of a planner. "Would you look at that. I have the evening free. Bring on the Moscato!"

In a few minutes, the sisters were seated comfortably on the porch, sipping Moscato from the "good" wine glasses that were normally reserved for special occasions. Autumn reckoned that if there ever was a special occasion, this surely must qualify.

After a few minutes of small talk, the conversation lulled, and the sisters sat silently. Autumn grabbed the Moscato from the ice bucket and refilled their glasses.

"Thanks," said Spring. "This stuff is really good."

Then Autumn got down to business.

"You will never guess who came into the gallery today."

"Tom Cruise?"

"No, although that would be pretty awesome. No, it was Gabe."

Spring was momentarily stunned.

"Gabe? What on earth for? Did he buy something?"

Autumn could not be certain, but she thought she had piqued Spring's interest more than she had annoyed her.

"No, he was just visiting. I gave him the cold shoulder at first, what with how things ended up with you two. And with him being married."

"He deserves more than a cold shoulder."

"Yes, I think he does deserve more," Autumn said seriously, looking Spring directly in her eyes.

"What on earth do you mean?"

"Let's just say he told me some things. Some things I think you should hear," Autumn explained.

"So tell me."

"No," Autumn protested. "Gabe should tell you. You will just have to trust me. Trust me when I say you will be glad I insisted he tell you what he has to say, rather than me. It has to come from him."

* * *

Sheriff Landry picked up the phone on his desk, took a deep breath, and dialed Teppy's number.

"Hello," Teppy answered.

"Teppy, it's Buddy. Look, we need to have a meeting about these letters. I want to do it this afternoon at three. Okay?"

"Sounds good to me. Want me to start the phone tree?"

"No," the sheriff said, with a little more forcefulness than usual in his voice. "Just the people who got the letters." Then he clarified with, "*Only* the people who got the letters."

"Okay," Teppy replied. "I can make the calls. It's slow right now."

"Thanks, Teppy," said the sheriff. "So just to be clear, just the people who received a letter. And we'll meet in the conference room at my office, not the community center."

"I'll take care of it," Teppy said confidently. "See you at three."

At about a quarter to three, Sheriff Landry took his coffee and sat down at one end of the oval conference table. He went over in his mind how he was going to explain to everyone that, contrary to what he told them at the last meeting, now he was going to need to know what was in those letters. It was the only thing he could think of to jump-start his investigation. Maybe the secrets themselves would point to who was sending the letters.

The sheriff gazed out the window and saw Kyle strolling up the street and was surprised to see him walk into the Borough Building. A few seconds later, Kyle was standing in the doorway of the conference room.

"Hey, Sheriff," Kyle said.

"Kyle," acknowledged the sheriff. "Nice to see you, but I've got a meeting starting in a few minutes."

"That's why I'm here."

"Don't tell me you got a letter, too."

"No, I'm just here for moral support. I want to help find the perpetrator any way I can."

The sheriff considered his options and then said to Kyle, "Okay, you can stay for the meeting. But it's supposed to be just the letter recipients. If they decide they don't want you here, well, I know I can count on you to be a gentleman."

"Absolutely!" Kyle assured the sheriff. "If they object, I will leave. No problem."

As the clock approached three, the letter recipients began to appear. First to arrive was Teppy, then Duncan, then Melissa Overholt, then Miss Elsie. The rest arrived at three on the dot, with Spring and Gabe pointedly ignoring each other.

But Sheriff Landry was surprised, and even a little annoyed, that many people who did not get a letter, in addition to Kyle, were also present. The conference room was overflowing. Autumn, Ducky, Samantha DeMuth, the owners of Number One Wok, and a few others from the Merchants Association had all come, too.

Sheriff Landry considered his options yet again and decided that everyone already knew about the letters, and some even knew what the letters contained, so what could it hurt to have everyone there?

The sheriff cleared his throat and declared in his most authoritative tone, "There are too many of us to meet here. Let's all head over to the community center. We'll have the meeting there."

A few minutes later, the sheriff stood in front of the group in the community center and began to outline his plan. "Look," he said, "my original idea was to have the meeting with just the letter recipients. But if you guys don't object to the people who did not get a letter being here, then it's okay with me."

None of the letter recipients objected and, in fact, seemed very glad to have the others present. The sheriff continued, "Cases like this are really difficult to solve. Almost impossible. I've been hoping all along for some kind of break in the case. Some clue as to who wrote the letters. But so far, well, the case is going nowhere."

Everyone was listening intently. The sheriff gathered himself and continued, "It occurred to me that the letters themselves, I mean the secrets they contain, might be the clue to figuring out who sent the letters. I know I told you before that no one would have to reveal what was in their respective letter. But, since the case is going nowhere, it seems logical for me to know what's in the letters. All of them. So I am going into the next room and would like the recipients to come in one at a time and tell me what's in your letter. I promise, absolutely swear on my grave, I will not reveal your secrets. I simply need to know what they are to help me figure out who's doing this. After all, those letters are evidence. Technically, I could get a warrant. I really don't want to do that. So I would greatly appreciate your cooperation." With that, Sheriff Landry walked into the next room and sat down in a chair.

Samantha stood up and walked over toward the next room and just stood outside the door, then addressed the sheriff. "We're going to discuss this privately before we make any decisions. Do you mind if I shut the door for a bit? Hopefully this won't take long."

The sheriff folded his arms across his chest and said, "Okay. Discuss. But just for a little while. Don't take forever."

* * *

Samantha stood in front of the group and stated emphatically, "I can't speak for everyone, but I am not going to reveal my secret. If he wants to know, he can get a warrant. Look, I love Sheriff Landry. We all do. But this is just a weird situation." Everyone was nodding their heads in agreement.

Samantha continued, "So, Melissa, do you want to reveal your letter to the sheriff?"

Melissa did not hesitate. "No. No I don't. I kinda see the sheriff's point, but I think I would rather never find out who wrote these letters than have to tell my secret. Not that it's anything that terrible. It's just, you know, personal."

Samantha continued to ask each recipient the same question, and all agreed that, as Melissa had said, it would be better to never catch the writer than to reveal their secrets. And several recipients made the point that it wasn't that they didn't trust the sheriff to keep their secrets. It's just that they really did not want to tell anybody.

"Samantha, can I chime in?" Kyle asked.

"Sure."

Kyle stood up and said, "Look, everyone. I didn't get a letter, but I can tell you if I had, I would be just like you. Every time I get the mail, I halfway expect one of those poison pen letters. I have secrets. Everybody has secrets. So I just want to say, I'm on your side."

"Thanks for the support, Kyle," Samantha said, looking relieved now that a decision had been made. "We really appreciate it."

Others in the room expressed their agreement, and Samantha walked over to the adjoining room, opened the door, and invited Sheriff Landry to join them.

Samantha and the sheriff stood before the group, and she turned to address him. "Sheriff, you know we trust and respect you, so this is not personal or about whether we trust you to keep our secrets. But we've decided, we've *all* decided, and it's unanimous, that we don't want to reveal the contents of our letters. We want to keep our secrets secret."

Sheriff Landry had a look of consternation on his face as Samantha continued. "We know you can get a warrant, but we all think it would be better not to ever find who wrote those letters than to reveal their contents, to you or to anybody."

Sheriff Landry thought to himself, *Well, on to plan B, whatever the heck that might be.* He turned to face the crowd, smiled, and began, "Since it's unanimous, what can I do? I tell you what. I will try to figure out another angle. You all must know, I really, really want to catch this guy. So if any of you change your mind, please come see me. And, God help us, if anyone else gets a letter, let me know right away."

CHAPTER 18

*S*PRING, AUTUMN, KYLE, and Bella Macken-zie, Autumn's hairdresser from Mt. Pleasant, sat in Spring's SUV, one block over and around the corner from Finch's Crossing's only post office. Spring was wearing all black clothing, including a strange watchman's cap she had dug out of a costume chest in the attic. Kyle had a set of bird-watching binoculars hanging from his neck.

A creature of habit, Meg took a break every day at ten in the morning, came down to Pittsburgh Street to grab a dough-nut and coffee from the lunch counter, then stopped at the post office to get her mail from the Ten Oaks Kennel post of-fice box.

"Don't you see," Spring had argued the night before as they

sat around Kyle's small kitchen table plotting their next move in their scheme to make Meg jealous, "it's a perfect plan. It's out in the open, totally casual. It will just look like Kyle's out for a walk with his new lady friend. Meg will be totally surprised. We just need to get a hot girl to walk down the street and hold Kyle's hand. Meg won't be able to not see you. You'll be right there out in the open."

Spring had practically ripped Autumn's cell phone from her hand and scrolled through her contacts until Autumn identified a "hot girl" to help them.

Now, sitting in the car with her partners in crime, Autumn felt a pang of guilt. She missed her old friend. What had started out as a mission to reconcile Meg and Kyle was turning into *Mean Girls* meets *Inspector Gadget*. What was she doing acting like a high school student on some dumb dare? Oh, why had she let Spring talk her into this ridiculous undertaking?

"Are you sure she won't know who I am?" Bella asked from the back seat, where she sat next to Kyle. "I mean, you've been best friends forever."

"Yeah, and in that time we have talked about beauty and fashion exactly zero times," Autumn said, holding up her hand and making an "O" with her thumb and forefinger. Even though no one could see. They were all sitting low in their seats so Meg wouldn't see them. "And I doubt she's been to a hairdresser in ten years."

"How does she cut her hair?" Bella asked, aghast.

"You don't want to know," Autumn answered.

"Shhh," hissed Kyle, who had kept his eyes peeled on the rearview mirror. "I see her."

"She can't hear us," said Spring, ever the voice of reason. "We're a block away. And how can you even see her?"

"Okay, so I can't, but I can hear her old truck. Her motor has a very distinct hum to it. Wait, now I see her. She's about to park," Kyle reported. "We gotta get out, now."

He opened the door to the SUV and practically dragged Bella out after him.

"Hold hands," Spring hissed, looking in the rearview mirror. "Now."

Kyle grabbed Bella's hand, just as they rounded the corner at the post office, nearly slamming into Meg as she approached the entrance.

"Oh, hello," Kyle said nonchalantly.

Meg folded her arms across her chest. "Hello," she said, looking at Kyle. "Going bird watching?" Then she squinted suspiciously at Bella. "I see you've brought your sister with you. Nice to meet you. I'm Meg." She stuck out her hand, which Bella automatically shook.

"But I don't have a sister," Kyle stammered, completely flummoxed. He looked at Bella, then looked back at Meg, who scowled at him for a second and then headed up the steps of the post office.

"What just happened?" Kyle said to the empty place Meg

had just occupied.

"Man, you got burned, that's what just happened," Bella said and tugged him back to the car.

They had barely closed the passenger door when Spring demanded, "Well, what happened? What did she say?"

Kyle repeated what Meg had said, reminding the group that he didn't have a sister.

"So what does that mean?" Spring asked. "That's totally crazy."

"And what about that thing about bird-watching?" Kyle asked. "Where did she get that idea?"

Autumn turned around in her seat and pointed to Kyle's chest. His hand flew up and he felt the binoculars that were still hanging around his neck. He could feel the heat rising in his cheeks.

Spring drove back to Mt. Pleasant to drop Bella off at her salon. Autumn spent a lot of time looking out the window, while Kyle and Spring tried to decipher what Meg had meant by the sister remark. But Autumn didn't need her friend's words translated. Meg was terribly hurt by what she saw. And instead of doing what any normal person would do—walk away, cause a scene, or be polite—she made a smart-ass remark and, as was her custom, got the better of Kyle. They all should have known better than to mess with Meg. Autumn should have known better. Because the only thing they had accomplished on their ridiculous mission was hurting her best friend in the world. She was going to have to do something to fix this, and fast, before it was too late.

* * *

Spring could skillfully avoid walking past Gabe's book-store by approaching the shops on Pittsburgh either from the north or the south, depending on which shop it was. Yes, it took her out of her way, and yes, she had to trudge up and down the hill on Chestnut Street, past the Methodist Church, and take the back alleys and enter the stores from the rear. But it was worth it. And she needed whatever extra steps she could get. She glanced down at her Fitbit, frowning at the measly four thousand steps she had walked that day. She needed more steps and less of Miss Elsie's pie and Martha's cookies.

"Yoo-hoo, Spring." She heard a voice coming down the block and turned to see Teppy waving at her from the side-walk outside her Et Cetera shop.

"Damn," Spring muttered. She'd have to pass Wellspring Books to go see Teppy. It would look very strange if she dart-ed behind Brilhart Hardware and took the alley to Teppy's back door. And did she want everyone in town to know she was slinking around hoping to avoid Gabe? No, of course not, and besides, she was better than that. She shook her hair, squared her shoulders as if preparing for battle, and struck the quintessential model's pose. Instead of slinking, she would glide, carefree and breezy, past Gabe's store.

Later at home, she was so engrossed in assigning the exhibit booths to each merchant and making a list for Duncan, that she didn't think to look in the peephole when she heard a knock at the front door. She rose from her chair at the dining room table and made her way to the front door humming the tune to *Here Comes the Bride*.

She flung the door open and was stunned to see Gabe, handsome in blue jeans and a light camel-colored sweater, standing on the door step.

"Please don't slam the door," he begged, holding out his arms. "I just want to talk to you for a few minutes. I promise I won't take up much of your time. And we could talk out here so Autumn won't even have to hear."

"Autumn and Ethan took Heather out for dinner," Spring said.

"So we're alone?" Gabe asked.

"Alone?" Spring echoed. "What does that have to do with anything?" She started to close the door.

"No, that's not what I meant," Gabe said. "I only want to talk with you without anyone around to hear."

"You mean you don't want anyone to hear your lies," Spring retorted.

"I deserve that," Gabe said. "No question about that. But I just want you to give me the chance to explain. If, after you've heard me out, you don't ever want to see me again, I will respect that and leave you alone."

"We can skip the part where you try and explain and go

right to the part where you leave me alone," Spring said and closed the door.

"Spring," Gabe said through the door. "Please hear me out. I know if you understood the situation, you would feel differently."

"Are you still married?" Spring asked through the door, trying to keep her voice from revealing that she was crying.

There was no response from the other side of the door, where Gabe had leaned his forehead. No matter what the piece of paper said, in a sense, he would always be married to Marla. He would never stop loving her or visiting her at Arbor Commons.

After a pause Gabe answered. "It's complicated," he said quietly.

"Then I don't feel any differently," Spring snapped. "Now please go away."

Spring waited until she heard Gabe's footsteps proceed down the sidewalk, and she listened for the slam of his car door and the revving of his engine as he pulled away from the curb.

Once he was gone, she stood with her back to the door and sobbed. She cried so hard that the sorrow of it all—memory, loss, fear, anger—made her double over with pain.

How could Gabe torture her like this? She had allowed her old feelings for him to surface. But what had taken her even more by surprise was the way he wouldn't let go. What else was there to say? He was married. Complicated or not, married was married. Why would he think that she would ever let him back into her life? She was many things, but an adulteress—a woman who would steal another woman's husband—she was not. And never would be.

CHAPTER 19

I'M GOING TO Pittsburgh," Meg called to Sammy two days after witnessing Kyle with a beautiful red-headed woman in front of the post office. "Will you take care of the second feeding and take Spike for a walk?"

She didn't wait for an answer, and knowing his boss as well as he did, Sammy knew she didn't expect one.

Meg drove north on the Pennsylvania Turnpike until she reached Pittsburgh. Scottie's gallery was in a fashionable part of town and easy to find.

"Meg, my dear, you have no idea how glad I was to get your call. Is it that time? Are you ready to go pantsuit shopping?"

"Not yet," Meg said. "Actually, it might not be at all."

She forlornly explained what had happened. "I don't know

244

what to do. I need your help," she finished.

"I have just the thing," Scottie declared. "Come on, get your purse. We're going for a ride."

Meg stared at him blankly. "I don't have a purse."

"Oh, for Pete's sake. Just come with me. Trust me. We'll get Kyle back for you."

Later that afternoon, the plan in place, Meg headed home. She had called ahead and told Sammy he could leave early. No one could see her if the plan was going to work. And Scottie promised—dramatically swearing on generations of his ancestors—that it would.

* * *

Kyle had been pleased to get Scottie's call asking him to meet him for dinner that evening at the Greystone to discuss publicity for his gallery. Kyle had been wanting to branch out to clients in Pittsburgh, and this would be a great start.

He walked into the restaurant fifteen minutes early and spotted Scottie already seated at a table. Kyle waved and joined him. Kyle didn't know Scottie well but liked him.

"So glad you were free to join me tonight," Scottie said, his eyes not quite meeting Kyle's.

"You pretty much insisted," Kyle reminded him. "But I'm glad you called. I'd love to do some publicity for you. Where should we start?"

"Hmmm?" Scottie asked distractedly. "Oh yes, publicity. Let's enjoy our dinner first, and then dive into it. I'm starving.

What's good here?"

As they looked at their menus, Kyle became aware that the dining room, though full of people, suddenly had become quiet. He looked up and watched a tall, willowy woman make her away through the dining room, accompanied by a man so stunningly handsome that it almost made Kyle cry.

"What?" Scottie asked innocently, noticing Kyle's distraction and turning in his seat.

"What a beautiful couple they are," Scottie remarked. "Don't you think so, Kyle?"

Kyle nodded absentmindedly, unable to take his eyes off them. "Mmhm."

There was something familiar about that woman. She was beautifully dressed in a black skirt and soft-green silk blouse with a matching cropped jacket that billowed as she walked. Her legs were so long, they reminded him of…

Kyle stood up, and his menu fell to the ground. He watched the beautiful woman link her arm through the man's as she gazed romantically into his face and gave him a coquettish giggle.

"Kyle?" Scottie asked. "What is it? Are you okay?"

Kyle sunk back into his chair. "That, that, was…Meg," he stammered. "That gorgeous woman with that man was Meg. My Meg."

Scottie put his hand to his chest in mock disbelief. "No. It can't possibly be. She was wearing a skirt. And makeup. But now that you mention it..." He pretended to study the woman as she sat down and her date pushed in her chair. "Well, I'll be and I never. Praise the Lord and pass the potatoes, it *is* Meg."

He turned back to Kyle, who looked as if he had been kicked in the gut.

"Looks like she's moved on," Scottie said. "But then so have you, or so I heard. You should be happy for her. She looks divine. Who knew it would take a breakup to bring out her feminine side."

Kyle had tears in his eyes and they started to spill over, and Scottie almost felt sorry for him.

"You don't understand," Kyle said. "I haven't moved on. I don't want anyone else but Meg. Autumn and Spring arranged for me to go on fake dates to make Meg jealous. But it didn't work. The plan just pushed her further and further away from me."

"Really?" Scottie replied, now genuinely shocked. "I don't know what to say." To himself he thought, *Now I've gone and done it.*

"I'm leaving," Kyle suddenly declared.

"You can't," Scottie practically yelled. "We haven't had dinner."

"I'm not hungry."

"Or discussed publicity for my gallery," Scottie added.

"I'll call you tomorrow."

Kyle stood up.

"Wait," Scottie said, jumping up to block his path. "You

should go over to say hello."

"No way. She's made her choice. It's obvious. I don't need to humiliate myself."

"Oh, for Pete's sake," Scottie hissed, exasperated, "she's on a fake date, too. That's my cousin Errol visiting from Florida. Now sit yourself back down while I figure out what to do."

Kyle did as he was told.

* * *

Meg was so grateful to be sitting down. She had barely made it through the dining room and had to clutch Errol's arm tightly to make sure she didn't fall. The blouse she was wearing was form-fitting, unlike her plaid work shirts that just hung on her, and she had so much gel and spray in her hair she thought she had entered some nuclear waste zone, the smell was so strong. Not to mention that her lips felt like they weighed ten pounds with all of the stain and gloss.

As promised, Scottie had lured Kyle to the restaurant just minutes before she made her appearance. She had the feeling as she walked past Kyle that he didn't recognize her at first, which gave her a little shiver of pleasure. She had no idea that she could look so good. Scottie had taken her to Carnegie Mellon University where he knew the creative director of the drama department. Scottie had selected an outfit, had her hair and makeup done, and given her a five-minute lecture on how to walk on heels and make an entrance. When she had looked at herself in the mirror, she couldn't believe it. Scottie had crossed himself dramatically.

"Well, slap my face and take me home," he said. "And to think, underneath your hobo clothes and cowboy saunter this beauty was waiting patiently to be let out."

More like forced out, thought Meg.

He reached up to put his hand on her shoulder. In the heels, she seemed a good foot taller. "I had no idea this was possible."

Meg started to tear up but he pinched her arm.

"Ouch! What did you do that for?"

"No crying. There is no crying in makeup. You'll streak your mascara."

"Do you really think I look good?" she asked, quietly, turning from side to side to examine every angle of the new Meg.

"Darling girl, you are a stunner."

"I didn't know I could look like this. I hardly recognize myself!" she said. "Growing up, I spent all my time with the dogs or horses. I never paid any attention to how I looked. It never seemed to matter."

"And now?" Scottie asked gently.

"I don't know," she replied. "It feels strange. Like I'm wearing a costume."

"Well, you sort of are."

And now, sitting in the restaurant with Kyle just a few feet away, Meg felt a surge of love for him so strong that it was all she could do to not rush over there and throw her arms around him. She'd have to take her shoes off first, though. But

Scottie had made her promise to sit tight until Kyle came to her. So far, Scottie had been right about everything, so she was inclined to listen to him.

She and Errol were just finishing their salads when she saw Kyle approaching. He looked so handsome in his immaculate jeans and white dress shirt. He was wearing the burgundy Pumas she had bought him for Christmas last year.

"Hi, Meg. You look nice," Kyle said, somewhat lamely.

"Thank you, Kyle," Meg answered politely. "I'd like to introduce you to my date…."

Before she could finish, Kyle had dropped down to one knee and took her hand in his. "Let's start again. I'm sorry I rejected your reconciliation attempt earlier. I was messing with you, trying to make you jealous on those fake dates."

"Fake dates!?" Meg screeched, the ladylike mannerism she had temporarily adopted disappearing.

"I wanted to make you jealous, but not anymore. I love you. I'm so sorry. Let's just settle this once and for all. Meg Overly, will you marry me? We can have a long engagement. As long as it takes. I'm not going anywhere."

By that time Scottie had joined them and was shaking his head. Meg's mascara was streaking down her cheeks. "Yes, of course. I'm sorry, too," she said. "This isn't a date either. Scottie set it up."

Kyle took Meg's face in his hands. "I know," he said, and kissed her.

* * *

Martha was looking through her freezer and noticed she still had a large plastic container of her famous chili that had been dodging detection behind all the other frozen goodies. *Hmmm,* she thought, *oughta get rid of that pretty soon. Need to free up some room. . . . Autumn loves my chili.*

"Hey, neighbor!" Autumn answered enthusiastically, seeing Martha's name pop up on her cell. "Need a cup of sugar?"

Martha chuckled, as it was usually Autumn who needed a cup of sugar.

"No, honey. I was just calling to see if I could interest you in some black bean chili tonight."

Autumn did love chili. Especially Martha's twist on it. "Well, let me see. I told Ethan I'd join him and Heather for dinner around six."

"I've got enough for everybody. Why don't you grab them and you can all come over?"

At six sharp the three made their way up Martha's front walk. Martha was standing at the front door holding it open for them, and as they entered, their nostrils were delighted with the tangy aroma of spicy cumin and chili sauce simmering on the stove.

After everyone had their fill and the dishes were clean and put away, the four settled in Martha's cozy den. Heather insisted on sitting in the love seat with Autumn, with Ethan and Martha occupying opposite ends of the couch.

The adults engaged in small talk, which seemed to always find its way around to Ethan and Autumn's upcoming nuptials. Autumn realized Heather seemed preoccupied, staring at the pictures framed lovingly on the fireplace mantel, and she watched as the little girl squirmed out of the love seat and took a couple steps toward the mantel. She pointed up at the photo she had been staring at and asked, "Can I also have a GI Joe doll for my birthday?"

"A GI Joe?" Ethan asked.

"Yeah," continued Heather. "Like Uncle Bryan."

"Sure," Ethan assured her. "We can get you a GI Joe. That's no problem." He wondered if there was a Marine version of GI Joe, guessing that there had to be.

Martha had been listening intently to this exchange. Now the room remained quiet for what seemed like forever.

Martha broke the silence, facing Heather and asking as kindly as she could, "Sweetie, what makes you want a GI Joe?"

"It would remind me of Uncle Bryan." She said this so sweetly.

Martha reluctantly allowed herself to go back in her mind to the terrible event that had taken Heather's parents. So much of it was just a blur of tears and pain and gut-wrenching agony. She really was amazed that she had survived it all as well as she had. Losing a precious daughter, Denise, and her wonderful husband, Troy, at the same time—it was just lucky Martha was a strong person. She remembered how her

CHAPTER 19

son Bryan had rushed home from wherever his unit was at the time for his sister's funeral. And now she remembered how kind and incredibly loving he had been to his niece.

Heather completely shut down when her parents were killed. She stopped talking altogether. When the dreaded black limo had pulled up in front of Martha's to ferry the mourners to the church, and later to the graveside, Heather had run upstairs to her grandmother's bedroom and flung herself face down on the bed, sobbing. She ignored Martha's gentle coaxing. "Heather, honey, I know you're upset, but we have to get into the limo so they can take us to the funeral," Martha had said.

It was Uncle Bryan who had climbed the stairs, at first just standing in the doorway, tears streaming down his tanned and weathered cheeks as he watched the little girl suffer. Eventually, he stepped over to the bed and sat down beside her.

With his presence, Heather's sobbing subsided, and she sat up on the bed beside him.

He lifted her up with his strong arms and sat her sideways across his lap, holding her tightly with both arms, both of them sniveling.

"Heather," he whispered, his lips close to her ear. "If I didn't have to talk, I wouldn't either."

He just held her for a bit, then he said, "I don't want to get in that limo either. But we have to. I'll make you a deal. You stick by me, and I will make sure nobody tries to make you talk. You stick by me, and you can be as invisible as you want to be. Deal?"

Heather stared at her uncle intently while he continued. "Sweetheart, I will always, always, always be there for you, whatever you need. Understand? I mean it. As long as I live, you will never, ever be alone. I might not be right here with you, or even in the same country sometimes, but my heart will always be with you, wherever you are, wherever I am. And when you need me, I will be there."

He could see a twitch at the corner of her mouth, the beginnings of a sheepish, sad little girl smile. He smiled sweetly back at her. "Remember, Heather, I will always look out for you, fight for you, protect you, and I will always be your biggest fan in whatever you do. And I will always and forever love you. Okay?"

Heather nodded her head affirmatively, and the two stood up. Bryan clasped her hand in his, and they walked toward the door, where Martha stood, wiping the corners of her tired eyes with a tissue, having just witnessed pure love.

When she was alone again after the delicious chili dinner, Martha retrieved the photo of Bryan from the mantel and looked at it lovingly. He was so handsome in his dress blue uniform, posing casually at the Marine Corps Ball several years ago. Martha thought about how much the Corps had transformed her son from a shy and gangly eighteen-year-old into a rugged Marine. Into a man capable of defending his country and soothing a shattered child. Martha put the photo back on the mantel.

He just has to get here in time for the wedding, she thought. *He just has to.*

CHAPTER 20

SPRING WALKED AROUND the grand ballroom on the third floor of the Greystone Manor, her measuring tape at the ready. There was little that Spring liked more than precise measurements. You couldn't argue with measurements. Feet, yards, inches, millimeters, these didn't have minds of their own. They could only be what they were. Better yet, they could be broken down into the minutest of parts and never once stray from their origins. She got on her hands and knees and examined the original wood floor. It was still beautiful, and the finish Duncan had put on it last week made it gleam. Using her measuring tape, she mapped out where all the merchants would put their exhibit tables during the Bridal Expo. Each merchant would have at least two six-foot skirted tables. Spring sat down and pulled a notebook from her purse. She did swift calculations and sketches, placing each table just so, and determining the order in which the merchants would appear based on the natural flow of a wedding ceremony. The first table would be Krop's Jewelers. After all, everything started with a ring. And the last table would belong to Miss Elsie's Tea Room. The cake was always a crowning glory at a wedding reception. And Spring noted satisfactorily to herself that this befitted the matriarch of Finch's Crossing. All was in its place.

Almost.

She rose and walked down the stairs to the restaurant. Looking at her watch, she decided it was five o'clock somewhere and seated herself at the bar, where Bert the bartender greeted her with a nod. After she ordered a glass of Chardonnay she brought out her notebook once again, turned to a clean page, and proceeded to take the measure of her own life.

She knew life could not be ordered and kept in line by a ruler. She could not order her heart with her measuring tape or tap out her decisions on a calculator, as much as she might want to.

She thought about what Autumn had said about giving Gabe a second chance to explain himself and remembered how she had turned him away from her front door. She examined what Autumn had said, and what she hadn't said. She hadn't told Spring, for example, that she should give him a second chance in general or let him back into her life. Autumn had said precisely that she needed to give Gabe a chance to explain himself.

What was it that Autumn wasn't telling her? What was Gabe's secret? And why did her sister believe that she should give Gabe another chance to win her heart?

* * *

Once again, Stan was tucked away in his office at the hardware store, but this time it wasn't to avoid Ducky. Yes, Ducky had been very much on his mind recently, but at the moment, he had bigger problems.

Sitting at his big wooden and time-scuffed banker's desk, he looked around his office at a lifetime of memories, accomplishments, and personal and professional contributions to the community. Above his desk hung fifteen framed photos of the Finch's Crossing Pee Wee baseball team, each smiling boy and girl sporting a white jersey with "Brilhart Hardware" emblazoned on the front.

To the right, a bulletin board spanned the wall, with thank-you notes, old calendars, and sticky-note reminders from his wife, Renata, that he didn't have the heart to throw away. Over the years, the baseball players grew up, and so many of them sent high school portraits, wedding pictures, and baby photos. Yellowed newspaper articles hung, curled and worn, at the bottom of the board, celebrating the twenty-fifth anniversary of the store or announcing that Stan had been elected as president of the Finch's Crossing Elk's Club and other assorted civic news. This had been his life's work, and he had been proud of it. But at that moment, only a coarse feeling of shame shot through him.

Behind him a row of battered army-green file cabinets stood vigil, silently watching over twenty-five years' worth of supply orders, customer locksmith requests, and other paper collections that he hung on to for no discernible reason, except they were a tangible expression of his life's work. Now everything was on the computer.

He turned back to his desk and stared at his laptop. Just a few weeks earlier he had been so proud to show Kyle how he had digitized his records. Now he cursed the machine's very existence.

Leaning forward, elbows on his desk, he hung his head in his hands. He was surrounded by a lifetime of service to his beloved hometown and, in return, the love and respect he had earned over the years from his friends, neighbors, and customers. And with a few strokes of the keys on that blasted machine, he had thrown it all away.

He sat back, his old chair creaking in protest, as if to chastise him for his awful mistake. He moved the mouse to wake up the laptop and clicked over to the sent box in his email account. He grew more and more horrified as he read on. Clicking on the emails that he had sent Nancy one by one, he scanned each one until he found the paragraphs where he had shared with her the secrets of Finch's Crossing.

Stan knew he wasn't handsome or refined. His fingernails were impossible to keep clean. Day in and day out, he worked with oils, scooped up handfuls of nails and picture hangers, and moved dirty bags of soil and mulch. He used words like "ain't" and "yun's." And when he wrote these words in his emails, and stumbled over grammar and sentence structure (he wished he had paid more attention in school), he felt like a bumpkin, compared to Nancy's beautiful, silky words. She told him about her career in sales, using phrases like "return on investment" and "core competency" and described herself with phrases like "forward-thinking" and "heavy-lifter."

He felt he had to offer something in exchange, something other than the details of his boring, blue-collar life. Before he started his foray into online dating, he had never felt ashamed of who he was. He was proud of his civic activities and of the locksmith and hardware services he provided. He loved it when he could go directly to a shelf in his hardware store, which he knew inside and out, and find exactly what someone needed. He was particularly happy when the ladies came into his store, and he could provide gentle instructions, without implying that they didn't know what they were doing. He showed them kindly that they were about to buy fifty dollars' worth of the wrong paint brushes, or told them that no, they didn't need a seventy-five dollar drill to hang a few pictures in their new home. People appreciated his honesty, even though it meant less revenue for him.

But for some inexplicable reason, he had let his correspondence with Nancy plant a seed of insecurity within hm. So he wrote about the next best thing, offering up the secrets he knew about his friends, which he had innocently stumbled upon over the years. He couldn't go into people's houses to change the locks on doors inside and out without overhearing things, or seeing a person's item or document placed in the very desk drawer he was unlocking with a skeleton key. In his defense, learning the secrets had not been his fault. And no one in Finch's Crossing knew he had discovered their secrets. He would never, ever, confront anyone. A person's secrets were their own. He knew and respected that. Until recently. But how could he know that Nancy would have turned an innocent correspondence into a campaign of cruelty against the people he cared about? It was unthinkable.

Through the door, he heard the sheriff's voice. Johnny was grinding keys for him and the two were chitchatting about the poison pen letters. Impulsively, Stan stuck his head out the office door and asked Buddy to come in.

"Sure thing," the sheriff said, looking first at Stan then at Johnny. "I'll pick those up on the way out."

Stan ushered him into the office and closed the door, signaling for him to sit in the visitor's chair as he took his own desk chair opposite.

"You okay, Stan?" the sheriff asked. "I always see a red flag when someone invites me into their office and closes the door. What's up?"

"The red flags are flying high today," Stand answered, deflated and defeated. "I know who the letter writer is."

"That's good to hear," the sheriff responded. "The whole town's been on edge for weeks, and I want to get this straightened out once and for all."

"It's not that easy," Stan answered, miserably.

"I don't follow, Stan," the sheriff said. "Why don't you start from the beginning."

So Stan told him about the online dating and how Nancy vowed to seek revenge on him for ending what she had come to believe was a romantic relationship.

"And so she got even with you by sending nasty letters?" Buddy asked, confused. "But how did she know what to write? How did she know all these secrets?"

There was a long pause as each man studied the other. "Oh. I see," the sheriff said, and leaned back in the chair. "You are the source of the gossip. And you fed it to Nancy."

Stan nodded his head miserably. "You know me, Buddy," Stan said by way of explanation. "I'm just an awkward old fool when it comes to women. I don't know what to say, or in this case, write in an email. And my life sure isn't interesting enough, so I just told her about the town and before I knew it, I was telling people's secrets. She seemed like such a nice person and she was so interested in what I had to say. And she promised she wouldn't tell anyone."

"Until you dumped her, and then all bets were off," the sheriff finished for him, and Stan nodded again.

"I'm so embarrassed and ashamed. I can't believe how badly I've hurt my friends and neighbors. And worse yet, I don't know what to do about it."

"It's a good thing you came to me then," the sheriff remarked, and was glad to see Stan perk up a little bit.

"Really?" he asked. "You can help make all of this go away?"

The sheriff nodded. "But first thing first. How did you know all of these secrets?"

Stan shrugged. "It happened over time, I guess. I've lived here all of my life and you hear things, you know. People are in and out of my shop all the time. And when they're off in the back surrounded by those tall shelves, not to mention the key maker and glass cutter, I think they forget that they're still in a public place. And with my office right there in the back... even with my door closed I could hear everything. Sometimes people would move to the back of the store to take a phone call. I think most people didn't even think about me being back there. It was like a regular beauty parlor, I tell you. And I go into people's homes all the time as a locksmith." He paused and shrugged. "People leave things around. Sometimes it's hard not to see something."

"But Miss Elsie?" the sheriff asked. "And Gabe? He just got back to town a few months ago."

Stan explained about seeing Gabe in Virginia, but was a little reticent about explaining how he knew about Miss Elsie.

"C'mon," Buddy encouraged. "I'm like your priest or a lawyer. I won't tell anyone."

"Really?" Stan asked.

"Well, no," the sheriff admitted, shifting uncomfortably in his chair, "but you should tell me anyway."

"It was long before you arrived here," Stan began. "I was newly married and had just opened the store. It was slow going at first, so I started doing furniture repair and restoration in the back of the property, before I expanded. Anyway, Earl Hixon brought in a bureau he wanted restored. He said it was a surprise for Elsie."

The sheriff made a motion with his hand to tell Stan to hurry along and get to the point. Buddy's wife wasn't due back for another few days, and it was lunchtime. Pie time.

"When I pulled out the drawers, there was an old letter stuck in the crevices," Stan continued. "It was from a police station in a small town in Quebec, Canada. I had to look it up on a map. The English wasn't very well written, but the message was pretty clear and not lost on me."

"Well?" Buddy asked impatiently.

"It read like a response to a letter that Earl had written. He was looking for his wife. The return letter explained that the whereabouts of his wife was unknown. It also said that his father-in-law would not give his permission for a divorce and to not write again. I guess he had written several times before."

Dumbfounded, Buddy didn't know what to say for a minute. "And you kept that secret and all the others all these years? You didn't even tell your wife?"

"Nope. I figured I had learned about them accidentally. I was never supposed to know, so I forgot that I did. I never told anyone."

"So what did you do with the letter?" Buddy asked.

Stan opened a desk drawer and handed the letter across the table. "I don't know why, but I kept it. But I'm glad I did. Maybe Miss Elsie might want to know how hard Earl tried to find his wife and get a divorce."

"And Earl never came back looking for it?"

Stan shook his head. "I'm guessing he was so disheartened after reading it that he wanted nothing more to do with it, so he stuck it in a drawer. Strange he didn't throw it away," he finished.

"Human nature isn't anything but very strange," the sheriff mused philosophically, all thoughts of pie momentarily gone.

"So what are you going to do?" Stan asked. "About me, I mean."

The sheriff stared at his friend for a long while. "I don't think we need to worry about that right now," he finally answered.

"Am I going to jail?" Stan asked, panicked.

"No, Stan, you haven't broken any laws. You're only guilty

of temporary bad judgment, completely forgivable. But right now, we have to stop this Nancy person."

"How are you going to do that?" Stan asked.

The sheriff pointed at Stan. "Not me. You. You are going to stop her."

* * *

Spring knew she had to do something. Things were getting out of control with Meg and each day Autumn grew more and more agitated. Either Meg could get Bryan to Finch's Crossing in time for the wedding or she couldn't. Spring had to boil everything down to its core, whittle what she knew down to brass tacks, and follow the realities to their logical conclusion. But the thing was, there just didn't seem to be any logic when it came to Meg. The woman lived and played by her own rules and it was anyone's guess as to what those rules were.

Spring steered her SUV down the bumpy driveway to Ten Oaks Kennel. Again.

Feels like I was just here, she muttered to herself, remembering the painful meeting where she exploded at Meg when she and Autumn had learned Meg had broken up with Kyle.

With a feeling of déjà vu, Spring parked in the dusty parking lot, went inside the kennel, walked down the long hallway of photographs demonstrating Meg's prowess as a businesswoman, and stopped to knock on Meg's office door, which was ajar.

"I come in peace," she said gently when Meg looked up,

eyes flashing.

Meg beckoned for her to come in. "You better sit down then," she said gruffly. Meg had known Spring for as long as she had known Autumn, and Meg begrudgingly admitted to herself that if she had a sister, she probably would be advocating for her as mightily as Spring was advocating for Autumn.

"I feel like we just had this conversation," Meg said, "right here in this office," and Spring nodded in agreement.

"I know, and I really should apologize for what I said. I was cruel," she said. "And wrong. And I hope you will accept my apology."

"I will," Meg said, "for Autumn's sake." She shuffled a few folders on her desk and produced the one she was looking for, waving it in the air in front of her. "Aha," she proclaimed, delighted with herself. "I've been waiting for you." She waved the file folder again in front of Spring.

"Okay, I'll play along," Spring said, trying not to sound exasperated. "What's that?"

"Not what, dear Watson," Meg said triumphantly, "but who."

"Not who," Spring shot back, "but 'whom.'"

"Okay, whatever. I'm not interested in getting a grammar lesson," Meg said.

"Obviously," Spring retorted and watched as Meg opened the folder and reached for the phone on her desk. Spring noticed that it was an old dial phone, and remembering what

Autumn had told her about Meg's technology shortcomings,
Spring laughed.

"Yeah, look *whom's* laughing now," Meg said dryly. "But
guess *whom* will have the last laugh."

Spring watched as Meg dialed. "I'm guessing that would
be you?" Spring asked, mesmerized by the phone dial rotating
back and forth. How long had it been since she had seen one
of those? She had had a pink princess phone in her room in
school, and she and Gabe had talked for hours into the night,
planning their future, whispering to each other, wishes and
kisses on their pillows.

"Yes," Meg was saying, "that *whom* would be me."

"Oh, give it a rest," Spring snapped, annoyed not at Meg's
deliberate grammar shenanigans, but at her own mind be-
traying her with memories she would sooner forget. Meg just
smiled a Cheshire cat grin.

"Yes," Meg said politely into the phone. Spring had never
heard her sound so, well, so nice. "This is Meg Overly, Ten
Oaks Kennel, in Pennsylvania. May I please speak with Staff
Sergeant Major Nichols? Yes, I'll hold."

Meg covered the mouth of the phone with her hand and
turned to Spring. "I'm on the phone with the Royal Canadian
Mounted Police K9 unit in Saskatchewan," she said in a false-
ly sweet voice. "You see, I have supplied German Shepherds
to them for more than six years now, and they're helping me
expand into other canine units. Interesting fact. Only seven-

teen percent of dogs that they train make it through their rigorous program. Do you know what the success rate is among my dogs?" She didn't wait for an answer to what Spring knew to be a rhetorical question. "Sixty seven percent of the dogs raised at Ten Oaks are among the seventeen percent of dogs that make it through the RCMP training. That's the highest rate of any German shepherd breeder anywhere. As in, the world."

"I didn't know that," Spring said, knowing exactly where this conversation was going.

"Of course you didn't," Meg said, apparently still on hold. "And neither did Ethan when he was eavesdropping on my private conversation and misunderstood what he heard, and then misled Autumn, who unwittingly misled you, you *whom* is now sitting in my office. Pretty soon, your tail will be between your legs."

Spring knew Meg was right. She thought back to the few times she had walked down Meg's photo gallery corridor and remembered that several officers in the photos sported the distinct red coat and trooper hat of the Canadian Mounties.

"Joseph," Meg was saying, back to being all business, and Spring snapped her mind back to the task at hand, which, she was quickly realizing, was getting her butt handed to her in a sling.

"Let me put you on speaker," Meg said sweetly. "I'm trying to multitask."

"Sure thing," Spring heard a deep male voice say as Meg hit the old-fashioned speaker phone contraption attached to her rotary phone. Spring surmised that Meg hadn't replaced any of the equipment, except for maybe the computer, since the Overly family opened the kennel in the 1950s.

Meg turned to face Spring. "You know when we were talking about a week ago about that little customs problem I was asking you about?"

"Yes," the voice said hesitantly, as if bracing for another one of Meg's tirades. "I remember. You told me your reputation was on the line if you didn't deliver and then slammed the phone down in my ear. How could I forget? If your shepherds weren't so damn good, we'd not be having this conversation." The voice broke off into laughter.

"Well, Joseph," Meg said, continuing in her false nice voice, "I want to apologize for that."

The voice was silent for a moment then asked, "Eh? Come again? Meg Overly apologizing? Let me just step out of the way so the lightning doesn't strike me."

"Ha, ha. Very funny," Meg said. "So enough of that mushy stuff. Gotta go. Call me when Zeus wins another award."

"Ten four," the staff sergeant said. Meg ended the call with a dramatic flourish on the disconnect button.

Spring was nothing if not a daughter of truth and honesty. She knew when she was beat, and she was big enough to admit it. "You're right," said Spring to Meg, whose grin had graduated into a smirk. "Ethan should have listened to your explanation instead of jumping to conclusions."

"He actually used the phrase 'nineteenth-century Canadian *Little House on the Prairie*,'" Meg whined, "when I told him that I was talking to a Mountie. That's their nickname, you know. Mounties."

"That's in the past, nothing I can do about what happened," said Spring, ever the pragmatist. "All I can do is apologize and hope we can move forward."

"And?" Meg prompted.

Spring got up to leave, desperately wanting to get out of the uncomfortable situation. "And go back and tell Autumn that everything is fine and she can go ahead with the wedding."

"And?" Meg queried again, leaning back in her chair and crossing her long legs on top of her desk.

Spring shuddered at Meg's dirty boots and the dried crusts of dirt that fell off the bottoms onto the file folders. "And tell her there really is a Mountie called Staff Sergeant Nichols who you chewed out on the phone about a customs issue?"

"Bingo," Meg said and got up from her chair. "Let me walk you out."

Spring followed Meg down the hall. And if she had had a tail, she thought wryly to herself, it would indeed be tucked between her legs.

Part of Spring was overjoyed by what she had learned. She

desperately wanted Autumn to marry Ethan, and she desperately wanted Heather's wish to come true. The other part of her chastised herself for not being on her game. She knew better than to take the word of one person when it came to establishing the truth. She knew there were two sides to every story, and somewhere in between was the truth. She had heard that truth today. But it shouldn't have come to this. She should have investigated for herself instead of taking Ethan's word. Of course she knew that Ethan meant well. And he truly believed what he overheard Meg saying was about his wedding. Above all else, Spring knew Ethan wanted to protect Autumn. And he thought he was doing that. Spring didn't blame him for misleading them. She blamed herself. She had let thoughts about Gabe and Chad distract her.

"Interesting fact," Meg was saying as she held the door open for Spring. "Did you know it was the RCMP who were the first K9 police unit in the world to train dogs to safely identify the presence of the synthetic opioid called fentanyl?"

But Spring only half-listened. It was time to set things right with Autumn. She could tell that her sister missed her friend. It was time to set things right between Autumn and Meg and to ramp things up a notch. She had a wedding to plan, and there would be no time for nostalgia and might-have-beens.

CHAPTER 21

*S*TAN PULLED UP in front of the Borough Building in his big red pickup truck with "Brilhart Hardware Store" emblazed in gold on both truck doors and the back of the truck bed. As he idled at the curb, waiting for the sheriff to emerge, he ran a finger between his shirt and his neck. Stan hadn't worn a suit since Renata's funeral. The collar of the white dress shirt was tighter than he remembered, and the dress shoes were starting to pinch his pinky toes, even though he had put them on less than thirty minutes ago.

By the time Sheriff Landry climbed into the front passenger seat, Stan had started to sweat. He reached for the temperature knob on the dashboard and turned on the air conditioner. He watched as the sheriff removed a black pen and a knot of wires from a paper bag.

"Is that it?" Stan asked nervously. "The recording device?"

"Yup," Buddy answered in what seemed to Stan to be a little too enthusiastically. "Had to borrow it from the Greensburg PD. I drove up there this morning to pick it up. All you do is put the pen in your shirt pocket."

He handed the pen to Stan, who did as he was told. It felt heavy, like the secret that had weighed him down for so many weeks. "Have you ever done this before?" he asked.

"Nope," Buddy said. "First time. Pretty exciting, huh?"

Stan stared at his friend. "For you, maybe." He patted his shirt pocket and fiddled with the pen.

"That's the last thing you want to do," Buddy scolded. "Don't call attention to it. There's no reason in the world for her to suspect that the pen is a recording device. Just leave it alone. Pretend it's not there."

"How does it work?" Stan asked, putting both hands on the steering wheel.

"It's voice activated to start recording when you start to speak. It has a twelve-hour battery life and a range of fifty feet. Once you're done, I'll take it back to the office and we'll download the audio files to the computer and give them to the prosecutor.

"Sounds pretty straightforward," Stan agreed, reminding himself not to pat his pocket.

"Okay then," Buddy said. "What are you waiting for? Let's

CHAPTER 21

go."

Stan felt like a chastised child sitting in the principal's office awaiting punishment. As he drove along the highway toward Mt. Pleasant and the Main Street Diner where he had arranged to meet Nancy, he wished he could just keep driving. His son, Stan Jr. and his family lived in a suburb outside Pittsburgh. Instead of taking the exit for Mt. Pleasant, he could keep driving until he reached Pepper Lane. Then Stan remembered that the sheriff was with him, and he forced himself to take the correct exit.

"I don't think I can do this," he told the sheriff, who gestured for him to keep driving, instead of turning onto Main Street.

"Drive two more blocks and turn onto a side street," Buddy said, ignoring Stan's comment. "It's better to be out of sight and approach the diner on foot."

Stan did as he was told and pulled up in front of a row of neat bungalows. Shifting the truck into park, he felt his shoes pinch him again, and suddenly his shirt collar seemed to be cutting off the air supply into his lungs. He felt his hands tremble.

"Look," Buddy said kindly, "I know you're nervous. That's to be expected. Just remember that all you have to do is get her to admit that she wrote the letters. After that, you can go. Ten minutes, tops. You can do anything for ten minutes."

"I don't even know where to start," Stan mumbled, staring

out of the windshield. "What if she won't even talk to me? Or worse, what if she's not there?"

"She agreed to meet you, didn't she?" the sheriff asked.

Stan nodded.

"First, you need to apologize," the sheriff continued. "Be sincere. You have to bring her back to your side. She might demur at first, but eventually she'll accept your apology."

"Demur?" Stan asked. "What on earth does that mean?"

"It means she'll probably hesitate," Buddy answered patiently. "She'll make you pay for what she considers your misdeeds and then eventually forgive you."

"That's crazy," Stan said. "I've done nothing that needs forgiving. I'm the injured party here. She's the guilty one."

"Not in her eyes," Buddy reminded him. "In her eyes, you acted very ungentlemanly-like when you broke off your correspondence out of the blue. She expects you to make amends."

"How do I do that?" Stan asked, exasperated and ready to bag the whole thing. Hadn't the merchants said in their meeting the other day that they didn't care if the letter writer was ever caught? It was more important to them to keep their secrets. And besides, once Nancy was arrested and revealed, he, and his role in the whole awful mess would also be exposed. He wasn't sure he could bear that humiliation.

"You're going to have to suck it up and be really sincere when you apologize," Buddy answered, and then added, "Maybe take her hand as a gesture of affection."

CHAPTER 21

"Then what?" Stan asked. "How do I bring up the letters?"

"You'll figure it out," Buddy assured him, leaning over to slide the power button to the on position on the side of the recording device. "Just go with it. When the opportunity presents itself, insert the subject into the conversation. Once she's admitted that she wrote the letters, you can leave."

Stan sighed and opened the truck door. He was so ashamed of the mess he had made of things, and he figured he owed it to everyone to make things right.

He began the walk of shame toward the diner. When he passed Brown's Candy and Bakery he was instantly overcome with the memory of Renata buying Easter candy for their children. He thought of his wife of thirty years combing through the chocolate Easter bunnies and colored candied eggs looking for just the right ones for the children's Easter basket. His mind then flashed to Ducky in her pretty pink sweater set at the Merchants Association meeting when she gave her presentation about the penalties of mail harassment. He felt his face flush as he thought how much he would like to see more of her, then he felt the blood leave his face as he realized that she wouldn't want anything to do with him once she learned what he had done. Then he thought of Nancy and her deviousness and deceitfulness. How dare she! As he walked, Stan's hesitation and nervousness turned to anger, and by the time he stood in front of the diner, he was more than ready to bring the whole business to a close. He straightened his shoulders and walked through the door.

Nancy had said she would be wearing a yellow shirt, and it was not difficult to spot her in a bright buttercup blouse that was tied primly at her neck in a tight bow. As he approached the booth, he grew more and more confused. Instead of the sleek and sophisticated woman Nancy had boasted to be, she was actually a mousy woman with a tight line for a mouth and small, dark sunken eyes magnified by thick glasses. Her hair, or what was left of it, was greasy and stringy. He looked under the table, as if he might find the real Nancy there, and saw that she was wearing thick black tights and brown oxford shoes.

"Hello," he said, standing at the end of the table. Then he sat down in a smooth motion, momentarily surprised that his bulk hadn't jarred the table or made the salt and pepper shakers jump. Typically, his size made him perpetually clumsy.

"Hello," said Nancy tightly without looking at him, and Stan groaned inwardly. He had his work cut out for him.

He remembered the sheriff's advice and reached out to take Nancy's hand, which was resting next to the placemat. "I owe you an apology, Nancy," he said in what he hoped was a voice that sufficiently expressed the regret he did not feel. "It was wrong of me to break off our correspondence. I know that now and I am very sorry."

"Well," Nancy said slowly. "It was awfully rude. You treated me terribly after we had gotten so close." She still had not looked at him. Stan figured this is what the sheriff had meant by "demur."

"Can you ever forgive me?" he asked and squeezed her hand. At this gesture she looked up and smiled at him, revealing yellowed teeth.

"I suppose I could try," she said coyly. "It won't be easy, though. You really hurt my feelings."

"How can I make it up to you?" Stan asked, willing her to get on with it so he could talk about the letters, though he still didn't know how he would work them into the conversation.

"If there's anything I can't abide it's disloyalty," she said primly. "I find it very unattractive in a man."

Stan saw his opportunity and grabbed it. "I promise to be completely loyal to you from now on, Nancy," he said, choking over the false words. "For example, I won't tell anyone about the letters."

Nancy pulled her hand away and put it in her lap. With her other hand she fiddled with the silverware. "I don't know what you're talking about," she said, but the red splotches that appeared on her cheeks betrayed her.

Stan reached for her other hand. "It's okay," he said. "It's no big deal and there's no harm done. Actually, it really was kind of fun to be the only one in town who knows everyone's secrets. Besides you," he added. "Now this will be our secret. Just between you and me. I promise."

Nancy let several seconds pass before she responded, a tight, smug smile on her lips. "It was fun, wasn't it?" she said, then giggled girlishly. "I wish I could have seen that Teppy's face when she opened her letter. And Duncan. Well, he deserved what he got, pretending to have a college degree. Why, that's not fair to the rest of us who had to work hard for advanced education, now is it?"

Stan nodded his head in agreement. To himself he was thinking, *I know I have enough to nail her, but I just want a little bit more, to make sure.*

"And Miss Elsie," she continued primly, "living in sin all of those years. I don't know how she could show her face in church."

That was it. Stan had heard enough. It was time to wrap things up. "Will you excuse me a moment?" he said, gesturing to the back of the restaurant. "All of a sudden my stomach is a little troubled. Probably just nerves."

"Of course," Nancy said. "But don't be long, dear."

Don't hold your breath, Stan thought as he made his way to the back of the diner, past the restrooms and out the back door. He almost walked into the side of his truck, which stood idling in the alley behind the restaurant.

"Thought you might want a quick getaway," Buddy said, smiling. "How'd you do?"

Stan hustled around to the passenger side and jumped in, barely closing the door before the sheriff screeched away.

He's enjoying this, Stan thought, and now mostly relieved of his heavy burden, he laughed at the absurdity of two middle-age men skulking around back alleys to pull off a sting operation. He patted his pocket proudly. "I got everything we need. She won't know what hit her."

"Where does she think you went?" Buddy asked, driving out of town and back onto the highway toward Finch's Crossing.

"I told her I was having some stomach trouble," Stan laughed. "She'll probably still be waiting for me when we're sitting at the bar at the Greystone and I'm buying you a beer."

* * *

With the letter writer safely in jail in Westmoreland County, Buddy Landry stewed over what to do next. His first move, of course, should be to tell the merchants that the letter writer had been caught and that their secrets were safe. He reflexively felt his breast pocket where he had stored his letter from Nancy. He pulled it out, unfolded it, and began to read.

What will everyone think when they find out the Big Sheriff has been to the Big House upstate? Why, they will think you're a big fat fake.

Buddy sat down in his desk chair and fed the letter into the shredder. Everyone in Finch's Crossing knew he had a long and illustrious career as a petty juvenile offender. It was no secret. Which got him thinking about secrets. Oftentimes, there was little difference between a secret and a lie. He thought back to the pies and greasy foods he enjoyed whenever his wife was out of town. But was that really a secret? He ate in front of plenty of witnesses at the lunch counter at Hoffman's

Drugstore. But Nina never found out. And that's where things went "click" in the sheriff's mind. He ate pie in front of all of Finch's Crossing. But no one knew he wasn't supposed to be eating sweets, so he wasn't really keeping a secret after all. Well, except from Nina.

All of this splicing and dicing of lies and secrets got him to thinking about Stan and their shared predicament. And their shared secret.

Stan was a lonely widower with a lot of life yet to live and a lot to offer. What good would it do to tell the whole town— to tell his friends and neighbors—that he had been the cause of their troubles? He couldn't think of a single reason to share Stan's secret. But he could think of a boatload of reasons not to.

Rising from his chair, Buddy steeled himself for the Merchants Association meeting. He left his office and walked through Gazebo Park and into the community center.

Looking at his watch, he saw that if he hurried, he could catch them before they left their regularly scheduled meeting.

Oh Lordy, he thought, *but there have been a lot of Merchants Association meetings. Maybe after the Bridal Expo I'll finally have some peace.*

He walked into the community center just as the group was preparing to leave, without, he noticed, the usual enthusiasm and spirit the Merchants Association members typically gave off, like rays of blinding sunshine. But he was about to give them the good news they'd all been hoping for.

He strode to the front of the room, hat in hand. "Everyone," he said sharply, "I need to say a few words, so if you could all please sit down I would appreciate it. I know you're all anxious to get home, but this is important." He paused, waiting until everyone had returned to their seats and the room was quiet. "Now I want you to hold your questions to the end, after I have my say. You're all going to want to leap around and wave your hands and shout out your questions, but there will be plenty of time for that afterwards. And then, after that, there's a favor I want to ask of you."

He surveyed the room, and when he caught Stan's eyes, he gave him an encouraging smile.

"We have apprehended the writer of the poison pen letters and they are currently in jail. The individual pled guilty in night court and will be incarcerated."

As predicted, everyone erupted into an uproar, shouting questions and talking among themselves.

"So who is it?" Teppy demanded, her face flushed. "When can we see him? I have a few suggestions of where he can go when he gets out of prison."

"That's where the favor comes in," the sheriff said, taking a deep breath.

He had pulled in a favor with the prosecuting attorney to keep the arrest so low-profile and ambiguous on the court documents that no one would know the true nature of the crime. Nancy had immediately confessed, and Ernest Wheaton, the prosecutor who owed him a favor, had dropped the charge to a misdemeanor with such a vague description of the criminal activity that no one would more than glance at it. Nancy would have to pay a hefty fine and would be sent to live in a halfway house for two years, monitored, and forbidden to mail any letters to Finch's Crossing again. Her outgoing and incoming mail would be read by the halfway house staff, and she was forbidden to use email for a year. It would take someone very industrious to figure out who the poison pen letter writer was. It was the only way the sheriff could think of to protect Stan.

"I want you to be satisfied that the letter writer has been fined and appropriately punished. And leave it at that."

The room erupted again and angry and confused voices hurled questions at him. Sighing, he waited patiently until they calmed down.

"I am asking you to trust me on this," he said.

"Why should we trust you, Sheriff, with all due respect?" Teppy asked.

"Do you have any reason not to trust me?" he asked. "Have I ever, in thirty years serving this town, given you any reason to doubt me?"

He watched as the assembled merchants shook their heads and looked at one another.

"You will never understand why I am asking this favor of

you. But know this. What I am asking is for the good of the town." He spread his arms to motion to the assembled group. "It's for your good."

Duncan Olack stood up and crossed his arms across his blue oxford cloth shirt. "That can mean only one thing. The letter writer is one of us. And you are trying to protect him."

Buddy raised his hands in front of him, signaling that he wanted quiet. "I swear to you, as an officer of the court and on the oath of office I took thirty years ago to protect this town, that the letter writer is not one of you. The letter writer is not from Finch's Crossing."

"But it's our right to know," Melissa from the Burnt Orange Antique Shop said crossly.

"It is," the sheriff agreed. "But if you knew who it was, what would you do about it? What would it change?"

Spring Hamilton, bless her, stepped forward and joined him at the front of the room.

"I, for one, grant this favor to you, Sheriff," she said solemnly. She turned to the group. "I don't know what your secrets are, and I don't want to know. And don't you see, if we pursue this, if we demand to know who the letter writer is, then chances are, all of our secrets will come tumbling out and everyone will know about them."

"Well now, dear, that's true," Miss Elsie said, and the room went quiet again, as was befitting the matriarch of Finch's Crossing. Miss Elsie stood and faced the room. "What good would it do to dig all of this up? Do we really want to hurt ourselves and each other by airing our dirty laundry? And the good Lord knows we all have secrets, letter or no letter. And besides, we have a wedding to plan, a Bridal Expo to arrange, and it's time that we put all of this nonsense behind us and get on with it."

Miss Elsie had spoken, and the group disbanded soon after, whispering and tittering with each other.

Sheriff Buddy Landry went straight home, right after he stopped at Hoffman's Drugstore for a piece of take-out lemon meringue pie, which he would finally enjoy in the peace and quiet of his own home.

* * *

Later that evening, Autumn pulled her jeep up in front of the community center and turned off the ignition. She looked around at the empty parking spots on the street. Even the municipal parking lot was almost empty.

"I thought you said there was a special meeting going on?" Autumn asked Spring, who was gathering up her gigantic wedding expo binder and getting out of her Jeep. These days it seemed Spring never went anywhere without it.

"There was. Is. C'mon. We don't want to be late." She gestured for Autumn to follow her and the two entered the building, which was dark and quiet.

"There's no one here," Autumn observed.

"You're always so observant," Spring quipped. "Guess it's that eagle eye that makes you such a great painter."

"I can hardly miss the fact that this building is empty. So what are we doing here?"

Spring ushered Autumn down the hall and opened the door to the main meeting room where the Merchants Association and other civic groups met. She flicked some of the lights and the empty room was eerily and partially illuminated. Spring walked up to the projector table in the middle of the room and flipped on the machine. She retrieved her laptop from her voluminous purse and connected it to the projector.

"What the..." Autumn asked, but Spring cut her off.

"Now that we are full steam ahead with the wedding, with no more talk of cancelling or postponing, it's time to get down to the business of your dress. And we're running out of time. We should have done this weeks ago. Take a seat."

Autumn did as she was told, taking a chair in the front row of the chairs and looking quizzically at her sister. "We're looking at dresses here? Now?"

"That's right," Spring said triumphantly. "If Mohammed won't come to the mountain, then the mountain must come to Mohammed. You're the mountain, by the way." She flipped a few switches and the screen came to life with a PowerPoint slide reading, "The Perfect Wedding Dress: An Analysis and Evaluation."

"You have got to be kidding me," Autumn practically

wailed, dropping her head into her hands. "A PowerPoint about wedding dresses? Really? We can't just go to a store and pick one out?"

"Of course we can, and that's what we'll have to do since you've put this off so long."

"What else would I do?" Autumn asked.

"I was going to get one custom made, but you ruined that plan."

"Spring, that's your thing. Not mine. I can go into a shop, try a few on, and pick one."

"That's good to know," Spring said, "because we're going shopping tomorrow afternoon with Heather and Martha. I've booked an appointment for us at Sheffield's in Pittsburgh."

"Are you kidding?" Autumn exclaimed. "That's the most exclusive bridal shop in the whole state. There is no way I'm dropping thousands of dollars on a wedding dress."

"You don't have to," Spring responded, picking up the remote clicker and pointing it at the projector. "The dress is my gift to you. I've been scratching my head trying to figure out what to get you, and I decided this was it. After all, I am a world-famous model. I do know a little something about fashion. Now let's get started. Because I am pretty sure that you have no idea what a Sabrina neckline is or how to drape lace over satin or what would flatter your figure. I'm narrowing down the options so when we go into the boutique, we'll have an idea of what you like. Very efficient."

"That does make sense," Autumn agreed. "I won't want to spend hours trying on dresses, sitting around sipping champagne like in those romcom movies you love so much. I'd rather be painting or making cupcakes with Heather."

"That's where you and I have something in common, dear sister," Spring laughed. "We both want to get down to business. Get 'er done, as the cable guy says."

"Ugh, I hate that phrase," Autumn complained, but Spring ignored her.

She hit the remote and the slide advanced to a gigantic picture of a woman in a body-clinging sheath gown.

"Oh my God, Spring," Autumn moaned. "That's me. How did you get pictures of me in a wedding dress?"

Spring could barely respond for laughing so much. "Easy," she proclaimed. "I had Kyle Photoshop your face over the models' heads." She hit the button to activate the laser pointer and traced the model's neck. "It's pretty much flawless. I wanted you to see how you'd look in various styles."

"You're right about that," Autumn said, walking to the screen to inspect the image closer. "Now I know why you were taking all those pictures at Easter. You were a regular shutterbug. I thought you'd lost your mind."

"That's enough commentary," Spring commanded, and Autumn returned to her seat like a chastised schoolgirl.

Spring pointed the red laser dot to the screen again and moved it up and down the length of the dress. "This is a silk dress. Look how beautifully it drapes. It's clingy, but not in a vulgar way. You've got a great figure and can pull anything off, but I know you are particularly modest, so maybe this isn't the way to go."

"It's gorgeous," Autumn agreed, "but a little skimpy. I don't think I want bare arms. Besides, it could be a little chilly."

"You'll be inside," Spring pointed out.

Autumn gestured for her to advance to the next slide.

"This one is also made of silk, but it has a Sabrina neckline, straight across the top of the chest."

"And I like the long sleeves," Autumn observed. "You'd actually look good in this, Spring,"

Spring advanced the slide, ignoring her sister, and an image of Kate Middleton, before she became the Duchess of Cambridge, sprang up on the screen.

"Oh, I had forgotten how beautiful this dress was," Autumn gushed. "All that lace on the bodice and sleeves. And I love how it continues up over the shoulders and the back of the neck."

Spring beamed with pleasure. "See, I knew you would get into it. I just needed to get you started." She clicked through the rest of the slides and the sisters discussed necklines, fabric, embellishments, and veils, finally deciding on satin, lace, and the modest Sabrina neckline.

It was at that point that Meg entered the building, and as she sauntered into the room, she said, "Spring Hamilton,

CHAPTER 21

I swear if you don't stop demanding to meet with me I will make you clean out dog cages at the kennel for a week."

She came to a halt as soon as she saw Autumn sitting in the room. "Oh," Meg said, having stopped halfway into the room. "Hi, Autumn. I didn't know you were going to be here." She glared at Spring, who just smiled back as she packed up her things.

"And I didn't know you were going to be here," Autumn replied, also staring at Spring.

"Okay then," Spring declared, leaving the room. "I'll leave the two of you to work things out. I'll be waiting in the car."

Autumn and Meg just stared at each other, then they both spoke at the same time.

"I'm so sorry, Meg," Autumn said. "I should have trusted you." And Meg said, "I know I've stressed you out and I'm sorry." The two laughed.

"I've missed you," Autumn said, holding out her hand. Meg walked the rest of the way into the room and took it, sitting down next to her best friend.

"I promise you, Autumn, on everything I own, that Bryan Kelly will be at your wedding."

"Okay," Autumn said simply. "I believe you. You've never, ever disappointed me. I should have known all along that I could count on you."

* * *

After Meg pulled away in her old pickup truck, surprisingly having given Autumn a big hug, Autumn slid into her jeep.

"You know, something just occurred to me," Spring said hesitantly as Autumn started the car and pulled into the street. "Will Meg be hurt if she isn't included in tomorrow's shopping trip?"

"Are you kidding?" Autumn asked, exploding with laughter. "She would rather be anywhere else than in a dress shop. She'd be too afraid I'd make her a bridesmaid after all and make her wear pink taffeta."

"Okay, good," Spring said. "I sort of figured that's what your answer would be, but I wanted to check."

"That's awful big of you," Autumn said and pulled away from the curb.

"That's me," Spring agreed, "big-hearted."

"Too bad you can't see your way to being that way with Gabe," Autumn said quietly.

Spring turned to look out the window and didn't answer.

* * *

The next afternoon, Spring collected Heather from school while Autumn and Martha got ready to go, and then they were off in Spring's Mercedes, four girls on the town.

At the bridal studio, Heather sat between Spring and Martha, admiring the latest gown Autumn had put on. Martha got up to help arrange the veil, and Heather snuggled closer to Spring.

Heather pulled something out of her Hello Kitty purse and handed it to Spring. "It's my Uncle Bryan," she said with pride. "He gave it to me after Mommy and Daddy died." Spring unfolded the picture as Heather talked on. "He told me that no matter where he was, he was always thinking about me. And that when I really needed him, he would always come home for me."

Spring sighed. Knowing how well-intentioned Bryan was, she understood that Heather's uncle had meant that when another emergency or catastrophe happened, he would be able to come home. But in her little girl mind, Heather needed her uncle to be with her as Ethan, whom she loved like a father, got married. Sure, Heather's life would change for the better. But it was still a change. Spring kissed the little girl on the top of her head.

"He's really handsome," she said, handing the photo back to Heather, who looked at it for a few long seconds before she put it back in her purse. "You really want him to come, don't you?" Spring asked.

"Oh yes, I can't wait," Heather bubbled in response. "And Ethan promised me that he would be here in time. I hope he wears his uniform," she continued. "I like the buttons, and sometimes he lets me wear his hat. And he wears those little white gloves," she giggled. "They're just like the ones I wear on Easter to go to church."

The two looked up to see Autumn, luminous in a lace and

satin gown, twirling in front of them.

"Is that the one?" Spring asked Autumn, already knowing the answer.

Autumn, Heather, and Martha all chorused a triumphant "Yes!" Autumn made one more twirl, holding out her arms, like she was making windmills, the way they had as children.

"Okay then," Spring said, "back to business. It's time to see what the rest of us are going to look like at this shindig!" She pulled out three dresses from a garment bag hanging on the back of a chair beside them, all in different styles and various hues of light green. She handed one to Heather and another to Martha.

"Oh, I didn't think the alterations would be made already," Martha exclaimed, fingering the chiffon of her dress. "Lila at Morris's said it would take another week."

"I wanted Autumn to see all of us dressed in our finery while she was wearing her wedding dress, so I brought them here last week. So, what are we waiting for? Let's try them on, then we'll get the sales girl to coordinate our shoes."

The three emerged from the dressing rooms at the same time, and Autumn clapped her hands in delight. Spring saw the tears that were forming in her sister's eyes.

"Okay, no crying," Spring commanded, but it was too late. Tears were streaming down Autumn's cheeks. And then they were all crying, laughing, and smiling.

CHAPTER 22

AFTER THE DRESS fitting, Spring pulled her Mercedes over to the curb in front of Autumn's house and parked and her three passengers got out and entered Autumn's house. As Spring grabbed her purse, she glanced into the rearview mirror and saw a male figure walking toward her up Loucks Avenue. She thought nothing of it. That is, until the male figure was standing directly beside her.

Startled, Spring spun around, only to discover it was Gabe standing beside her.

"Gabe? Are you stalking me now?"

Gabe smiled, although weakly. "Hardly. I was just hoping we could talk."

Spring could feel the heaviness of Gabe's mood. She felt

annoyed with him and sorry for him at the same time. But Autumn had encouraged her to hear him out. Maybe it was finally time to listen. Then she could move on once and for all.

Spring stood there and stared at Gabe for at least five seconds before she finally said, "Okay, Gabe. Do you want to come in?"

Gabe gave Spring the saddest, most forlorn look she had ever seen and said meekly, "Do you think we could just take a walk?"

"Okay. Sure."

Spring pulled her purse over her shoulder, locked the Mercedes, and asked, "Where should we walk?"

"I don't really care," Gabe said, matter-of-factly. "I just need to talk to you."

The pair started walking down Loucks Avenue. They both remained silent at first. Spring, sensing Gabe's suffering, broke the silence. "Autumn told me you had some monumental revelation for me. So what is it?"

"I am now divorced."

"Wow," Spring mocked. "How convenient. Did you just kick her to the curb for me?"

"Spring, listen. I was married to a wonderful woman. Her name was Marla. Her name *is* Marla. I loved her dearly. In fact, I still do. But she has early-onset Alzheimer's. And it's bad."

Spring's brain struggled to process this revelation. "I am

very sorry to hear that," was all she could think of to say.

"Thank you," Gabe replied. "There is something I would like you to read, if you don't mind." He pulled Marla's letter out of his pants pocket, unfolded it, and handed it to Spring.

By now they had walked downtown and stopped at Gazebo Park. Spring took the letter from Gabe and sat on an empty bench while Gabe remained standing a few feet away, trying to give Spring privacy as she read Marla's letter.

Spring began to read. She sped through the letter once and then went back to the beginning. She needed to read it again. When she read it for the second time, her mind began to race. She had so many emotions coursing through her. Spring struggled to process the letter. She was immediately struck with intense admiration for Marla. She thought of the courage it took for her to set Gabe free in this remarkable manner. Feeling the smooth surface of the paper, she was struck by the balance that had just been restored to her world. It had been a letter that had taken Gabe away from her a few weeks ago, and it was a letter that had brought him back to her. She folded the page and put it back in the envelope.

As tears welled up in her eyes, she motioned for Gabe to come sit beside her, which he did.

She took his hand in hers. "Gabe, I am so sorry," she whispered, overcome with emotion. "I had no idea."

Gabe smiled sadly at Spring. "I know. There's no good way to tell someone about something like this."

"So is she still in the ... place?" Spring asked, suddenly ashamed at how petty and mean she had been with Gabe, when all along he had been suffering under the weight of these terrible circumstances.

"Yes. She's in the care facility. I visit her twice a week. Her disease has really progressed. She has no idea it's me when I visit. She's in her own little world. But I think she's happy, if that makes any sense. She smiles a lot and sings."

The couple sat silent for a moment, until Gabe sensed it was the right time to tell Spring how he felt. He turned to her on the bench and began, "Spring, I am sorry for what happened all those years ago. I loved you with all my heart, and still do. Back then, I was afraid that I would hold you back. I was just a small-town schmuck. And I was scared. I mean, I was no match for Spring Hamilton!"

Spring squeezed his hand and stared into his face.

Gabe continued. "Until these last few weeks, I never allowed myself to believe that, despite our separation, despite all the years, despite my marriage to a wonderful woman who was so brutally robbed of her life, I never, ever thought we would have another chance. But the universe thought otherwise. Now I know I have another chance with the girl I worshipped in high school. The wonderful woman she became. I never stopped thinking about you. I am convinced that our time is now. I will do whatever it takes to be with you. I love you so much, with all my heart. I love you now more than I did in high school, and believe me, that was a lot of love."

Spring was struggling. Her emotions were raw. She began to realize that Gabe had always been at the back of her mind since their breakup, all those years ago. She had never given up on him completely. She had always loved him. Chad was just a guy she allowed into her life because she thought she needed a guy. Ridiculous. Gabe was the man she needed to spend the rest of her life with. It was so obvious now. She began to cry.

Gabe put his arm around her, and she leaned into him, resting her cheek on his shoulder. They were both crying softly now. Neither spoke for a few minutes.

Then Spring said, "I don't know, Gabe. My world is just a whirlwind of change right now. Leaving California and moving to New York. Breaking up with Chad. You know, we were together for a long time. Everything is moving so fast."

"I know it's a lot to take in. But just know that I am prepared to commit the rest of my life to you. To us. I believe with all my heart we would be great together. I believe we both would be very happy. So please, Spring, give us another chance. Let's reignite that fire that I almost extinguished."

Spring continued, "I do love you, Gabe. I really feel it strongly. I don't think this time you'll break up with me."

"No way would I do that."

"My life is in flux right now, so what better time to embrace change?" Spring mused. "Why not strive for a new beginning? It's simple. I love you, and you are obviously crazy about me."

They both laughed. "I think we'll be very happy together, too."

Gabe added, "Look, I know you like to plan out everything. It's that logical mind of yours. But sometimes, maybe the craziest thing is the right thing."

Gabe stood up, and Spring followed his lead. They embraced in front of the bench, and Gabe's heart almost jumped out of his chest as Spring leaned in and kissed him. And when the thoughts about the logistics of two households and a long-distance relationship threatened to enter Spring's mind, she booted them out. The world, she decided, had a way of working things out.

* * *

It was six days before Autumn's wedding when Meg received a call from the Washington, D.C. police chief saying that he didn't think he would be able to get Bryan back to Finch's Crossing in time for the wedding.

"I'm doing everything I can, Meg," he promised, but she didn't hear any certainty in his voice. Deflated, she didn't even have the energy to bang down her office phone. Instead, she placed the receiver down quietly, grabbed her knapsack, and headed into town.

As she pounded on the door to Kyle's apartment, Meg mused that one good thing about having a fiancé was you could go over to his house and pound on his door and he had to help you.

"Kyle! Kyle!!" she yelled. "Let me in. I've got a huge problem."

Dressed in his customary dark blue jeans, white dress shirt with the cuffs flapping, and black and white Pumas, Kyle greeted Meg at the door and practically dragged her inside.

"What's wrong?" he asked frantically, reaching for her arms, then turning her face one way and then the other. "Are you hurt? What happened? Are you all right?"

Meg practically shoved her way past him and into the apartment. "No, nothing like that."

She settled on the navy-blue Ikea couch in Kyle's small living room and looked uncomfortably around at the decorative throw pillows, scented candles, and plethora of plaques and small paintings with pithy sayings, such as "Live, Love, Laugh" and "Bloom Where You're Planted." Kyle had grown up with parents who were not exactly abusive, but who were at odds with each other so much that they failed to give Kyle a loving, nurturing home. So as an adult, Kyle had done that for himself. Or overdone it, as Meg had come to think of it. Once they were married and moved into her house at Ten Oaks Kennel, she was going to put her foot down about all those sappy sayings.

Kyle pushed a "Live Simply, Dream Big" pillow out of the way and sat down next to her, taking her hand in his. For once, she didn't pull away, which made him especially nervous. Although Kyle knew Meg loved him, she wasn't into what she called "that touchy-feely stuff."

"What's wrong, Meg? It can't be that bad."

"It's worse," Meg wailed. "I don't think Bryan is going to make it home for the wedding."

"Oh," was all Kyle could think to say.

Meg threw a "Choose Joy" pillow at him. "That's not very comforting," she accused.

"It does put you in a precarious position, especially after all these weeks of confidently promising you could deliver on your promise. So what happened? Did the police chief bail?"

"No, nothing like that," Meg said. "It's something to do with the request not making it up the ranks to the right person."

He looked at his watch. It was just after seven.

"C'mon," he commanded. "Let's go."

"Go where?" Meg asked as he stood, grabbed her hands, and pulled her off the couch.

"To Washington, of course. Where else?" He pulled out his cell phone and poised his fingers over the screen. "Call Sammy," he commanded, "and ask him to watch the kennel until we get back. We can be in D.C. in less than four hours." He looked at his watch again and asked Siri, "What time is it in Afghanistan?"

"It is 6 a.m. in Afghanistan," said the computer-generated voice.

"Do you know where the chief lives?" Kyle asked Meg.

"No, but isn't it a bit late to be going to his house?"

Kyle ignored the question and dialed another number. He

didn't care if it was two in the morning when they arrived on the chief's doorstep. He had made a commitment to Meg, and Kyle was going to make sure he honored it.

"The sheriff owes me a favor," he said. "I helped him out with an uncomfortable Facebook situation. But you didn't hear that from me."

Meg held up both hands in front of her. "Hey, that sounds like something I don't want to know about."

"Buddy, this is Kyle," he announced and got straight to the point. "I need some information. I need the home address of the Washington, D.C. chief of police. Hello? Sheriff, are you there?"

There was a long stretch where Kyle didn't say anything, then he hung up. He looked at Meg. "He told me to call back in fifteen minutes and he'll have the details. For now, we need to hit the road."

"Wait," Meg said. "What are we doing here? What's your plan?"

"We're going to make this right. There is plenty of time for them to pull this off. How hard can it be? It sounds like the equivalent of a phone message not being delivered. It's just a matter of passing on information."

"That's what I thought, initially," Meg said. "But what if he says he won't push it up the chain? What if he says no?"

Kyle turned and pointed to a ceramic plaque sitting on the fireplace mantle. It read "Never Take No For An Answer."

* * *

With Meg trapped in Kyle's car for four hours, she was treated to his vision of their wedding.

She listened patiently as he droned on an on. Now was as good a time as ever to share her feelings with him. The thought made her want to spit out the window.

After Kyle had finished talking about the ice sculptures and the bridesmaids, Meg said, "Okay, so is it my turn now?"

"Of course. This is our wedding. I've just thought of all this stuff because I knew you wouldn't be into it. You know, being, well, being you."

Meg felt a glimmer of hope surge through her. "So you thought of all this stuff just because you knew I wouldn't, not because you have your heart set on it?"

"God, no," Kyle said. "I don't care anymore about the wedding details than the next guy," he said. "I just want to marry you."

"Really?" Meg asked, still doubtful. "I was so sure you wanted a big poufy wedding with all that tulle and crepe stuff."

"I'm a guy," Kyle said defensively. "Guys don't care about that stuff. I don't even know what that stuff is. Why on earth would you think I wanted a big wedding?"

"For starters, all those goofy pillows and plaques in your house," she responded. "Those platitudes just scream 'girly wedding with all the trimmings.'"

"Now you know that isn't the case," Kyle said. His voice

became wistful. "I have all those pillows and wall hangings around me because they make me feel good. They remind me how lucky I am to be alive and to be grateful for all I have."

Meg rolled her eyes. "Oh. My. God. I am going to barf."

"Okay then," Kyle said, ignoring her. "If you don't want a big white wedding, what do you want?"

"For starters, I am not wearing a dress." Meg looked intently at Kyle's profile to gauge his reaction. He continued to stare straight ahead.

"All right. I can live with that. I've already seen you in a skirt once, which is one time more than I thought I would. So I can check that off my bucket list. What else?"

"I am going to wear a white pantsuit with my Doc Martens. And Spike is going to be in the wedding. And I don't want any flowers. Maybe there can be a tree somewhere. Or something. We'll have to see. And I'm not going to say anything mushy at the altar. I'll get my vows from the internet."

Kyle did not respond but turned to look at Meg.

"Oh my God, are you crying?" she asked his tear-stained face.

"I can't help it," he sobbed. "I just love you so much and I can't wait to be your husband."

"Okay, well, me too," Meg agreed grudgingly. "Now can we get off at the next rest stop because I have to pee."

* * *

SPRING

Four hours later they were standing on the doorstep of Chief Butler's home in Georgetown. He had not answered the bell, so Meg was pounding on the door.

"Okay, Matthew, open up. I've come to collect on your promise. You know what'll happen if you don't let me in."

In response, the front porch light flicked on, and a balding, rotund middle-age man opened the door, tying the belt of a dark blue terry cloth bathrobe. "Meg?" he asked sleepily. "Is that you?"

"No, bozo, it's the Ghost of Christmas future come to tell you what's going to happen if you don't get Bryan Kelly to Finch's Crossing by April 29."

She shoved past him and Kyle followed. "Sorry, man," he said and shrugged. "I'm just the driver."

Chief Butler closed the door but didn't invite them in past the foyer. "My wife and kids are sleeping upstairs," he whispered. "Why are you here?"

Meg stepped closer to him and responded icily. "You told me five years ago that you owed me and you would do anything for me. No matter what."

"I tried," Butler said lamely.

Kyle pulled his phone from his pocket and held it out to Butler. "Try again," he said.

Butler took the phone and, turning away from them, dialed a number he was warned not to call unless it was an extreme emergency. He spoke in hushed tones, grimacing occasionally. Meg and Kyle could tell he was basically selling his soul to whomever was on the other end of the call. He turned back to them and held out the phone to Kyle. "Okay, it's done. Now will you please leave?"

"See, now wasn't that easy?" Meg asked sarcastically. Yawning, she added, "Do you have a guest room, we really could use a good night's sleep before we head back."

"Are you out of your mind?" the chief hissed.

When they heard a floorboard creak upstairs, they all froze, like statues. "You have to go," the chief hissed and pushed Meg and Kyle out the door. "Bryan Kelly will be in Finch's Crossing on April 29. Never contact me again."

"You better hope I don't have to," Meg responded matter-of-factly, while Kyle gave the chief a shrug, as if to say, *Hey, man, your best bet is to do exactly what she says.*

Meg and Kyle found themselves on the chief's doorstep once again, the door having been slammed in their faces. But their mission was accomplished, and that's all that mattered.

CHAPTER 23

SPRING AND GABE walked hand in hand along the streets of busy downtown Pittsburgh. There were no longer any secrets between them, and Spring felt free to let herself fall deeper and deeper in love with Gabe. With every step they took toward their destination, she counted a blessing. Step. Gabe. Step. Second chances. Step. You can always go home again. Step. A loving family.

Dressed in a simple, elegant cream suit she had bought at Morris Ladies Wear, Spring admired Gabe's dark blue pin-striped suit. As always, his dark curls just skimmed his shoulders, and she had to resist the urge to run her fingers through them.

They slowed as they entered the city's vibrant cultural district lined with art galleries, performing arts centers, bistros, and trendy boutiques. Spring pulled a sticky note from her purse and read aloud.

"Scottie's gallery is called 'The Space,'" she said. "It should be along here somewhere on Eighth Street. Hey," she cried, as if it had occurred to her for the first time, "we should look at some of Autumn's art! Wouldn't that be fun? Maybe I can buy a piece for our new home."

Gabe looked at her lovingly. "That's not a bad idea. But maybe we could get married first?"

"Oh right," Spring agreed as they stopped in front of the gallery, a glass-fronted building with a remarkable aluminum and glass sculpture out front.

Gabe gave it a second glance as they walked in.

"Be right there," a voice sang from somewhere in the back, and then Scottie appeared, dressed in his traditional seersucker suit, bow tie, and white bucks.

"Well, I declare," he said in that dramatic way he had, and put his hand to his chest. "What on earth are you doing here? And why on God's green earth are the two of you together?" He turned to Spring and threw a very indiscreet stage whisper. "I thought he was the devil's spawn?"

Spring took Gabe's hand. "He was." She smiled up at him. "But it's all worked out now."

Scottie crossed his arms on his chest and tapped his foot. "I guess if that's the way you roll, I can't judge."

"Scottie," Spring groaned, "we'll tell you all about it later, but right now, we have a favor to ask you."

"Oh boy," Scottie said, "here it comes. First Meg and her insane wedding logic and now the two of you with God knows what you have up your sleeve. I had to give that girl a 180-degree makeover. It about killed me, I have to say."

Gabe chimed in for the first time. "It's not as bad as that, but it is wedding related. We've snuck over to Pittsburgh to get married. And we would love for you to be our witness."

"We don't want to upstage Autumn," Spring rushed to add. "But we can't wait any longer." She squeezed Gabe's hand and looked into his eyes, seeking the same deep love she was feeling.

"We've waited almost two decades," Gabe added. "We don't want to waste even one day."

Scottie feigned some sort of overheated reaction and fanned his face with his hand. "Well, you have me all aflutter. I just don't know what to say."

Spring took a step toward him and took his hand. "Just say yes," she whispered.

"Okay then," Scottie responded, suddenly recovered from his attack. "Let me just grab a few things and we'll be going." He paused. "Where are we going? Don't tell me you're getting married at the courthouse?"

Gabe nodded and looked at his watch. "Yep, and we've got about twenty minutes to get there in time for our appointment."

"Well, why didn't you say so?" Scottie rushed past them to the front door, apparently forgetting the things he needed to collect. He withdrew a ring of keys from his suit coat pocket and beckoned them forward. "This is so exciting. Two weddings in one week! Maybe I'll catch the bouquet."

The trio walked quickly down the street, across the pedestrian bridge over the Alleghany River until they arrived at the Allegheny County Courthouse. The Romanesque Revival monstrosity rose above them, all stone and turrets. Gazing up at the oddly threatening architecture, Spring thought to herself that this medieval-looking building, where she would link her life forever to her high school sweetheart, symbolized the days gone by when their love had been strong. It symbolized their first chance. As they approached the side entrance where they had been instructed to go by the clerk of court, she saw the bridge that attached the monolithic courthouse to a more modern building on the other side of the street.

How fitting, she thought, absorbing the metaphor of the building around her. *We've come into another world, with a bridge that takes people from one world into another.*

She felt Gabe squeeze her hand, and she emerged from her reverie as they walked through the arched doorway and into an entryway that reached two stories high, ending in a painted ceiling depicting a night sky.

They walked lightly up the marble stairs, flanked by the

dark wood paneling on the walls and staircase rails, with Spring's heels making the only sounds, echoing softly around the curves and angles of the interior.

"You have to swear that you won't tell anyone, especially Autumn and Ethan, until after their wedding," Spring implored Scottie as they emerged on the second floor. "This is her wedding week. Her big day. I would never want to do anything to take away from that."

Scottie mimed locking his lips with a tiny key, which he then dramatically pretended to throw over his shoulder.

"You don't have any flowers," he observed, suddenly absorbed again in the details of Spring's wedding, forgetting all about Autumn's. "You can't get married without flowers. Tell me at least you have rings!"

"We do," Gabe acknowledged. "I stopped at Krop's Jewelers. We're set."

Spring watched in horror as Scottie stepped away from them and approached another couple descending the same grand staircase they were climbing.

"Excuse me," he said and gestured over to Spring and Gabe. "My friends are getting married at the last minute and don't have any flowers." He paused for dramatic effect and very pointedly looked at the bouquet of daisies, roses, and light pink lilies the woman in a short wedding dress carried. "Do you need these anymore?" And with that, he reached out and snatched the bouquet from the bride's hand and bounded back up the steps.

"Scottie!" Spring scolded. "You go right back and return those flowers. How could you!"

"It's all right," the young woman called up the stairs. "We've already had our pictures taken. I don't know what I would have done with the flowers anyway."

And with that, the couple turned and continued down the stairs, and Spring, Gabe, and Scottie continued up.

"See," said Scottie, shoving the bouquet at Spring. "All's well that ends well."

"Oh my God," Spring chimed in, and the three broke into laughter, sobering only when they reached the courtroom where the judge and a clerk stood waiting for them.

They stopped laughing and stood straighter as they entered the chambers with the tidy row of wooden church pew–style seating, the wooden dais, and witness box before them.

The judge in his dramatic black robes was reviewing a sheaf of papers as they approached. They were greeted only by the clerk of the court, who passed Gabe the marriage license for him and Spring to sign. When that was done, they took their places in front of the judge, facing each other, hands clasped together as to make a bridge between them. If either the judge or clerk recognized Spring, who was, after all, a face that was known the world over, neither said anything, for which she was grateful. Today, she felt like her seventeen-year-old self, before she had been discovered, and was bursting with an anticipation of a frenzied future so often reserved for the young.

The judge went through the marriage vows, but Spring barely heard anything. She remembered saying the "I dos" in the right places and slipping the gold band on Gabe's finger, just as he did for her. And then they kissed, and it was done. She was who she always thought she would be, from the time she was fourteen years old. Even during her years with Chad, she now realized, she had, deep in her soul, secretly longed for this day. She was, finally, Mrs. Gabriel Vignaroli.

* * *

Stan had the key in the lock ready to twist it shut when Kyle ran up and banged on the glass door of the hardware store. Always glad to see Kyle, Stan let him in and then flipped the sign to "Closed" and locked the door.

"Hey, Kyle, what do ya need?" Stan asked in a friendly voice.

"It's time," Kyle declared.

"Time for what?"

"It's time for you to make the move on Ducky," Kyle said emphatically.

"Oh, Kyle, I just don't know," Stan said, leading Kyle toward his office in the back.

Stan sat down at his desk, rubbing his chin, a look of both worry and consternation on his face.

"I just don't know. What if she says no?"

"Are you serious?" Kyle asked, emphasizing his incredulousness. "There is no way she'll say no. She likes you, dude!"

"She likes me? How do you know for sure?"

"Stan, my man, have you seen the way she looks at you?"

"I haven't noticed."

"You should pay attention. When you stood up for her calligraphy at the Merchants Association meeting, well, that got you lots of points."

"Really?"

"Really."

"But where would we go? What could we do? I don't know how to go on a date," Stan lamented.

"Come on, man. Just take her out to dinner. Easy as pie. Take her to the Greystone. Everybody loves the Greystone."

"Okay," Stan said halfheartedly, now rubbing his temples. He sat silent for at least a minute, as Kyle gazed down on him, intent to make this Ducky and Stan thing work.

"Will you ask her for me?" Stan pleaded, obviously leaping outside of his comfort zone by even agreeing to go on a date with Ducky.

Kyle opened his mouth to speak but, not liking what he was about to say, closed it. Kyle liked Stan and hated to see him suffer like this.

"Okay," Kyle started. "But I am not going to 'ask' her, per se. More like arrange an evening out for two of my friends." He didn't know if Ducky considered him a friend or not, but

Kyle had a feeling that if he could just get them started, things would work out, and Ducky would definitely think of him as a friend then.

"What is today, Stan?"

"Tuesday."

"Tuesday," Kyle repeated. "Perfect. If I call today, I am sure I can get a reservation for Saturday. I suggest you go about seven. That's when the restaurant will be really crowded, so you won't feel like you are so alone with her. If you go too early, you guys could be the only table in the whole place. Awkward for a first date."

"Awkward," Stan repeated. "Awkward is the story of my life."

"Okay then. Stan, my man, be at Greystone, Saturday at seven." Kyle thought a minute, then said, "If it would help, I'll make a point to be there too, somewhere in the background."

"Yes!" Stan blurted. Then, more softly, "That would be very kind of you, Kyle. I would be much obliged."

* * *

Kyle called the Greystone and made the reservation on his way home from Stan's. The next day he caught Ducky as she slid his mail through the mail slot and called out "Marketing company. Mail call."

"Hey, Ducky!" he called as she hustled down the street.

"Oh, hi, Kyle," she said, seeming genuinely glad to see Kyle standing there. "What's up?"

"You have plans Saturday night?"

Ducky always had plans on Saturday nights, but they involved sitting in front of the television at home, so she thought she should reply in the negative.

"Nothing pressing. Why?"

"Have you ever heard of a blind date?"

"Of course."

"I'm trying to arrange a blind date with Stan." Ducky's eyes sparkled a bit when Kyle mentioned Stan's name.

"If I know who the guy is, it's not really a blind date, is it?"

Kyle wished he had thought through this whole situation a little better.

"You're right. Truth is, Stan has been such a good customer of mine, I wanted to treat him to a meal at the Greystone. You know, just show my appreciation for his business. But I couldn't stand the thought of him eating alone. I mean, I could go with him, you know, two guys enjoying a nice dinner out. But then I thought, wouldn't it be better if he was out with a nice lady. Someone like you?"

"He was too chicken to ask me, right?" Ducky said, smiling cutely.

There was nothing else Kyle could say. "Yes. But . . ." Kyle started. "Given time, I am positive he would have asked you out. It's just that I was the one getting impatient. I really, really think you two would hit it off."

"Okay. I'll go. What time and where?"

"Greystone. Seven sharp."

Ducky repositioned her mail sack on her shoulder, giving Kyle the brightest smile he'd ever seen on Ducky. She was obviously on board.

"I'll be there." With that, she turned abruptly and continued on her route, with a new spring in her step.

* * *

"But the wedding is in just a few days and I haven't been able to get a hold of Meg. Or Kyle. I think she's avoiding me," Autumn complained as she and Spring sat in Autumn's studio on Pittsburgh Street sorting glass pebbles according to color, adhering to Teppy's strict instructions.

"They just got back together," Spring pointed out. "They're being all lovey-dovey somewhere. I think you're overthinking it." She mentally crossed her fingers. It was easy to say the words, but she didn't believe them.

Spring tried to distract Autumn with cheery conversation. "The good news is that we pulled this wedding off. Everything is practically done. One hundred and fifty of your favorite friends will be with you as you start your new life with Ethan and Heather."

"I just wish Summer could have come," Autumn mused.

"Yeah, but she can't travel with that broken foot. At least not from as far away as Oregon," Spring responded. "I tell you what, why don't we call her later? We'll Skype and it will be just like we're all together again."

Autumn smiled in agreement. "We haven't talked about Win yet," she observed, referencing their older sister.

"I'm guessing she's not invited?" Spring asked.

"Luckily, it didn't come to that," Autumn said. "She sent an email when she got the invitation and said she has an important client meeting in New York that she can't get out of."

CHAPTER 24

AND THEN, THE day was upon them, and all of Finch's Crossing was abuzz as the town's golden girl prepared to marry the man of her dreams. Autumn heard footsteps hurrying down the hallway near the dressing room at the back of the church. Meg—at least she thought it was Meg—was entering the dressing room wearing a black pencil skirt and a green silk blouse. And high heels. And pantyhose.

"Don't say a word," Meg commanded. "This is what I wore on my fake date and Scottie arranged for me to keep it. I had to buy the hose myself at Hoffman's Drugstore. Man, but they chafe like a…"

Spring, who was staring at Meg, still transfixed by the

CHAPTER 24

transformation, interrupted her. "Thank you, Meg, for that commentary, but despite our collective surprise, we have to get Autumn ready. So go back to the guest book and make sure everyone signs in. And see if you can't get them to write a note or sweet sentiment."

Meg raised her arm as she walked away, indicating that Spring need say no more. They both knew that Meg would not encourage anyone to do anything other than sign the book. If that.

Spring stood beside her sister and they gazed at each other in the full-length mirror, sharing a smile. Spring fussed with Autumn's veil and made sure the clasp on her necklace was tight.

Autumn would be the first of the four sisters to get married. Well, the first to get married in a big public setting. As of now, only three people knew Spring and Gabe were married. Spring let her thoughts drift to the day she never thought would come, as she stood next to Gabe in her simple cream silk suit. It was so different than the designer clothes she normally wore. And so, it was perfect. If she had been in Los Angeles, marrying Chad, there would have been a cadre of paparazzi waiting for her, tipped off to the time and location of the wedding by Chad himself. Until a few days ago, she had been of the opinion that the Hamilton sisters were like satellites circling in their own singular orbits. Now, at least two of the satellites were in similar orbits.

SPRING

How far she had come in just a few weeks, Spring mused. She had successfully organized and orchestrated a large—by Finch's Crossing standards—event. She had put her painful past with Chad behind her and was pursuing a new career. Most importantly, she had learned that sometimes people deserve second chances, even if the pain they caused seemed undeserving of forgiveness.

The world lay before Spring and Gabe. She knew Gabe was sitting in a church pew, probably alone, waiting for her. Neither of them wore their wedding rings. Hers was tucked away in her purse and Gabe had put his in his wallet. They would bring them out in a few days, as they gradually announced their news. It made her sad to think that her friends and neighbors still harbored ill feelings for Gabe. Oh, she knew it was born out of love for her. Gabe was a real trouper, coming to the wedding when everyone around him was whispering and tsk-tsking about him.

But today was Autumn's day. Outside, springtime sang its lovely song, loudly enough to spur the ladies of Finch's Crossing into wearing their Easter hats. The town was in bloom—greens, pinks, and yellows heralding the new life that would emerge from its deep winter sleep.

Spring stood and faced her sister, clasping her hands. "You look beautiful, Autumn. Now let's go get your married."

"Don't cry," Spring commanded as tears welled up in Autumn's eyes. "There's no crying in makeup."

* * *

Meg stood nervously by the podium, upon which sat a guest book that she pretty much had been ignoring. When she spotted a small anteroom in a corner, she headed that way, slipped in, and closed the door, squashing herself against the shelves stocked with extra hymnals.

"Oh no you don't," a familiar voice called after her and Kyle followed her into the room, leaving the door ajar.

"Close the door," Meg commanded Kyle in a harsh whisper. "I don't want anyone to see me."

"I don't blame you," Kyle whispered back, "skulking away like this with your tail between your legs. No one wants to see you like this."

"Oh geez, if there is anything I hate more than your inspirational throw pillows it's your dog metaphors."

"Meg," Kyle said gently, taking her face in his hands. "This is not you. You don't run and hide when things get tough. You are not a quitter. Now get your butt back out there and do your job." He looked at his watch. "There's still half an hour until the ceremony starts. As far as I'm concerned, it's not over until the organ plays the opening chord of 'Here Comes the Bride.'"

With that, he turned and left. Meg had never seen Kyle so assertive. Obviously, he was reacting to the fact that everything had started to go south regarding getting Bryan to Finch's Crossing for the wedding. After all, he had made it his mission, too, to get Bryan there. Meg sort of liked this new Kyle. Doing as she was told, she slipped out of the tiny room and back to her post.

As wedding guests streamed past her, Meg imagined the various ways she might make Chief Butler pay for what he had done. Or what he had not done. She didn't like to think of herself as a violent person, but she felt, if the opportunity arose, she could be capable of bodily harm. She looked down at her tight skirt and wished she was wearing her Doc Martens and jeans. As soon as Autumn and Ethan said "I do," Meg would jump in her truck, hightail it to northern Virginia, and kick some police chief butt. She knew just how she would do it. She would surprise him at work and embarrass him in front of his subordinates. Then she would force him into a headlock, yank his arm behind him, and escort him to her car...

"Meg. Meg!" Spring's voice interrupted Meg's daydream. She returned to the present moment and looked into Spring's eager face.

"Autumn wanted you to know," Spring was saying, "that it's okay that Bryan isn't here. I'm sure that once we explain it to her, Heather will understand. Autumn is not mad at you. She wanted you to know."

As she was finishing her sentence, and as Meg was preparing to return to daydreaming about how she would make Chief Butler pay for ruining Autumn's wedding, there was the unmistakable sound of helicopter blades coming from above them. Spring and Meg looked at each other, wide-eyed, then both looked up, as if they could see through the ceiling.

"Is that?" Spring started to say.

"Sure is," Meg responded and grabbed Spring's hand. "Let's go."

* * *

The morning of April 29, a United States Air Force C-130 touched down at Marine Corps Base Quantico in Virginia and taxied to a halt in front of the expansive hangars. After a couple of minutes, the door in the forward part of the fuselage swung open, and a set of stairs folded down and came to rest on the tarmac. Nearby, the base commander sat in the back seat of his staff car with his aide, watching the door of the plane. Shortly, a disheveled Marine disembarked, at which time the base commander told his aide to move, which he did quickly. Almost as soon as the Marine stepped on the tarmac and shouldered his pack, the aide executed an especially crisp salute, relieved the major of his pack, and ushered him to the base commander's staff car, guiding him into the back seat beside the colonel. Before sliding in, the Marine also executed a crisp, perfect salute to the colonel.

The base commander smiled broadly and extended his hand toward the Marine, and the two officers shared a hearty handshake.

"Welcome home, Major."

"Thank you, Colonel," the Marine replied. "It's great to be

home."

The base commander continued, "I'm not sure who the hell you are, but you must have friends in high places."

The major smiled and said, "I just wish I knew who they were."

Both men laughed heartily.

"Your bird is all warmed up."

"Not sure how to thank you. Or exactly who to thank, truthfully."

"No need," said the colonel.

The base commander's aide followed the major across the tarmac to the waiting Huey helicopter and handed the major's pack to one of the two crewmen occupying the small passenger compartment toward the rear of the chopper. The major climbed up into the chopper and turned to face the aide, also a major, who offered his own crisp salute, which was returned respectfully and enthusiastically.

The Huey lifted off the tarmac, gained altitude, and initiated a northeast heading.

The pilot and copilot of the Huey, along with the crew and their single passenger, gazed down on the Virginia countryside, which soon gave way to the eastern panhandle of West Virginia, and then a sliver of Maryland, and finally settled on a path above Pennsylvania, directly in line with the small town of Finch's Crossing.

Just over an hour from leaving Quantico, the Huey began

descending toward Finch's Crossing. As Major Bryan Kelly looked out the open doors of the chopper, he was amazed at how his hometown looked from the air. It occurred to him, apart from Google Earth, he had never seen his town like this. And then he had an idea.

He leaned over to one of the crew members and yelled over the churning rotor blades, "Do you think I could do a fast rope?" This was a technique Marines used to put personnel on the ground fast, especially when it was unsafe for a chopper to land, and consisted of dropping a thick rope to the ground, which the Marines would grab onto and slide down to the ground.

The crewman pressed the button on his headset to talk to the chopper pilot.

"He wants to do a fast rope."

The pilot smiled broadly. "Okay. I don't see why not. I didn't really want to land there anyway."

The crewman gave the major a thumbs-up and handed him a pair of leather gloves.

As the chopper glided over Finch's Crossing, Bryan recognized the Methodist church where the wedding was about to happen.

Bryan prepared himself. The chopper hovered over a field next to the church. Major Kelly stood in the hatch as the thick rope was tossed out the door. A crewmember smiled at the major and helped him shoulder his pack, making sure it was secure.

Bryan stood in the doorway, then reached up with leather-gloved hands, grabbed the rope, and leaped out of the chopper, his legs and feet expertly clenched around it to slow his descent. Four or five seconds later, his combat boots touched down on Finch's Crossing soil. He ducked his head to avoid the rotor wash and ran toward the church as the Huey reeled in the fast rope, gained altitude, pointed itself back toward Quantico, and after a few moments, disappeared over the horizon. A few more moments later, the sound of its spinning rotors faded until inaudible.

By now, everyone who had been inside the church had spilled outside and gathered around the field, encircling the newly arrived wedding guest.

No one said anything. Bryan scanned the crowd but didn't see Martha or Heather. So he did the one thing he was trained to do: he saluted.

"Major Bryan Kelly, U.S. Marine Corps, reporting for duty."

Relieved, he watched as two women rushed toward him. He recognized them immediately because he had gone to school with both Meg and Spring.

Meg was ecstatic. She knew this day was Autumn's day. And it would be. In just a minute. For now, this moment was hers. And she was going to savor it. As Spring bounced up and down giddily, Meg stood before Bryan and saluted.

"Major," she said, in her best commanding voice. "Glad you could make it."

Spring stopped jumping up and down and ran to stand next to Meg. "Hey, Bryan. I'm sure you've got a lot of questions, but they'll have to wait. Right now this wedding's about five minutes off schedule. So move out, troops."

The crowd, still buzzing with the excitement, returned to the church, passing a bewildered Autumn, Martha, Ethan, and Heather as they ran toward Bryan. Heather laughed and screamed as she jumped into her uncle's arms. "I knew you'd be here," she said, nuzzling her head into his neck. "I just knew it."

Autumn, holding her dress up over her ankles, hugged Bryan with one arm, and Martha grabbed her son around his waist and squeezed.

"Hi, Mom," he said. "I have no idea how you did this, but here I am."

"Oh, it wasn't us," Martha responded, and they all turned toward a beaming Meg, who stood beside a proud Kyle.

"You must have some kind of pull, Meg, because you pulled off the impossible." Bryan turned to Ethan to shake hands.

Martha could tell her son was feeling overwhelmed and was probably jet-lagged. She took Heather from his arms and told everyone to get back into the church. "There will be plenty of time for all this later," Martha instructed. "Right now, let's take our places and get this wedding going!"

SPRING

* * *

Reverend Frye took his place at the front of the congregation. He had decided to forgo the traditional formal robes of his office, opting instead for a smartly tailored light charcoal three-piece suit, with a white boutonniere pinned to his lapel matching that of Ethan, who was standing at the reverend's side. Both men were smiling broadly, as soft music from the pipe organ swirled around the happy guests. The church was filled to the brim with many of Finch's Crossing's finest citizens, all excited to be getting ready to witness the marriage of their own Autumn Hamilton.

Jack escorted Martha down the aisle and she held to the crook of his arm proudly. They looked nothing like a couple that had recently finally found each other. Jack bowed slightly as Martha took her seat in the first pew of the bride's side, and then took his place at the front, standing with Ethan and Reverend Frye. Kyle was next down the aisle, obviously ecstatic to have Meg, who looked gorgeous, on his arm. As the couple approached Reverend Frye, Kyle released Meg who joined Martha on the front pew, and he took his place in the best man position beside Ethan.

All the guests strained their necks looking back excitedly at the next couple—Heather and Bryan, whose spectacular arrival would find its way into Finch's Crossing mythology. Bryan, still in his Marine fatigues, had to take tiny steps to remain by Heather's side, who was tossing rose petals gracefully to either side as they made their way to the front. The wedding had just begun and already most of the ladies were dabbing the corners of their eyes with tissues. Some of the men, too. When they arrived at the front, Uncle Bryan leaned down and gently kissed Heather on the top of her head. Heather smiled and squirmed into the pew between Martha and Meg. Bryan slid into formation between Jack and Kyle.

Recognizing his cue that the wedding party had all taken their proper places, the organist enthusiastically began playing the "Bridal Chorus," and the congregation stood and turned to face the back of the church. Their eyes fell upon two beautiful women. Spring was glowing in her light green chiffon gown with sprigs of baby's breath in her hair, and holding tightly onto her outstretched arm was her stunningly beautiful sister, Autumn. The two did the traditional stutter steps down the aisle as the music played, all eyes glued to them as they made their way forward. Once in front of Reverend Frye, Autumn released Spring's arm. Spring stepped slightly to the side, assuming the maid of honor position. With everyone in place, the organist brought the music to an end, and Reverend Frye indicated for everyone to be seated.

As the ceremony progressed, it was obvious to all that Ethan and Autumn adored each other. There was a song, Reverend Frye said some kind words about both Ethan and Autumn, and then he invited Martha to do her reading. Martha stood proudly and confidently, and as she approached the side podium she touched Jack on the arm as she passed, and he smiled, grateful in his heart for Martha.

Martha stood behind the podium. "A reading from First Corinthians, Chapter Thirteen." She paused, took a deep breath, and continued, "Love is patient, love is kind. It does not envy, it does not boast, it is not proud. It does not dishonor others, it is not self-seeking, it is not easily angered, it keeps no record of wrongs. Love does not delight in evil but rejoices with the truth. It always protects, always trusts, always hopes, always perseveres. Love never fails." She glanced at Jack, and then over to Ethan and Autumn, and repeated that last line, "Love never fails." She then glanced up at the congregation, smiling at all, and said, "The Word of the Lord," to which the congregation replied, "Thanks be to God."

The couple had decided not to write their own vows, laughing that maybe they would do that in twenty or thirty years when they renewed their vows. Reverend Frye took them through the traditional vows, led them through the exchange of rings, and after a beautifully sung version by one of Teppy Tartel's daughters of "Forever and Ever, Amen," he brought the proceedings to a cheerful finale with the familiar words, "You may now kiss the bride." No sooner had they kissed than Heather let out a little girl shout of glee and rushed toward the newlyweds. Ethan grabbed her up in his arms, kissed her cheek, and held her while Autumn joined the group hug, and the congregation broke into applause. The organist immediately started the recessional, and the happy trio walked toward the front of the church, Ethan holding Heather in his left arm and Autumn clinging to his right.

* * *

Wedding guests were steadily streaming into the reception hall at the Greystone. Meg, happy to have changed out of her pencil skirt into a more comfortable beige pantsuit, stood with Kyle surveying the dance floor, which had filled up remarkably quickly.

"Hey, look!" Kyle exclaimed. "That looks like fun!"

"Dancing is not my idea of fun," Meg said, "and I think you already knew that."

"I know," Kyle agreed, not yet defeated, but aware that he was close. "I just thought, it being a wedding and all, and everyone so happy and excited, we might take a spin on the dance floor."

Meg turned to Kyle and took his face in her hands. She was smiling, but also serious, when she said, "Kyle, you know I love you. But I just don't dance. I just don't." Her voice had been firm, but loving.

"Okay. That's okay," Kyle said softly. "We don't have to dance. Ever. Besides, it's just as much fun sipping wine and watching everyone else. As long as I am with you, I am perfectly content."

They both turned back to watch the happy dancers twirl and swirl around the floor.

Heather and Martha took turns dancing with Bryan, and then the three of them danced together until Bryan was so tired he had to sit down so he didn't fall down.

"Oh, look," Meg said, obviously done with the dancers. "There's no line at the buffet. I'm starved. Let's get some more shrimp."

Kyle rolled his eyes and shook his head as Meg began piling food onto a plate. *Where on earth does she put all that food?*

* * *

Even Gabe and Spring were twirling and swirling, smiling brilliantly at each other.

"I can't believe how much has happened," Spring said, speaking with her lips brushing Gabe's ear so he could hear her voice over the music and happy voices filling the reception hall. "Just think about it. About where we each were just a few weeks ago. And a year ago, where Autumn was. And Heather. And Ethan. So much has happened."

Gabe smiled widely at his new bride. "I know, my love. You're so right."

"So what are we going to do?" Spring asked.

"What do you mean?"

"I mean, where will we live? Are you sure you want to come to New York?"

"I'm sure I want to be with you."

"So you will come to New York?"

Gabe paused to gather his thoughts, then stopped dancing, causing Spring to stop also. The two stood motionless in the middle of the dance floor, their hands in perfect ballroom dance position.

Then Gabe said sweetly, "Look. You are the most important thing in the world to me. I will not lose you again. We will make this work. We will figure out the details as we go along. We'll figure out living arrangements, work stuff, everything. I will do whatever it takes to be with you, to make you happy, to make us happy, whatever that might turn out to be."

Spring squeezed his hand, wiped a tear from her eye, and then reached up to swipe a tear that was meandering down his cheek. She leaned forward and kissed him, with purpose, on the lips. The two then embraced tightly, and as the music continued, they began to dance again, as if they owned the world.

* * *

Suddenly, the music stopped, and the DJ's voice boomed on the PA system. "Ladies and gentlemen, what better way to start off a wedding reception than with a birthday!" Everybody clapped and smiled and laughed. "May I present to you, the lovely Miss Heather Christianson, who is celebrating six years upon God's green earth today! Please join me in singing happy birthday to Heather!"

Everybody sang at the top of their lungs, while Martha guided a slightly bewildered Heather up to the cake table. Not only was there a lovely wedding cake for Ethan and Autumn, but a smaller chocolate layer cake with birthday candles and

"Heather" beautifully written in white and pink icing. When the birthday song was over and the candles extinguished by Heather's breath and a secret birthday wish had been sent heavenwards by a now six-year-old girl, the DJ invited all the kids in the crowd to have a piece of cake first, with Heather insisting on doing the serving.

Once the pieces of cake were distributed, Martha grabbed Heather's hand and squeezed it. With a loving smile, she asked, "Are you ready?"

Heather didn't speak, but just nodded her head and smiled so brightly that it made Martha's heart jump.

The two walked hand in hand toward the bride and groom's table where Ethan and Autumn had finally sat down to eat some real food. Martha and Heather stopped and stood behind the newly married couple, and Martha reached down and picked up the microphone the DJ had pre-placed for this moment.

Ethan and Autumn turned in their seats, and were pleased to see Martha and Heather behind them, but weren't quite sure what was going on.

Kyle had noticed Martha and Heather walking toward the newlyweds' table and immediately glanced around looking for Meg. He saw her at the shrimp table, which she had visited many times throughout the reception. Kyle caught her eye, and with a gesture of his head, pointed her attention to Martha and Heather. Meg smiled and shrugged her shoulders, as if to say, "Beats me." She then made a beeline across the dance floor, glided into her chair, planted a kiss on his cheek, grabbed his hand, and held it on his knee.

This night had been special for Kyle and Meg, too. Watching Ethan and Autumn take their vows, exchange rings, kiss each other, and become husband and wife in front of all their family and friends had made them both realize and appreciate the gravity of their own love for each other. Meg had whispered to Kyle at one point early in the reception, "Okay, now I am sort of looking forward to it."

"To what?" Kyle had asked playfully.

"You know. Don't make me say it, or I might change my mind."

"Ladies and gentlemen," the DJ began. "I invite you to turn your attention to the bride and groom's table, where an important announcement is about to be made."

The room became quiet. Everyone stopped what they were doing and gazed toward the table where Martha and Heather stood nervously smiling.

Martha looked at Heather, who held a scroll of paper tightly in her hand.

Martha made sure the microphone was on and began to speak. "Good evening, everyone," she started. "Heather and I have something we would like to give the newlyweds." Everyone was intrigued, and Martha could feel the room fill with a buzzing anticipation.

Spring and Gabe had just slow-danced to the last song and were now at their table just in front of the newlyweds. Gabe was seated, Spring sitting on his left knee, a glass of wine in her hand. When Martha began to speak, Gabe's gaze met Spring's, and both raised their eyebrows inquisitively. Gabe was thinking how amazing it was that after all this time, after all that had happened, he was now married to the love of his life. He was amazed at how things had turned out, and extremely grateful. He told himself over and over that he was going to do everything right this time.

And Spring was happier than she had been in years. All the modeling accolades, mansions, fancy cars and clothes, and high-society friends in the world couldn't compare to what she had with Gabe. She, too, was so grateful that she had decided to come back to Finch's Crossing. It was almost as if she and Gabe were meant to happen. She never in her life would have imagined she could completely forgive Gabe, much less fall back in love with him more deeply than when they were both so young.

"Last month, Heather and I did a little research," Martha was saying. "Heather wanted me to find out how she could make sure Ethan, whom she loves dearly, and Autumn, whom, quite obviously, she also loves dearly, become her new mommy and daddy." She paused and then added, "Officially."

Everyone in the reception hall sucked in a breath.

Unable to wait any longer, Heather thrust out her arm and

CHAPTER 24

handed the rolled-up papers to Autumn. Autumn took the papers from Heather, who smiled euphorically, as if she had just managed to save the whole planet from extinction.

Heather had rehearsed her part over and over. Martha held the mic for her, and Heather began, "I had a great mommy and daddy, but they got taken away from me and all of us. Now I need a mommy two and a daddy two to take care of me." She was speaking in a precious little girl monotone, as if reciting a book report before her teacher, staring straight ahead. She continued, "Ethan is a great daddy two, and I know Autumn will be a great mommy two."

Martha continued. "We went down to the clerk of court to learn about adoption proceedings. We got the paperwork started. I, well, we, Heather and I, filled in all the information we could. But we realized, Ethan being a lawyer and all..." Everybody laughed. "We figured maybe he should take care of it. Anyways, what is mainly the point is that Heather needs a mommy and daddy, and she knows, as do I, how much Autumn and Ethan love each other and how much they love Heather. So..."

She didn't have to say anymore. As Martha spoke, every couple in the room clasped hands. Most of the women in the room had placed a palm on their breastbone, an involuntary gesture of intense pleasure, of knowing deeply that something that was absolutely supposed to happen had just happened.

Autumn was balling and sobbing as she bear-hugged

Heather and pulled the little girl onto her lap. She whispered into Heather's ear, "Nothing in this world would make me happier than to be your mommy. Thank you, my sweet little girl."

Ethan stood and slid his arm around Martha and kissed her forehead. Everybody in the reception hall stood and began to offer their heartfelt applause. Spring led Gabe by the hand toward Autumn, who was standing now, holding hands with Heather. Spring hugged her sister, kissed her warmly on the cheek, and whispered, "You will be the best mommy ever."

Meg grabbed Kyle and brought him up, too. She hugged and squeezed Autumn, and for perhaps the first time in her life, could not think of a single cute, sarcastic, or pithy thing to say. She just smiled at her friend and nodded, then turned her attention to Martha and Heather, hugging and kissing them both. Kyle gave Ethan a congratulatory handshake, followed by an enthusiastic bro hug.

Scottie had been taking this all in with great joy and enthusiasm. He and Autumn had a special relationship, a deep bond rooted in his appreciation of Autumn's artistic talents, which he considered genius. The two had become extremely close, and Scottie could hardly hide his delight with what had happened. He knew Ethan was a good man, and he also believed with all his heart that Autumn would be very happy with Ethan, and with Heather, and he was confident that her inner beauty would continue to flow forth from the delicate strokes of her artist's brush.

Scottie glanced over at the DJ and held a fake mic up to his mouth, as if to say, *May I say a few words?* The DJ understood immediately and motioned for Scottie to proceed, which he did. Autumn glanced behind her as Scottie reached around her to pick up the mic. She smiled at him, sensing he was about to make a toast, or something equivalent.

Raising the mic to his mouth, Scottie began. "Hi, everyone. I'm Scottie, for those of you who don't know me." There were few there who didn't know Scottie or at least know of him. "What an incredible evening!" He had the crowd's attention.

He moved around the side of the table. "Autumn and I have been, well, together, for a long time now," he said, smiling fondly at Autumn. "I have had the pleasure of witnessing the blossoming of an insanely talented artist. I have had the pleasure of representing her work at the highest echelons of the art world. I have seen her grow and mature. I have seen her struggle. Sometimes mightily. But I have seen her persist. Also mightily. But in all the years I have known her, through everything a career as an artist has to throw at you, I have never seen my dearest friend so very happy. I am serious. And she deserves it."

All the guests' eyes were on Autumn as Scottie continued. "I would like to propose a toast." He raised his half-full champagne glass to the air, first holding it up toward the on-looking faces in the crowd and then turning to directly face Autumn.

"Dearest Autumn, may this happiness never lessen. May your life with Ethan and Heather unfold before you like one of your paintings, a masterpiece of color and light, of form and substance, of movement and stillness, of meaning and grace. Autumn, Ethan, and Heather, please accept this wish for your happiness from someone who cares deeply about you all." He turned back to the crowd and gave an extra-hearty "Cheers!"

Autumn stood and walked over to Scottie, giving him a bear hug, sobbing with happiness.

Scottie hugged her back, then remembered something else he wanted to toast.

"Everyone!" he shouted, recapturing the crowd's attention. "I have another toast that I want to make. I will make it quick and simple. Please join me in congratulating Spring and Gabe on their recent nuptials!"

Blank stares all around. And a look of shock and confusion on Autumn's face, as everyone's gaze turned toward Spring and Gabe.

Scottie knew this was going to be a shocker. "It's true!" he exclaimed. "They swore me to secrecy. I wasn't to tell anyone until after Autumn and Ethan got married. Well, Autumn and Ethan just got married. So now I can tell. And with so much happiness in the air, why keep such good news a secret any longer?"

He paused for a second, letting the crowd try to catch up. "Now, I know some of you might have a slightly skewed opinion of my good friend Gabe. And not in a good way. But let me assure you, Gabe here is one of the most honorable men I know. When the whole story comes out all of you will understand. I encourage you to get to know Gabe. Find out what really happened before you rush to judgment. I am sure you will conclude, as did I, that Gabe is completely worthy of Spring's love and affection. Finch's Crossing should be glad to have him. Or to have him back, I should say."

Scottie paused again, hoping he hadn't embarrassed Gabe and Spring too much. And then, with great gusto, he loudly declared, "So, Spring and Gabe, here's to you. Cheers!"

Spring and Gabe walked quickly over to Autumn and Ethan's table. Autumn, who was still standing from her embrace with Scottie, reached out to her sister, gathering her in for a hug.

"Why didn't you tell me?" Autumn asked.

"I didn't want to take away from your big day. Besides, you didn't need any distractions," Spring explained.

"Are you kidding me? You are not a distraction. You're my sister!"

Autumn stepped back from Spring, still holding both her hands, staring into her face. She could see Spring was beaming. The happiness was just oozing from her pores. Then Autumn embraced her again, whispering into her ear, "I am so happy for you, sis. I am so happy for us."

CHAPTER 25

*S*PRING WAS UP before dawn the morning of the Bridal Expo, and she knocked on the door to Duncan's apartment in the Greystone at six in the morning. A grumpy Duncan opened the door. Spring handed him a cup of coffee she had brought with her from Autumn's Keurig.

"Wakey wakey, eggs and bakey," Spring declared and pushed past him. She was wearing a new buttercup-yellow business suit with a cream silk blouse and matching flats. "I've given everyone the run of show sheet with all instructions, the timetable, and all contact information. But here are some extra copies. Someone is bound to forget theirs. Happens every time."

Spring shoved some papers toward Duncan, oblivious to

the fact that he was still in his pajamas.

Duncan took a sip of the coffee. "Spring, just take a breath," he said calmly. He was not unfamiliar with large special events with lots of moving parts. He had held the hands of plenty of bridezillas and nervous grooms. "Everything is under control. All the vendors set up their exhibit tables yesterday. We are turnkey ready. My staff will be here at seven to put the finishing touches on the parlor and refreshments. The event doesn't start until ten, and we will be ready at nine, when people will start to arrive. Okay?"

Spring smiled wanly. "Thanks, Duncan. I don't know why I'm so nervous. I guess I never knew how much planning went into big events like this. I can't even imagine what all went into those fashion runway shows I was in. All I had to do was show up, get my hair and makeup done, and walk."

"You have nothing to worry about. You got this."

"Wait. What?" Spring asked, half-panicked. "You said people will start to arrive at nine? But we won't be ready with the trolleys until ten."

"It's all right. Remember, you're serving coffee and doughnuts at the gazebo for early birds, and you have those walking tour pamphlets to hand out."

"Oh, right. Okay. I remember."

Duncan spun her around and gave her a little shove out of his apartment. "It's time for you to go back to command central while I take a shower."

SPRING

Walking back to Gazebo Park, Spring willed herself to calm down. This was so unlike her. Why had she lost her confidence all of a sudden? Could it be because, for the first time in a long time, there was so much at stake? Finding her way. Her love for Gabe. Their second chance. Her determination to do right by Marla.

A block away from Gazebo Park she noticed that one of the trolleys had its hood up, and Vic the trolley owner and Ethan were bent over inspecting the engine. She quickened her step.

"What's happening?" she asked breathlessly as she arrived beside them.

Vic and Ethan raised their heads at the same time, and Vic banged his on the engine hood.

"Ouch," he complained, while Ethan said, "Just a little engine trouble. Nothing to worry about."

Vic rubbed his brow and frowned deeply. "My business partner was the one who really knew how to keep these old trolleys going," he said. "But he died two years ago. I only know basic maintenance."

Spring was about to implode when Autumn and Meg approached.

"What's going on?" Autumn asked, giving Ethan a kiss.

"Just a little engine trouble," he responded. But Vic revealed, "It's a total shutdown."

As the four stared dumbfounded at the engine, Meg elbowed her way in.

"Oh, for goodness sake, get out of the way," she growled, peeking under the hood.

Stan came to stand next to her and she commanded him to run and get his tool kit. No one said anything as Stan ran to the hardware store and back. Meg was glaring at all of them, so they all averted their gazes.

Stan handed Meg the tool kit and she extracted a few items, ducked under the hood, and after tinkering for a bit shouted, "Well, don't just stand there, go start it up!"

Vic obeyed and scurried aboard the trolley. At the turn of the ignition key, the trolley roared to life and everyone clapped. Meg emerged from under the hood and slammed it down dramatically. She handed the tools back to a thoroughly impressed Stan, then in an exaggerated motion, wiped her hands together to indicate she was done.

"How did you do that?" Ethan stammered, and Spring and Autumn chimed in behind him with words of awe and praise.

Meg pierced them with her legendary deadly gaze and rested her hands on her hips. "If I told you, I'd have to kill you. It's on a need-to-know basis, and the four of you," she swept one hand back and forth, "definitely do not need to know."

"You really haven't forgiven us, have you?" Autumn asked, adequately shamed.

"Nope, not yet," Meg said without hesitation and strolled away.

Kyle came up to them just then. "I hope you are all adequately chastised for doubting her," he said sternly.

Autumn looked at him incredulously. "Us? How about you? You're the one who thought she wouldn't marry you!"

"Not for a second," Kyle responded. "It was all part of my grand plan. I knew what I was doing. You all, on the other hand, did not."

And with that, Kyle jogged away from them, caught up to Meg, and threw a protective arm over his fiancée's shoulder.

"He's right, you know," Autumn said. "I have known Meg two decades. I should never have doubted her."

"Well," Ethan said, halfheartedly, "she did cut it pretty close. You were really white-knuckling it there at the end."

"Uh, excuse me," Spring exclaimed. "Can you please save all of this self-flagellation for later? Now that the trolley is up and running again, I need Ethan to get aboard and coordinate with Vic to make sure they have the route and schedules synced." She turned to Autumn. "And you're my floater. I need you back at the Greystone to monitor the vendors." She handed her sister a small walkie-talkie, which Autumn accepted reluctantly.

"Can't I just text you?" she asked Spring, who appeared not to hear.

Spring showed Autumn how to use the walkie-talkie, then shooed her away.

Even though all the merchants were at the Greystone,

CHAPTER 25

Pittsburgh Street was alive with activity. Spring watched as volunteers, including Kyle and Meg, Martha, Heather, Teppy's daughters and Ducky, guided visitors from the parking lot to the trolleys. When the first group was loaded and the trolley pulled away from the curb, Spring heaved a sigh of relief.

All those years of modeling, she hadn't considered that she was capable of doing anything else.

Gabe sidled over and quietly slipped his hand into Spring's. She rested her head on his shoulder.

"You done good, Mrs. Vignaroli," he whispered in her ear.

His words sent shivers down her spine. She wanted nothing more than to ride off into the sunset as his wife.

"That sounds so good," Spring whispered back. "All these years, I had never allowed myself to hope."

But for the time being, she had a Bridal Expo to finish. And finish it she would. She gave Gabe a peck on the check and walked toward the gazebo and a small group of volunteers who looked suspiciously idle.

"Okay, people. Chop, chop!" Spring commanded.

* * *

Spring made her rounds on the top floor of the Greystone Manor. There had been an issue with the single elevator, but Spring didn't really care. That was a good problem to have—too many people for only one elevator. There were enough people taking the stairs, so it mostly evened out.

As she took in the crowd, she noticed that many generations had come together to learn and plan. *Most likely grandmothers, mothers, and brides-to-be*, she thought. It made her think of her own family and the home that had passed from her grandmother to her mother and then to Autumn. Spring had never considered living in the family home. Autumn was the best suited to it and she lovingly cared for it with regular maintenance and seasonal and holiday decorations, which Spring knew made her sister's heart sing.

Spring wondered what it was that made *her* heart sing. Had it been all those years of modeling and living the high life of photo shoots at exotic locations and parties at the home of A-list celebrities? Why had she earned her MBA? Was it because she was looking for something of substance to fill an otherwise shallow life? Chad had, of course, denigrated her academic endeavors. To make him stop chiding her, she had actually told him that she quit the MBA program, when, in fact, she had carried on and graduated at the top of her class.

Spring trusted that knowing what would lift her heart was yet to come. And somehow, this was all right. She had stopped in Finch's Crossing and ended up drawn into a life she didn't even know she wanted. Her heart would sing with the future that she and Gabe would make for themselves.

Spring watched as three brides-to-be admired Samantha DeMuth's flower arrangement, complete—Spring was glad to see—with the once-maligned pussy willows.

"These will look so nice with an assortment of mums in orange and yellow, don't you think, Mother?" a young woman asked a middle-aged woman next to her. She pulled her mother by the arm and motioned toward the Merchants Association exhibit table. "Let's see when that lovely gazebo is available for the wedding."

"Oh, Spring," Miss Elsie called urgently. "I'm out of cake samples. Be a dear and run down to the shop and collect the second batch. My assistant baker should be finishing them up around now."

Spring took in the empty plates. "Wow, Miss Elsie. They really already ate all of your samples?"

Miss Elsie nodded enthusiastically. "That's what they're there for, dear," she remarked smartly. "I already have orders for five weddings in September. They all want autumn themes, with leaves of all colors."

Beaming, Miss Elsie came around the table and took Spring's hand. "You did this, Spring. Oh, we all had a hand in it, but it was your organization and ideas that brought it all together. Autumn told us you were the perfect person for the job. Now shoo. Go get my samples. And you need to move along—you're creating a bottleneck."

Spring did what she was told, enjoying the ten-minute walk back to the heart of the shopping district, very content with all that she had accomplished and excited about all that was to come in her life. She felt like she was in charge now, like she had been given a second chance, and she was determined more than ever to make the most of it.

* * *

As Stan had requested, Kyle appeared at the hardware store that evening at six thirty.

"Turn around," Kyle instructed.

Stan held his arms out and slowly spun in a circle for Kyle to inspect his "date" clothes. "I gotta say, Stan my man, you are looking extra-sharp."

Stan managed a smile. "You really think so?" Stan was wearing a baby-blue dress shirt under a casual khaki suit. He had on cordovan loafers to match his maroon belt, with baby-blue socks to match his shirt and the baby-blue pocket square that Kyle had insisted he wear.

The two exited the hardware store and headed to the Greystone. The streets of Finch's Crossing were now empty of the throngs of brides-to-be and their cohorts who had descended upon the town earlier that day, all smiles and happiness and jubilation. Kyle had a feeling the infectious hopefulness of the day's proceedings would carry over into Stan's big night with Ducky.

* * *

"I'll go in first and just sit at the bar," Kyle told Stan as they lingered at the entrance of the Greystone. "I'm meeting Spring and Autumn anyway, to celebrate the success of the

Bridal Expo. If you need anything, I'm there for you. Just come find me," Kyle said.

"Okay," Stan said nervously. As Kyle started to walk off, Stan grabbed his elbow.

"Thanks, friend," Stan said.

To himself he thought, *You can do this. Just go in there and be yourself.* Stan stood up to his full height and walked with purpose through the front door.

"Stan!" Duncan said, pleased to see him standing there.

"Hello, Duncan," Stan said, feeling a little calmer with each passing minute. "I have a seven o'clock reservation."

Duncan scanned the reservation chart. "I see you have reserved a table for two. Would you like to be seated now, or would you like to wait at the bar for the rest of your party to arrive?"

"I'd prefer to be seated, if you don't mind."

"Very well," Duncan said in his best official maître d' voice. "Please follow me."

Duncan led Stan through the middle of the crowded dining room to a lovely table against the far wall. He laid down first the dinner menus, and after Stan seated himself, Duncan handed him the wine selection. "Enjoy your meal, Stan. Great to see you."

Stan was startled when somebody leaned over from behind him and said, "I forgot to tell you, I did some research. Order her a glass of sparkling rosé."

Stan turned around to see Kyle swiftly walking back to the bar.

When the waiter arrived, it was five minutes before seven. Stan was habitually early for things. He ordered a Guinness for himself and for Ducky—he trusted Kyle's research—a house sparkling rosé. Within two minutes, the drinks arrived.

Stan picked up his menu and glanced at his watch. Seven on the dot. *I bet she's not coming,* he thought. *Don't be silly. It's only seven. Maybe she's running late.* Stan let his mind go back to the intense crush he had on Ducky in high school. He thought she was the most beautiful creature God ever created. He thought about her all the time. But he could never muster the courage to do anything about his crush. It was his secret.

And it was a secret he was glad he kept. Had he acted on it, he might not have met and married Renata. He might not have had the wonderful first chapter of his life, which had ended so abruptly, and so permanently, with Renata's death a few years ago.

* * *

Ducky practically beamed as she entered the Greystone.

She had chosen her outfit with care, just as she had done the evening of the emergency meeting of the Merchants Association, wanting Stan to see her best side. She had chosen a pair of cream-colored slacks with a beautiful but subdued light blue stripe, complemented perfectly by her light blue sweater set. She had completed her ensemble with a string of pearls and matching earrings and brand-new cream pumps. As soon as Ducky learned she had been matched with Stan, she had started taking better care of herself. Back in high school she had worn petites, but after high school her size gradually progressed from petite to what she called "dumpling." But the keto diet she had been following for over a month now had relieved her of ten pounds. She felt like she looked better than she had in a very long time. She hoped Stan would notice.

She was greeted by a pleasant hostess.

"Hello, ma'am. Do you have a reservation?"

"Actually, I am meeting someone," she said, as she scanned the dining room to see if Stan was already there. Her eyes landed on a very well-dressed and handsome Stan. Ducky thought he must have gotten his fashion cues from Kyle. She could see he had on a baby-blue dress shirt under a very fashionable khaki blazer.

"I see my date," Ducky said to the hostess, pointing with her head to where Stan was sipping his Guinness and going down memory lane. Ducky thought to herself, *Wow, that felt good to say "I see my date."*

She strolled over to Stan, feeling better than she had in a long time.

Stan caught her coming across the dining room in the corner of his eye, and by the time she got there, he was standing beside the table.

Ducky walked up to Stan and said shyly, "Hi, Stan."

Stan smiled and instinctively held out both hands toward Ducky, palms up. She softly grabbed Stan's hands, squeezed them gently, and let them go.

"Ducky, great to see you. I am so glad you came." He pulled her chair out for her and held it as she sat down. Stan seated himself across from Ducky and said confidently, "I hope you don't mind, I took the liberty of ordering you a sparkling rosé. But you may have anything you like."

"Thank you, Stan. How on earth did you know that was my drink of choice?"

"I did some research," Stan said, smiling slyly.

"I'm impressed."

Ten minutes into the date, both Stan and Ducky were completely at ease, laughing, talking, and soaking up each other's company.

The couple talked and talked and talked. Stan was on his second Guinness and Ducky on her second sparkling rosé. The dinner plates had been cleared from the table, and they were reading the dessert menu together, when Stan decided it was time to let his secret out.

"You know, Ducky, I had a terrible crush on you in high school."

"Terrible?"

"Terrible in a good way. I was terribly infatuated with you."

"Why didn't you tell me? Why keep it a secret?" Ducky asked.

"I was afraid. I can't really explain it. It was almost as if I loved the secret as much as I loved you."

"You loved me?" Ducky asked, surprised but pleased with Stan's explanation.

Stan didn't mean to use the L word. It just came out. He thought a bit and then said, "Yes, Ducky. I suppose it was love. Naive, high school love. But love, nonetheless."

They both sat there smiling at each other for what seemed like a whole minute.

Ducky broke the silence first. "I have a secret, too."

"Let's hear it."

"I knew you had a crush on me," Ducky revealed.

"Really? Did it show? Did I stare at you too much or anything like that?"

"Oh no!" Ducky exclaimed, laughing. "Nothing like that! One of your friends told me. I really can't remember who. It was at lunch in the cafeteria. He told me that you were crazy about me."

"I was. I only told a couple friends, so it's a short list of who spilled the beans."

"Doesn't matter who. I thought you were pretty cool. And handsome. I always hoped you would show interest in me. But you never did. Eventually, I just convinced myself that your friend didn't have his facts straight. I guess it worked out, though," Ducky continued. "I mean, you married Renata, and I am sure you guys had a good life, up until, well . . ."

"It did work out. Renata was a wonderful wife and person," Stan agreed. "We were very happy together. We made a great team."

"I am so glad you had that, Stan. You deserved it." Ducky extended her hand to Stan, who took it gently. "You never know. Maybe we could make a great team, too."

* * *

Spring looked around the table at her sister and at her friends, some new, some old, and all dear.

"So what's next for you two?" Autumn asked, winking at Gabe.

"I was wondering when you would get around to asking that question," Spring teased.

Autumn picked up her wine glass. "Give me some credit," she insisted. "I waited as long as I could."

Spring took Gabe's hand and a jolt of memory took her back momentarily to the first time he had taken her hand in the gazebo so many years ago. His hands had aged, of course, and in the lines and calluses, she saw a life well lived. She squeezed his hand and said, "We're still talking about it, but I have some ideas."

"It's more than an idea," Gabe insisted to Spring. "And it's brilliant. It fits your personality perfectly."

"I'm starting an online enterprise called Spring Hamilton Solutions: Where Life Meets Pretty." It's part lifestyle blog, part retail. I'll create content based on my experiences and recommendations based on my expertise."

"She's being modest," Gabe insisted. "Her name is recognizable enough to get things started. And her lifestyle blog and recommendations will have people flocking to her."

"Sort of like Gwyneth Paltrow and her company," Autumn said. "What's it called? Something strange."

"It's Goop," Kyle offered, and the group looked at him.

"What?" he asked, feigning irritation. "So I've been doing a little research for Spring. She's going to need a New York City firm to do the publicity, plus a brand manager and social media expert."

"Whoa there," Spring said. "First things first. I need to finish my business plan, then proceed in a logical order, step by step. Branding and strategizing are fun, but first things first. And Kyle, you know how much I appreciate you getting the ball rolling for me. I'm so glad we're all going to be family."

Meg groaned and rolled her eyes. "Oh, geez, don't get all sloppy on us," she whined. But Spring stopped her by reaching for her hand. She was surprised when Meg didn't withdraw hers.

"If there's anything I've learned in the past few weeks it's that family is something you create, not necessarily something you're given. And you—mean as a snake you might be—are my family. You too, Scottie," she finished, lifting her glass in his direction. He smiled and blushed.

"Ahem," Kyle cleared his throat. "I'd like to give you your

wedding present now, Spring." He pulled his phone from his pocket and powered up the browser icon.

"But there isn't anything Gabe and I need," she said, smiling at her new husband.

"Actually, there is," Kyle insisted and held the phone up for her to see. "I bought a few domains for your new endeavor," he explained. "Springhamilton.com, springhamiltonsolutions. com, wherelifemeetspretty.com and spsolutions.com."

"Oh, Kyle," Spring clapped, and the table followed suit.

Spring was happy—relieved, really—to see Meg beaming with pride and tucking her arm in Kyle's. "That's my guy," she said. "He's always got some plan or another in the works."

Spring couldn't even think about another wedding right now, but something told her that within a year, there would be at least one more wedding in Finch's Crossing.

* * *

The next morning, Gabe responded to an urgent call from Spring and was at her doorstep in minutes. She was waiting on the front porch.

"I want to talk to you about something," Spring said as he sat next to her on the top step. "I want us go see Marla together. We need to keep going, again and again until, well ..." Spring's voice cracked and a tear escaped her left eye, cascading down her cheek.

"My love," Gabe said, tenderly kissing the tear away.

Spring continued, "I know Marla is not, well, really herself.

CHAPTER 25

But whatever part of her is left needs to know that you and I, that we, will always take care of her. She needs to know that we will never leave her, will never let her be alone, never leave her unloved. It's important for me that Marla feels loved. Forever."

Gabe stood up and held his hand out to Spring. "No time like the present," he said quietly. "We'll go now."

"Thank you," Spring managed as she stood. Too shaken with emotion, she handed her keys to Gabe.

"You're gonna let me drive?" Gabe asked playfully.

"I guess so. It's just a car."

Gabe shot back, "A Mercedes Benz GLS 550 SUV is not just a car, love."

As they headed toward Arbor Commons, the conversation drifted from light-hearted banter to more serious matters.

Always the planner, Spring asked, "So where do you see us in five years?"

"Hmm. Five years. I will just say I see us as happy and together."

"Too generic," Spring challenged. "I need specifics."

"Okay. Why don't you go first, so I can get a feel for what you are looking for."

"Okay." Spring cleared her throat. "Here goes. In five years, I expect to be the highly accomplished CEO of my own highly successful company. I expect both of us to be doing something we love, with someone we love. Meaning each other. I am not saying you will be working for me, just that you will always be a part of whatever I do, with no secrets or hidden agendas, and I will always be a part of what you do. And Marla will always be a part of us, together."

Gabe smiled a wan smile. "Thank you for that," he said.

"How about you?" Spring asked. "What's your vision?"

"Honestly, I have been so alive in the present that I haven't thought much about the future. I mean, to have the opportunity to reunite with your first love—well, hardly anybody gets that in life. It's pretty overwhelming. But I like the future you've mapped out for us. And I'm so grateful that you've accepted Marla into our lives."

Smiling, Spring slid down comfortably in the passenger seat, enjoying the sound of her husband's voice, soothed by the hum of the engine as they sped toward Marla.

"I guess I could finally write that book I've been wanting to write," he said a moment later.

"What book?"

"I've had this fantasy of writing a thriller, you know, based on things I covered when I was a crime reporter in Virginia."

"That's a great idea! And Spring Hamilton Marketing Solutions could help you sell it!"

"Spring Hamilton Marketing Solutions? How many companies are you gonna have?"

"Many. Many, many," Spring mused.

The couple was silent for a few minutes, both recognizing landmarks signifying that they were approaching Arbor Commons.

Spring thought of the notion of family—what it was and what it wasn't. She thought of Miss Elsie and the secret she had kept for all those years. She thought of the small family Autumn had made for herself, instantly gaining Martha and Heather in the bargain. Families were made, she knew that. But family was also a decision. She had decided to make Gabe her family, and he and Marla were a package deal.

Spring wished she knew more about early-onset Alzheimer's and vowed that she would research the disease, so she could help and support Gabe and be a full partner in caring for Marla. Gabe was dedicated to Marla, and along with her doctors, had devised the best treatment plan. He did everything in his power to keep her comfortable and cared for and, most of all, loved.

Gabe looked over at Spring. "You must know I still love Marla with all my heart," he said, as if reading her thoughts.

"I know," she responded and touched the side of his face. "That's part of why I love you."

"My love for Marla has changed," Gabe explained. "But you must know that I love you the same way I used to love Marla. Marla was the love of my life, for a time. That time ended. I didn't want it to. If she had not been struck down with this horrible disease you and I wouldn't be where we are now."

Gabe pondered a moment, then continued, "I love two

women, with all my heart, at the same time. One woman had her potential and future snatched from her, through no fault of her own. And had this disease not descended on Marla with such force and venom, no one knows what she would have been capable of, what she could have accomplished. And then there's this other woman. You. Beautiful. Resilient. Kind. Brilliant. Forgiving. Full of love, for me, for Marla, for everyone. To see your heart break for Marla makes my heart break. To witness your deep understanding of the human heart, whether you realize it or not, thrills me. I am truly the luckiest man on the earth. I get to have two loves of my life."

Spring dug in her purse for a tissue and handed it to Gabe, who had steered into the Arbor Commons parking lot and turned off the ignition. From the car, they could see Marla sitting in a chair on the small patio outside of her room overlooking the garden. She was holding a large children's picture book. Bea, ever the faithful caretaker, hovered in the doorway watching her charge.

As Spring and Gabe got out of the car and approached the patio, Spring could hear Marla's laughter as she took in the pictures in the book on her lap. Today was a good day for Marla. And so it would be a good one for Gabe, too.

In the garden, surrounded by the roses and geraniums that made Marla so happy, Spring knelt beside Marla's chair and took her hand. Gabe sat in the chair opposite.

"Marla," Spring whispered. "I promise that we will always

take care of you. Nothing will change. Gabe will still visit you, and I'll come, too, if you don't mind. And when we visit, we can sit with you and look at the roses or eat cookies or go for a walk. Whatever you want."

Marla, whose eyes had not left the book while Spring was speaking, looked up slightly and turned her head from Spring to Gabe. Marla took them in with her huge, empty eyes. She smiled ever so slightly before bowing her head and returning to the book.

Spring knew that somewhere behind those eyes was the woman who had selflessly given her a second chance at love. She would probably never meet that Marla, but Spring would be forever grateful to her.

The End

Did you enjoy *Spring*? Please support indie authors and write a review on Amazon.com, Goodreads, and elsewhere so others may enjoy it, too. Thank you.

ABOUT AMY RUTH ALLEN

I'm an American girl who grew up overseas, riding elephants in Thailand, dancing around the Maypole in Sweden, drinking tea in the United Kingdom, and touring castles across Europe. In these foreign (to me) and exotic locales, books were both my anchor and my escape. They connected me to my native land (and English-speakers in general), while introducing me to worlds even more awesome than the ones I lived in.

Fast forward to present day in Minneapolis, Minnesota, where I am the author of the small town fiction series *Finch's Crossing*, the young adult novel, *Stealing Away*, and seven non-fiction books for young adults. In addition to writing fiction, non-fiction, and my blog, I support fellow indie authors by reviewing indie books.

PLEASE CONNECT WITH ME!

- www.amyruthallen.com
- amyruthallen@yahoo.com
- facebook.com/amyruthallenauthor
- @AmyAllenWrites
- pinterest.com/amyruthallen

THE *Finch's* *Crossing* *Series*

✧ WWW.AMYRUTHALLEN.COM ✧

Finch's Crossing Book One: Autumn

Artist Autumn Hamilton is stuck in a creative block so strong she wonders if she will ever emerge. Inwardly determined to find her way back to painting, she puts on a brave face and pretends all is well, even fooling her best friend, Meg. But then a distraction—in the form of hard-hearted Ethan Rasmussen—pulls her into a complex family saga. Autumn must stop Ethan from making a huge mistake, regardless of his good intentions, and no matter how handsome he is.

Meanwhile, online shopping and big box stores have taken their toll on the once vibrant shops and restaurants in downtown Finch's Crossing, a small town nestled in the Laurel Highlands of western Pennsylvania. Major Peggy Brightwell has hired entrepreneur Kyle Oswald to bring the merchants into the world of internet marketing and social media, in time to entice Black Friday shoppers to Finch's Crossing. The eccentric and loveable merchants fall instantly in love with Kyle, but it's Meg he wishes would notice him. But Meg is hiding a fierce loneliness from everyone, including herself. Kyle is determined to find a chink in her armor, no matter how grumpy and resistant she is.

Finch's Crossing Book Two: Spring

At thirty-six, Spring Hamilton has reached a crossroads in her modeling career. No longer young, but still beautiful, she has severed ties with her controlling and unimaginative manager, and for the first time must figure out her future, alone. The only thing she knows for certain is that if she doesn't transition her career she will end up as a grandmotherly model in mail-order catalogs. As she relocates from Los Angeles to New York she detours to Finch's Crossing for a quick visit with her sister, Autumn. But a chance encounter with Gabriel, her high school sweetheart, rekindles their love, launching Spring into unbelievable circumstances she never could have predicted. She never thought of herself as the kind of person who would fall in love with another woman's husband.

Finch's Crossing Book Three: Summer

Free-spirited, thirty-two-year-old Summer Hamilton has worked as a chauffeur, waitress, obituary writer, and house painter. But when she is fired from her job as a nanny because she rebuked her employer's advances, she points her pink VW bug east and travels from Seattle to Finch's Crossing. After a ten-year vagabond life, she yearns to decide what she wants to do when she grows up. Upon arriving in Finch's Crossing, she meets carefree Trevor Banks, whose job building adventure parks takes him away for weeks at a time. She is torn between the kind of life she has just abandoned and the one she has begun to make for herself in Finch's Crossing. Having just tamed her wanderlust and opened a yoga studio in the town's shopping district, Summer must decide whether or not to hit the road again with Trevor in order to be with the man she loves. But as their relationship blooms, a nagging voice in her head keeps asking, "Just exactly how 'carefree' is Trevor?"

Finch's Crossing Book Four: Winter

Winter "Win" Hamilton's high school nickname, "The Ice Queen," has followed her all throughout her life and she is, in fact, just that—cold, selfish, and emotionally detached. But her steely demeanor helped her achieve a full partnership, at age thirty, in a prestigious international architectural firm. True, she doesn't have many friends, but she lives in a beautiful penthouse, has a fat 401K, drives a brand new Porsche Cayenne SUV, and dresses flawlessly in designer clothes. When she breaks her leg in a skiing accident she reluctantly returns to her childhood home to recover. As the broken bones heal, with the help of the handsome local doctor W. Armistead "Trip" Harrison, she rediscovers the traditional values she grew up with, and wonders how on earth her life got so out of balance. As her strength returns and she embarks on a self-improvement campaign, Win realizes that the unflappable and aloof doctor is the one man in town who isn't rendered tongue-tied in her presence. Accustomed to getting her way, she bristles at his lack of interest in her. Realizing she's met the male version of herself, she knows she has her work cut out for her.

Martha: A Finch's Crossing Holiday Novella

A delightful holiday novella featuring the loveable and unforgettable characters from "Autumn," the first book in the Finch's Crossing small town fiction series.

Love is ageless! Just ask seventy-two-year-old Martha, who has set her cap on Jack Staub, Finch's Crossing's most eligible senior bachelor. But Jack is painfully shy, and nothing she does seems to get his attention. And much to Martha's dismay, some of the other Golden Girls in Finch's Crossing have Jack in their cross-hairs. Martha must up her game if she's ever going to get Jack to notice her. With the help of her friends and neighbors, Martha begins her strategic pursuit. But is she going too far? And will she end up pushing Jack away, and into the arms of her competition?

Made in the USA
Monee, IL
11 November 2020